CURING TIME

Tim Swink

To Christy —
Thank you for
coming to the
coming!

All
Best!

T.S.

PEGASUS BOOKS

D1715248

Pegasus Books
3338 San Marino Ave
San Jose, CA 95127
www.pegasusbooks.net

First Edition: November 2013

Published in North America by Pegasus Books. For information, please contact Pegasus Books c/o Caprice De Luca, 3338 San Marino Ave, San Jose, CA 95127.

This book is a work of fiction. Any resemblance to actual persons, living or dead, events, or locales is entirely coincidental.

Library of Congress Cataloguing-In-Publication Data
Tim Swink
Curing Time/Tim Swink– 1st ed
p. cm.
Library of Congress Control Number: 2013953525

ISBN – 978-0-9910993-1-3

1. FICTION / Historical. 2. FICTION / Family Saga. 3. FAMILY & RELATIONSHIPS / Interpersonal Relations. 4. HISTORY / United States / State & Local / South (NC). 5. BODY, MIND & SPIRIT / Angels & Spirit Guides.

10 9 8 7 6 5 4 3 2 1

Comments about *Curing Time* and requests for additional copies, book club rates and author speaking appearances may be addressed to Tim Swink or Pegasus Books c/o Caprice De Luca, 3338 San Marino Ave, San Jose, CA, 95127, or you can send your comments and requests via e-mail to cdeluca@pegasusbooks.net or Tim Swink at tj.swink@yahoo.com.

Also available as an eBook from Internet retailers and from Pegasus Books

Book Cover Art by Michael Ringer

Printed in the United States of America

Reaping Life

"Curing time" is tobacco's season of harvest, a time of transformation, when the leaf is made golden by subjection to fire and heat. Tobacco farmer Hume Rankin endures his own curing time in the summer of 1959. When the rains won't come and the crops wilt in the field, he solicits the magic of an old, blind black woman. She warns of the dangers of calling on the middle world and tells him once those spirits are unleashed, it is they who decide when and how the spell unfolds. Hume dismisses her warning, to his peril.

When his life-long nemesis, Worth Baker, who has always had his eye on Hume's land as well as his wife, is found dead, all eyes are on Hume. He faces the all-too real possibility of losing his land, his family and even his life. Sitting in a jail cell, uncertain of his own innocence, he finds himself lost and a long way from home.

Recalling the old woman's warning, he is haunted by the possibility that he may have played a part in his own demise.

Acknowledgement

Giving birth to a novel is a long, lonely and arduous task. Rejection is something a writer must go through. We try to grow a tough hide to lessen the sting, but we are never, really, able to do so. Close calls, rejections and eventual disappointment become a way of life.

That said, the first person I want to thank is my wife, Renee. Your creative, literary eyes looking over my shoulder were invaluable. Because I listened, the novel and I are the better for it. You always believed in me and were my rudder that kept me righted and on course through rough seas. You were, and are, my constant... my North Star... my way home.

To my Editor, Marcus McGee and Pegasus Books, thank you! I am indebted to you for your conviction in me and my novel. You "got" it, and that was all I asked for. Chris Moebs, Pegasus Books Art Director... thank you for your patience and your ear... you nailed it Chris! I am also indebted to Author Lee Smith, who read parts of the novel in the early stages, and let me know I had something worth working for. Thank you for the push.

Thanks and gratuity to artist Michael Ringer and Michael Ringer Galleries in Alexandria Bay, New York, for graciously allowing me to use your enchanting painting, "North Woods Campfire" for my cover. It encapsulates the soul of my novel.

To those dear friends who kept me close during this journey, thank you! There were many times, I knew, you weren't sure whether or not to ask (again) about the progress of Curing Time, but you did. You asked. And for that I will forever be grateful.

To my sons, Evan and Darin, my daughter-in-law, Andi, and my granddaughter, Mary Lacy, thank you for your love and support. You make me proud. Because you are in my world, all is complete.

For

Renee

The Balance

After he had journeyed
And his feet were sore
And he was tired
He came upon an orange
grove
And he rested

And he lay in the cool
And while he rested
He took to himself an orange
And tasted it
And it was good

And he felt the earth to his
spine
And he asked
And he saw the tree above him
And the stars
And the veins in the leaf
And the light
And the balance

And he saw magnificent
perfection
Whereon, he thought of
himself in balance
And he knew he was

And he thought of those he
angered
For he was not a violent man
And he thought of those he
hurt
For he was not a cruel man

And he thought of those he
frightened
For he was not an evil man
And he understood...
He understood himself

Upon this he saw
That when he was of anger
Or knew hurt
Or felt fear
It was because he was not
understanding

And he learned...Compassion
Then he was answered

Just open your eyes
And realize
The way it's always been
Just open your mind
And you will find
The way it's always been
Just open your heart
And that's a start.

— The Moody Blues

CURING TIME

Curing Time

The curing process when the tobacco, after enduring the summer heat, drought, and rain, matures and stands tall in the field, waiting for the last of the process when the tobacco leaves are plucked from the stalk and put up in the barn to be cured and transformed into perfected, golden leaves.

Prologue

The ponies were the first to notice the odor, pitching the two young riders forward when they balked.

The older boy popped the animal's withers with the crack of excess leather at the end of the reins and his pony stumbled forward along the path that ran beside the creek. At a dip in the bank where the stream was shallower, the rider pulled right, leading them across. The younger rider followed, both ponies breaking into staggering trots over the rock that lined the creek-bed.

Sunlight filtered through the changing October leaves, sprinkling the rushing water with shimmering slivers. Half blinded from the light-play, the older boy spotted something in the creek up ahead. He stopped in mid-stream and stood in his stirrups, straining to focus.

"You see that?" He turned back to look at his companion.

"Yeah, I do. What is it? And what's that smell?"

"I don't know. I never smelled nothing like this. Come on let's go look."

The object was lying long-ways across the creek, backing up the water until it found its way around and swirled on by at either end. As they came closer, they made out what looked to be a piece of red cloth hung up on part of a tree that had fallen across the creek. Both pulled their tee shirts up over their noses to stave off the odor.

They eased their ponies on until the cloth took on the shape of a shirt draped around what appeared to be the upper torso of a body, the back of its head slung sideways and down. An arm hung lazily over the back.

"What the hell..." the younger one said.

"Oh lord, it's a man! And he has a hole in his back the size of a cantaloupe!"

Chapter 1

Summer 1957

At the end of the row, Hume Rankin pulled up on Rhody's reins. It had been a long day for both him and his chestnut-colored mule. The summer sun had started its downward journey and the central North Carolina landscape had taken on a mellow hue, when the colors mute and the shadows from the tree line begin to grow long, reaching out to provide some solace to the parched bottomland. Didn't hurt that the breeze had picked up, rustling the boughs, giving sway to the pines that lined the south end of the tobacco field. Rankin held partial to this time of day. As the breeze cooled the sweat-soaked back of his khaki shirt, he lifted his stained wide-brimmed hat and wiped the sweat from his forehead.

Almost in the same motion, he lifted a brown bottle to his lips, taking a long pull of Southern Comfort. He kept the bottle stashed in the tobacco sled for moments like this. The brown liquid had long ago lost its sting. His gullet now comfortably accepted its welcoming rush of numbness. The solitude and peace of the ending of the day was what Hume Rankin lived for now. It kept his mind off the brood of nine awaiting him back at the house.

"Got a restlessness inside me, Rhody," he said, wiping the remaining dribble off his lower lip with the back of his hand. "And I ain't exactly sure where it's coming from, either."

Hume took another long pull before re-capping the bottle. He straightened, arched his back and winced.

"Maybe it's the young-uns... or the amount of em. The dollar to the pound of tobacco is getting less and less every year. Sometimes I feel like providing for them's taking more'n I have to give. Comes a point where a man just don't know where he stands anymore. And if he does, he don't know how he got there," he said to his mule as he scanned his land that lay before him.

"Times are changing. Some people say that's good, but I've never been one to take to change. I just don't know..."

The thoughtful moment dissolved with the sudden start of his mule.

"Whoa, Rhody, whoa," the farmer admonished, pulling back on the reins. The animal neighed and danced sideways in the row. "What's bothering you? Whoa now, settle down."

The mule calmed and he surveyed the green stalks gently swaying in the breeze. He'd experienced this before. It usually happened late in the day, about this time, when for no certain reason he felt a presence, as if he was not alone. The feeling was accompanied by the tingling of his hair as it rose on the nape of his neck. A sense of serpentine movement through the field and the sound of swishing leaves on swaying tobacco stalks followed, and then an eerie stillness took over. He felt it in the woods at times too...as if someone or something was with him, peering at him from behind the trees. His momma and daddy had talked of such things, of entities that inhabited the earth and dwelt in the fields and woodlands.

"Hume, now you be mindful when you're out by yourself," his mama used to admonish him.

"Them woods are full of mischief... specially late in the day... around twilight. There's changlings out in them woods that would love to get their hands on a little boy bout your size and carry him home with them... down under the roots of big old oak trees. That's where they make their home. That's where they do their mischief and change young-uns into one of them."

Just old wives tales, told by old folk who were too superstitious and sot in their ways to begin with, he told himself. Still, what bothered him most was the mule's reaction. That, he could never explain.

Looking across the field, he noticed the breeze was still softly blowing across the land, but the tobacco stalks now stood dead still in the fading, evening light.

———

Ellen Rankin lifted the sweat-stained, white linen shirt from around her neck and fanned her shoulders. The oppressive heat of the day seemed to have finally broken. As she glanced in the full-length mirror on the back of the bedroom door, the glass revealed that she had retained, somehow, something of the figure that had pleased her husband years ago. The child bearing years and rearing of nine children had not affected her body as one might have expected. Even at mid-life, her skin retained the smooth, olive glow of her younger years, and her dark eyes still contained the deep, pensive pools that Hume had fallen in love with.

They had married in 1937. Twenty years of hard life had not taken a hefty toll on her physically, or on the love she felt for her husband.

The telephone rang its familiar two short rings. Ellen ran down the stairs and lifted the phone from its cradle. She heard her sister's voice at the other end of the party line.

"Ellen! I declare, hon. Are you all right?"

"What do you mean, Clara?"

"Well, I haven't seen you or talked to you in a month of Sundays. Ed and I were just saying we haven't seen you or Hume at any of the Grange dances lately. And we never see you at church anymore. I know Hume isn't big on church, but the Grange dances... I don't mean to be sticking my nose where it doesn't belong, but I *am* your sister and... it's just that he and I were just talking about that, wondering if anything was wrong?"

Silence followed before Ellen answered.

"Clara, I'm sorry. I didn't mean to alarm you and Ed. And you're right. We haven't been to a Grange dance in a while... it's just that we... it seems we're going through a time right now," Ellen said.

"A time? What do you mean by that?"

Again, silence filled Clara's ear-piece, save for breathing on the other end.

"Is that you breathing so heavy, Ellen. Are you crying?" Clara asked.

"Yes and no," Ellen responded. "The no part is the breathing. That's not me. Earlene! Will you please hang up? This is not a party conversation. It's private and I wish you would stop listening in on my conversations. You know, they say you never know when the operator is listening in for people eavesdropping on other people's conversations," Ellen said.

They heard a soft click.

"Who was that? Was that Earlene Wyrick?" Clara asked.

"It was. She does that a lot, the old busy body. I've been tempted to get a private line, but Hume would hit the ceiling if he found out I'd gotten one... what, with the expense of them," Ellen said.

"I believe she hung up. Go on with what you were saying," Clara said.

"I just don't know, Clara. Hume's distant right now. His mind seems to take him to places where I'm not allowed. He's gotten more sullen. Hume's just not the same man. He used to get so much joy playing and teasing me... and was such a flirt. I hate to admit it, but I miss that attention. And his time in the field seems to stretch out longer than before. The amount of tobacco he's planted hasn't changed. We haven't added any additional land in the past ten years, other than the New Ground—that little plot down at the north end of the field that he bought from his brother. The workload's the same, but his time spent out in the field takes up more of his day. I used to look so forward to him coming in at the end of the day. Now, for reasons I don't completely understand, all that's changed."

"Well, one of the reasons I called was, Betty Johnson retired from the Grange's social committee and I thought it might be good for you to put your name in. You'd be a shoe-in for it. And after what I'm hearing, it would get you out of the house some... give you and Hume some space. Who knows, might get y'all back to Grange dances and re-kindle some interest in you two for slow-dancing," Clara said.

"I don't think he would go for that. I don't want to stir up the water. And slow-dancing is just not in Hume right now," Ellen said.

"Ellen, I'm sorry y'all are going through a hard time. But I guess that's natural. Me and Ed had ours, a few years back. Didn't touch each other under the covers for several months," Clara said.

"Several months? I'd be grateful if ours was only several months. Except for the children being around, I feel as if I've been living in a convent for the last year. I know how nuns must feel when they first declare their celibacy," Ellen said.

A familiar creak of the screen door returned Ellen's attention to the darkening room. Hume was in from the fields. Used to be, he was like clockwork, a creature of habit. His entrance in the house at the end of his workday had been without deviation for 20 years. He'd stop by the wash sink on the back porch, bend his lanky torso over the sink as he peeled off his stained work shirt and let it fall in a rumpled heap around his boots. He'd then commence to wash the day's sandy soil and sweat from his sinewy arms and chest. After toweling, he'd remove his work boots, amble across the kitchen floor and give his wife the familiar one-word greeting, simply, "Ellen," followed by a kiss on the cheek, and a playful slap on her hind side, before heading upstairs to complete the change.

"I've gotta go. Hume just came in," Ellen whispered.

"Call me back when you can, Ellen."

"Okay. I will. Love you.

"Love to you too," Clara said.

Ellen put the phone back on the cradle and turned to find Hume in the hallway, staring at her.

"Hume! You frightened me. I didn't hear you," Ellen said.

"Who you talking to?" Hume asked, holding the stare.

"Clara called. I haven't talked to her in so long... I need to do better..."

"You always talk to your sister bout our sex life?"

"What? No! Oh that... that was just women talk. She and Ed..."

"Ellen, I don't take to you talking to your sister, or anybody, about our *private* life. You understand? That's the damndest thing I've ever heard. You talking about how often we do it... or ain't doing it. You know it takes two, Ellen, and you ain't showed much interest yourself," Hume said.

The two stared at each other for several seconds, saying nothing, their stares filling the space between them, before Hume said, "I'm gonna go upstairs and lie down. Call me when supper is ready. "

Ellen started to turn and walk away, but then she turned back around and faced her husband.

"Hume. What is wrong? I love you, but I feel like we're like strangers in our own house. You're not happy. This has been going on for some time now, and I just don't understand what is wrong with you. With *us*!"

When Ellen turned to walk away, Hume caught her arm.

"I'm sorry Ellen. I'm just..."

"What Hume? Tell me! Please talk to me!"

Hume paused.

"Nothing, Ellen. Call me when supper's ready."

Chapter 2

"Are we still feasting on Miss Piggly Wiggly? Thought we'd be finished with her by now," Hume said, taking his place at the head of the supper table. "By the time we're done with her, we'll have eaten everything but the squeal."

"Daddy! That's not nice," Mary Ellen said. "Miss Piggly Wiggly was our pet."

"Mary Ellen, she's nothing but a pig. A *dead* pig, that is," Alford said.

"That dead pig is the one I won in the greasy pig contest at the county fair. Y'all can just thank me for this meal," Emmaline said.

"Can't wait for the day you decide to be a girl, Emmaline," Alford followed. "How old are you now? Ten? Eleven?"

"I'm fifteen and I *am* a girl, in case you haven't noticed! Open your eyes, Alford. You might learn something," Emmaline responded.

"Yeah, I guess that's what Butch Cole thought just before you broke his nose and gave him two black eyes," Alford said.

"Well, he shouldn't have said what he said about me."

"You know, Emmaline, Butch Cole used to be one of the toughest boys around. Notice I said *used* to be. I bet that poor boy ain't never gonna live down that whuppin. I reckon his man-hood took just as bad a beating as his face," Alford finished.

Alford Humley Rankin, Jr., seventeen and the namesake of this father, was more like his daddy in nature than the rest. The first-born, he was spoiled by his aunts on his mother's side and had a tendency to be lazy. Being the oldest and most able, he spent time in the fields with Hume, particularly during the early planting and the later priming season. Both bore elegance in their manner. While some observers believed it to be gentlemanly sophistication, others saw arrogance. Either could be charming and endearing one minute and spew a verbal slashing the next. Alford and his daddy honed the latter trait on each other. Both, when in the fields under the hot southern sun, could let it fly against each other, rough as a cob.

"You lucked up when Billy Lucas slipped and fell, Emmaline," Fredericka joined in. "Or else we'd be eating more like white people."

"Fredericka..." Ellen started.

"Well it's true. The only people I know that eats as steady a diet of pig as we do are the coloreds. We may as well invite Walt and Daisy Neal over for dinner every night."

The female version of Alford was sixteen-year-old Fredericka. Although more aggressive and not at all lazy, she was spoiled by her aunts as well. Like all the Rankin girls, Fredericka was dark haired and of olive-complexion. But her inner hardness seeped through to her outer features, forfeiting a depth of inner beauty the others retained. Fredericka carried an agenda and was not the least bit timid in arranging the universe around her in order to get what she wanted. As she grew older, the younger female siblings became intimidated by her nature. Their mother was among those who bowed to her passing.

"That reminds me, Alford. Don't let me forget to talk to Walt about us pulling those plants from the beds as soon as the weather looks to break. We've got a new banker down from up north and he must be something else. I haven't had the pleasure of meeting the fellow yet, but some who have say he's lien crazy. Wants to put all the farmers under secured notes. They say times are a changing. A new winds blowing, and it ain't a pleasant breeze. Sounds like we're gonna have to step it up in the future. I ain't gonna lose my land to some Yankee. We did that once already, down here," Hume said.

"I'll see if I can remember to do that," Alford answered. "Now can we say grace and pass the gravy?"

Suppertime in the Rankin kitchen usually consisted of fare closely related to the farm. Cured pork shoulder and ham from the November hog killing season remained a mainstay during the dark months, usually lasting the family through spring, along with daily-baked biscuits, smothered in red-eye gravy—a concoction derived from the juice of the ham, mixed with strong coffee, to produce a thin, reddish-looking liquid that Southern folk called gravy (not to be confused with the thick, white gravy made with milk and flour and normally poured over chipped beef and biscuits, which the Rankins consumed in the morning along with ham and fresh sausage). Very little of the hog went to waste. Backbone and spare ribs had to be eaten early on, while still fresh, as there was no way to preserve the delicate, tasty meat. Ellen made liver pudding out of hog liver, and souse meat from the pig's feet and tongue. She usually saved the chitlins for Walt Neal and his family.

In the summer, when daylight lasted longer, the bounty consisted mostly of earthborn fare taken from the garden. Tomato sandwiches—with slices of cucumber added, sprinkled abundantly with salt and pepper and encased between two slices of white bread, both sides slathered with mayonnaise—were common. Summertime side dishes included beans, usually half-runner green beans that Ellen set and staked in early spring. A bowl of sliced cucumbers, mixed with cubes of spring onions, floating in a pool of vinegar and water, a little sugar and salt and pepper added to the mix.

The chicken house provided fresh eggs each morning, and sometimes for supper. Fried chicken was a year-round offering. It was never fancy fare, but as Hume called it, "Just good honest eating."

Feeding such a gathering of children was, at times, a burden for Hume. It had to be for Ellen as well, although she never complained. Her dedication was admirable. Hell, he loved all his young-uns, but any rational reason for having such a large brood had escaped him. As he recollected, it was just a matter of Ellen saying "yes" more often than "no," and Hume's eagerness to oblige. A new Rankin had come into the world once a year for eight years straight—that was the pattern. There was one four-year glitch however, that being the birth of John, the youngest and eventually the last of the Rankin brood.

Hume sat at the head of the long wooden table, Ellen at the other end, with the two youngest seated on either side of her, John and Jack.

"John, watch your elbow! Your milk... watch your..." Ellen said just as John's glass tilted over onto the table and the milk ran down onto his lap.

"I wondered when that was going to happen," Mirabelle, age fourteen, said pushing her chair away from the table. "You seem to have such a talent for that, John," she complained as Ellen started up out of her chair as well.

"I'll get it mother. You sit," Mirabelle called back as she walked over to the sink to retrieve a drying towel. "He's six now, and should be doing better than this. It's almost a nightly thing. With his coordination, I'm amazed he started walking when he did."

John turned toward his mother with a questioning look.

"John, you must try to be more careful," his mother comforted.

"It's okay, John. I used to spill mine too when I was your age," Jack commented with a grin. "You're too small to get a whuppin. Me, I gotta watch my step because I'm almost a teenager now..."

"Oh stop it, Jack. You *just* turned ten," Fredericka contested.

"Well I am, almost... got two numbers in my age now," Jack said.

"Still doesn't make you a teenager," Mirabelle chimed in.

Jack, next to the youngest, sat to Ellen's right and for good reason— he was the most playful of the brood. A simple, sweet boy who enjoyed life, he had a habit of disappearing during the meal to the tunnel-like recess underneath the long, wooden table where, deftly crawling on his hands and knees around everyone's feet, he attempted to make his way to the head of the table where his father was stationed. Along the way he pulled the peach fuzz on each of his five elder sisters' exposed legs. Most times he never made it clear to the end. While passing each of his sisters, their one-by-one knee jerks slamming against the bottom of the table alerted Ellen of Jack's exact whereabouts.

The progression of nine children continued down the table in chronological order with Thomas, Etta, Mary Ellen, Mirabelle, and Emmaline, ending with Alford sitting to the right of Hume, and Fredericka the eldest female, to the left, where the nightly discussion usually centered around the day's work.

"Speaking of Walt," Hume reported to the elder members of the table, "Sam and him went at it again yesterday. If that boy don't learn to keep his mouth shut, I swear, Walt's gonna kill him one of these days. And Walt's got just the temperament to do it if that boy gets him riled enough."

"Goodness! I thought Uncle Walt and Sam were doing better, since their fall-out the end of last summer," Ellen followed.

"Momma, why do we call Uncle Walt, Uncle Walt?" Mary Ellen asked.

"Because that is the way we show respect for an older negro man. It's as if we were addressing him as Mr. Walt."

"So then why don't we just call him Mr. Walt?" Mary Ellen asked, unsatisfied.

"Those two ain't never gonna do any better," Hume waded in impatiently "They just patch it up after each feud and keep on going. Somebody's gonna end up prone on the ground, permanently, before it's all over."

"Sam is just standing his ground," Alford said.

"Yeah, maybe so," Hume grumbled, laying his fork down, starring at his oldest boy, "But it never hurts for a son to show a little respect for his father."

"That can be a two-way street, you know. Doesn't hurt for a father to show a little respect for his son, either." Alford responded.

The two remained fixed on each other and silence descended on the table like a mantle, until Hume softened.

"Still, I'm afraid that when the man upstairs commenced to handing out traits, Sam got most all of Walt's temper. I gotta admit though, Sam does have some of Daisy's kindness, but that temper still boils just under the surface."

"Why's he like that?" Thomas asked. "Whenever we go down to the creek or have to cross over where they live, we always have to call out and let him know who we are. Some days, he sits out there in his yard with his shotgun across his lap with a scowl on his face. When I call out and yell, 'Walt! It's me. Thomas Rankin! Hume's boy,' he'll break out into that toothless grin he has and waves his arms, tell me to come on across and becomes all syrupy as molasses."

"That's best you do that. All of you," Hume said to his children. "Don't be sneaking up on Walt. Even if he don't have that twelve gauge across his lap, you need to let him know who you are. He won't ever knowingly hurt a Rankin. But knowing is the key. Let him know who you are before you cross over where they live."

"But why's he so mean? He's nice to us, but I've heard tales," Mirabelle said.

"I guess it's just his and his family's condition," Hume replied.

"What do you mean, Daddy? "Thomas followed.

"His condition. His situation. I guess if my situation was that I had no say over my life, I might feel a little mean too. Might feel caged in and wanna do some harm to them that keeps me caged in. Might mistake that situation for some*one* or some*thing*."

"That don't seem *right*," Thomas said, thinking.

"It's not, son. But that's just the way it is. But y'all have nothing to worry about with Walt. Just let him know you're a Rankin, and he won't harm a hair on your head. He's beholding to this family for his and his family's well-being and the roof over their heads."

Though he never spoke of it, there was a part of Walt's world that worried Hume, a dark corner where he could sometimes go. Hume felt that when Walt dwelt in that place, he was capable of most anything. Community folk and church folk alike believed it was Walt who dynamited the windows out of Oak Grove A.M.E Church. Rumor had it, the congregation shunned him and his family by letting it be known that their membership into their church fold was not desired because of his past.

Not that Walt ever had any intention of darkening the church doors. But his wife, Daisy, felt church might be a cure for the bitterness between Walt and Sam. Wouldn't hurt her daughters Bessie, Dorothea and Nettie either, seeing as how strange boys had started showing up around the place, calling the girls out at all hours of the night, causing Walt to fetch his shotgun whenever their noise awakened him. Daisy had even heard Nettie, just fourteen and the youngest, return to her bed after a late-night sojourn.

"It's a good thing Walt done lost some of his step," Daisy was once heard to remark, "Or else one of em boys might not be goin back home, come one of these nights."

"Pass the gravy, Mirabelle," Alford demanded of his younger sister. "Or is that your personal bowl?"

"You'll get it when I'm through with it."

"Well, I believe you've had your fill of it, and I'll just take that, thank you," Alford insisted, reaching across the table. He bumped Emmaline, who was seated beside him, in the head with his elbow in the process.

"That hurt," she yelled as she swatted his arm.

"Today's the twenty-first, Midsummer's Eve," Mary Ellen suddenly offered, mesmerized and in her own world, while staring into her plate. "The nature fairies will start to be more active."

"I've had it with your stupid imagination," Fredericka thundered. "You think it's cute and you think everyone else will think you're cute, but you're not. You're just trying to get attention and everyone *knows* that, Mary Ellen."

Gentle Mary Ellen, thirteen and the fifth child in line, was named after her mother. From the beginning, she was the antithesis of Fredericka. Mary Ellen danced and sang her way through life. Thus early on, she was easy prey for Fredericka's manipulative skills. Hume always felt that Mary Ellen, being her mother's namesake, might have created more problems with Fredericka than with the other siblings. A namesake was something Fredericka could not change or take away.

"Ouch, Jack! Stop it," Emmaline yelled, banging her knee on the underneath of the table. "Mother, he's doing it again. Make him stop!"

Hume's attention settled on Mary Ellen for a pensive moment before shifting down the table to Ellen. Understanding her husband's silent intent, she announced, "Jack! Come out from under the table right now! And the rest of you all, stop right now or you can leave the table. And there won't be any supper for any of you, if that happens. And you can forget about seeing the Jackie Gleason show too, for that matter."

"Well, tell him to stop..."

"Right now, Emmaline. Stop it right now."

"Yes Ma'am."

"And that goes for the rest of you as well," Ellen directed toward Alford and Fredericka. "The fussing and bickering at this dinner table has got to stop. It's getting out of hand and I won't have that in this house. Suppertime is not a time for bickering. It is a time for *family*! And it will remain that. Does everyone present understand?"

The silent response indicated it was by all, except for Mary Ellen, whose attention remained far away, while fixated on her plate.

———————

Daisy Neal sat by her night fire, periodic gusts of wind whipping the flames. She poked the embers with her fire stick, thinking out loud.

I got me a feeling and it ain't a good one. There's a bad moon coming. I can feel it. Maybe not this summer... we bout done with this one... but a-comin it is. I'm afraid it's a killin moon, this one. I won't know for sure till they show up. Them little people have a mind all they own.

I knows about such things. Momma and grand-momma done passed it down to me... bout potions and spells... bout the killing moon. It's right there in the bible, and it told that someone's death was nigh—can't nothing be done about it. Sometimes I wished they hadn't brought me into their world. The folks down in the Raw Hut community came to my momma and grand-momma for them to tell em the future, get their revenge or cure a spell that had been put on them.

That was back when we all lived in Burlington, though. Hadn't been much of a call for it here in Brown Summit. The colored folks round here don't know I have such powers. But the little people do. And them's who matters most.

Chapter 3

Late Summer 1957

Tobacco farming revolved around seasons. The spring planting gave way to the monotonous daily chore of cultivating and weeding the crops, which continued until the end of June, when the tobacco stalks were about knee-high and able to *lay it by*.

Hume never could understand what was meant by "lay it by," only that his daddy always used the expression, meaning the tobacco stalks had matured to the point they no longer needed to be tended. Hume continued farming in the tradition that his daddy and his granddaddy had done generations before. He saw no need for change.

The last cultivation required a farmer to throw all the dirt he could on the rows in order to make as big a ridge as possible. That done, all that was left for the month of July was to pick the sucker leaves by hand, remove the blossoms from the tops of the stalks, pull the thick, green tobacco worms from the plant, and pray for rain so the crop makes it to the August *priming*. That's when they pulled the tobacco leaves from the stalks, bottom to top, and took it to the barn to be tied onto tobacco sticks and put up in the barn to cure and in time, transforming it to become the desired, golden leaf.

Late August was curing time and meant nights by the fire, staying with it all night and all day, feeding wood to the flues that brought curing heat to the tobacco hanging from the barn's rafters.

Come fall, after the priming and curing had all been attended, Hume would hitch up Rhody and steer from behind as the big chestnut pulled the dragging plow through the sandy soil, turning the land under, preparing it for the long winter slumber ahead. Around the same time, late fall or early winter, he worked up a new plant bed where he placed the seeds for the next season's crop. Hume never used the same bed in consecutive years, for fear of ruining a new crop right off, due to disease or contamination that had set up in the old bed over the hot steamy summer. He always took up a new place in the woods for his beds. After he turned the new bed, he and Rhody hauled out the lumber, took it to the barn where he would spend the winter cutting and splitting the timber to use in the flues in August.

The fire crackled and danced, forming plumes of fiery red anger. Hume sat on the fallen log he'd dragged from the edge of the field earlier, while it was still light. Across from him sat Walt Neal, a leather-faced Negro, whose hair was snow white.

Studying Walt, Hume thought, *a man would have a right to think him to be younger than he is, solely by the way he worked in the field. And the way he could endure the heat, bugs and long hours in the rows better'n any man half his age.*

But his work stamina belied the truth. Walt was in his mid-fifties and had himself a passel of young-uns, too. He, his younger wife Daisy, and his brood of four lived in a cabin that was provided by Hume, one that overlooked the tobacco field. Their front yard was a sandy patch, save for a few scattered bunches of yellow daffodils that bloomed every spring. Daisy, rendered sightless since childhood by smallpox, planted the flowers she would never see when they first arrived on the land. It was her humble attempt to add a bit of beauty and color to her family's otherwise drab world.

They received a stipend of three dollars a day. Rent was ten dollars a month. Walt had one boy, Sam, a big, strapping nineteen-year-old, and three daughters.

"Walt, go over'n add some wood to the fire in the flues, and check the thermometer inside the barn... needs to hold steady around one ten for an even cure."

"Yessa, Mista Hume."

Walt pushed his wiry, worn body up with one hand, while steadying himself with the other. He shuffled over to the low fire contained in the metal flue outside the barn wall, just to the right of the door. Then he began feeding the red-hot coals more hardwood to keep the steady supply of heat, needed by the tobacco hanging in the barn. Walt opened the wooden-plank door and walked into the dark smoky den, striking a wooden match to read the thermometer that hung on the pole in the center of the barn.

"One-o-five, Mista Hume!" Walt called out. "Good timin!"

"Yeah, good timing is everything, I suppose. Just seems now days, the time ain't so good," Hume muttered to himself while sitting by the main fire.

Walt settled back at the fire onto the makeshift-sleeping pad of old quilts Daisy had patched together by touch. Beads of perspiration dotted his forehead. Hume took a long swig from the bottle. Walt eyed the brown liquid enviously, and the look was not lost on Hume. Feeling somewhat gluttonous, Hume held the bottle out to Walt, saying nothing. Walt met the gesture and took the bottle to his lips, taking several short swallows, and then returned it to Hume, making sure not to over extend its stay.

"Thank ya, Mista Hume. The heat in that barn sure can dry a person out in a hurry."

Hume silently studied Walt's weathered face through the fire. "How long've we been out here doing this now, Walt? What's it been ten, twelve years?"

"Fourteen, to be sure, Mista Hume. I knows, cause Nettie was born just a'fore we came here."

"Damn! Where's the time gone," Hume asked, more to himself than to Walt.

"Time gone to live in the past I reckon, Mista Hume. Hear tell *that's* a place where the livin ain't supposed to go to."

"I don't know Walt. Seems the past holds more for me than the future. Times are changing. And I ain't so sure the changes are for the best."

Hume let the moment sit, contemplating what he'd just said, before continuing his thought.

"Take the barn there. My daddy built that with his own hands. Felled and notched the trees himself. Built it to withstand season after season, out in the elements. That's a work of art, sitting there. Nowadays, some of the farmers over in Brown Summit and Monticello are talking about putting up these new, fast curing bulk barns that are made out of tin! Put the tobacco in and leave it— come back when the tobacco's finished curing. No more need for nights like tonight, out here by the fire. And they talk of putting a tractor out between the rows instead of a mule. That ain't right. A man can't talk to a tractor like he can a mule."

"Nawsir, that's fo sure," Walt said.

"And the banks. Used to be they'd lend a man the money on the front side to put his crops in. They were willing to extend credit based on the farmer's *word* that he'd pay em back. And they *knew* whose word was good and whose weren't. Now, the bank says they're gonna change the way they do business and put liens on our land, our barns, our tools and our crops, so they can take near about everything away from us, if we have a lean year. My daddy had bad years, but back then, they gave them *time* to get right," Hume continued.

"Seems to me your world is a-changin. Fast, too. My world... it don't work that way," Walt replied.

"How's that?" Hume responded as he gazed into the fire.

"Well... change don't seem to be something that's got no place in the colored man's world. We be *waitin* on some things to change, but seems like it never come. Not in my lifetime, anyway. Change seems to be stuck in one place."

"Be careful what you wish for, Walt," Hume replied as his gaze returned. "It might come true. Might wake up one morning and find a big, hungry wolf, sitting on your front steps, instead of that lazy coonhound of yours."

Sitting in silence, contemplating what Walt had just said, Hume leaned his head back on the log, taking a deep breath of night air, mixed with pine and hardwood smoke. He caught sight of the crescent moon, hanging over his left shoulder, and exhaled. The cicadas hummed, just out of sight of the firelight. Hume loved the sound of late August. *Curing time*—and with it, the first remote feel of a shift in seasons coming on.

Even though the August sun still burned hot over the fields, the slight change in the afternoons and evenings that time of year— the ever so subtle chill in the night air or the slant of the late afternoon sunlight—foretold a change to come.

Chapter 4

During the 1940s and 1950s, there were several families in the northern Piedmont of North Carolina who owned large tracts of tobacco. One, the Clapps, was a big family over in Monticello. Another prominent tobacco family was the Bakers. All, including the Rankin family, were mainly of second or third-generation Protestant Scotch-Irish descent. The early settlers began arriving in the mid-1800s, from the province of Ulser in Ireland, most by crossing the Canadian border to avoid the Immigrant Tax.

They settled in the southern Appalachian Mountains because of the resemblance to their homeland, and in the central Carolina Piedmont, where the land was cheap and the soil was rich. They continued the same agricultural techniques they used in Ulster. Hume and his brothers, Mose and Sanders, were considered small, family farmers. Hume owned and farmed about fourteen acres by himself. His land was considered prime bottomland that was rendered sandy and highly nutrient, compared to the red clay so prominent in the Piedmont. Its finer quality was due to the seasonal flooding of the creek, when it swelled out of its banks and deposited its rich sediment in the bottomland.

The families, for the most part, co-existed well, each tending to business and staying to themselves. There was one exception however—an exception that had been a gnat in Hume Rankin's eye for most of his adult life. Actually, it was more like a festered briar in his thumb. And that briar went by the name of "Worth Baker."

Baker farmed a large tract, just to the north of Hume, that he inherited from his daddy, with plenty of farmhands to help him. Most were local Negroes, with the exception of a few dirt poor, white farm boys, who served as Baker's immediate family. He had neither married, nor sired any offspring—at least none that he claimed. But he had let it be known over the years that he had his eye on Rankin land, if the chance should ever present itself.

Hume Rankin and Worth Baker had a history. Both had attended the one-room schoolhouse in Brown Summit, followed by a short stint at Monticello High School. That "short stint," however, had been Hume's short stint, since he attended high school only until his daddy took sick the summer after his second year. It was understood, due to the fact his older brothers were married and had families, that Hume would forgo his education in order to help provide for his mother and daddy.

It was a matter that would remain stuck in Hume's craw for years to come. He had been a good student and enjoyed school. He took a special liking to math, an advantageous subject when deciphering matters concerning farming, such as how many bushels of corn would be produced in a planting. Or the yield of tobacco per acre from the number of plants that were put in.

The fact that he and Ellen had been in the same class added to the embarrassment of having to quit school early. Hume had become sweet on her several years before, but only during that first year of high school had he let it be known that Ellen was his girl. But that meant nothing to Worth. To Worth Baker, perhaps largely because she was Hume Rankin's girlfriend, she became another of Hume's possessions he desired.

Hume never forgot the senior dance.

———————

"Hume, please come! This is my senior dance. I know it's not something you want to do, but would you do it for me? Please."

"Ellen, I don't go to school there anymore. Didn't graduate either. I don't think they'd let me in, even if I did come."

"Yes they would, Hume. They would if you were my date."

"Ellen, you know I'd do anything..."

"Please Hume. It would mean a lot to me."

Her pleading brown eyes caused his falter.

"Well, I reckon I could... I mean I guess..."

"Oh Hume, thank you. We'll have a good time, I promise," she said and sealed it with a gentle kiss on the side of his cheek.

———————

"Daddy, I gotta go now. I got you all set up, and you can call Momma if you need anything else. I'm already an hour late and Ellen will think..."

"Well, you go on then, boy. Go on! Leave me here all stove up and miserable. Go on! I don't matter to you no-how. Go on!"

The drive to the schoolhouse took about fifteen minutes in his daddy's pickup truck, and by the time he arrived, everyone was inside. Music lilted across the yard that Hume crossed while clutching a bouquet of gardenias he had plucked from his mother's bush. As he got closer, he could make out the tune, a soft waltz. The butterflies stirred in his stomach as he thought of Ellen and what she would look like all dressed up. Being over an hour late caused his heart to quicken as well. Through the thick, leaded glass of the schoolhouse windows, he could make out the movement of couples as they danced close, in the golden glow, round and round the room, in time to the music.

Mr. Scott, the principal of the high school, met his first stride onto the schoolhouse steps.

"Oh... Mr. Scott. Ah... I'm here to... nice evening ain't it?"

"It is, Hume," he answered coldly, adding nothing more to the conversation.

Slow, heavy seconds passed.

"Well, ah... Mr. Scott... Ellen Reston... she... I know I'm late and I'm sorry, but I had to settle things with my daddy before I could come, what with his condition and all."

"Yes, I know about your daddy, Hume. How is he doing?"

"Well, he's still cantankerous as usual, but I guess I really can't blame him for that. I might be just as ornery if I was in his shoes."

The principle held his position as Hume advanced up the steps, arriving at the one just below the top one that Mr. Scott occupied.

"Now Hume, this is the senior dance for the graduating seniors. I don't mean to be rude, but just what is your business here tonight?"

"Oh yeah, well... see, Ellen Reston invited me as her date. I told her I didn't really feel comfortable coming tonight, seeing as how I didn't graduate and all."

The principle was caught off-guard, and relayed that by saying, "*You* are Ellen's date? I'm sorry, but I thought Ellen's date was already here."

With that said, he moved aside, looking over his shoulder as Hume's gaze followed his, and settled on Worth Baker, who at the moment was turning the corner of the dance floor, closest to the door where Hume stood watching. Baker was facing Hume, and when he saw him outside the doorway, his condescending face broke into a snide smile, accompanied by a victorious wink of his eye.

The woman in his arms had her back to Hume, but there was no doubt who she was, her shiny black hair, worn up in an elegant bun.

"I'm sorry Hume, but it's best that you leave," brought Hume back to Principle Scott on the steps.

Hume took one more look over the principle's shoulder. Ellen was circling back up the dance floor and this time her face was exposed to Hume. He couldn't help but notice the giddy laugh directed up and into her dance partner's face.

"Yes sir, Mr. Scott. I'm sorry. I didn't mean to..."

"No, *I'm* sorry, Hume."

Hume backed down the steps and walked across the yard the same way he came. He set the flowers on the hood and turned, pushing himself up and sat next to the bouquet on the front of the truck.

Oh hell, Ellen's gonna think I stood her up, he thought to himself. *I'd better hang around until the dance is over and at least let her know I was here. I told her they wouldn't let me in, but damn if she didn't insist. And I'm gonna let her know I saw her and Worth together, enjoying themselves out on the dance floor.*

Hume lay back and looked up into the night sky, the big dipper above him. The still warm hood was relaxing to his tense back muscles. The music from the dance and the warmth of the truck melded into one. He became drowsy and soon drifted off.

"Rankin! You still here? I heard old man Scott told you to leave. You don't take a hint very well, do you?" Worth Baker thundered, waking Hume from his little sleep.

"What hint is that, Worth?" Hume asked calmly.

"That you don't have a place here anymore. Or maybe the problem is that you just don't follow instructions. Is that it, Hume? You're too dumb to follow instructions. Maybe that's the reason you flunked out."

"Go to hell, Baker! I didn't flunk out and you know it. Daddy got sick and I had to..."

"Your daddy! Your daddy and his brothers lost most all their land to the bank..."

At that moment, Ellen broke through Worth's laughing entourage. Worth looked over at her and finished with a snide smile.

"And you ain't no better. You come from the same stock, Rankin."

Hume's face flushed red, more from embarrassment than anger, though the latter was in there as well. Hume slid off the truck and moved toward Worth.

"You wanna do something about it, little man," Worth scoffed, as he slid a gold Masonic ring off his finger. He had taken the ring off his daddy's hand the day he passed away.

"Y'all stop it, right now," Ellen shouted, stepping through the crowd.

Hume obeyed, but Worth continued toward Hume, pushing his large face in front of Hume's.

"How about it, little man? You wanna *make* something of it?"

Hume glanced over at Ellen and when he did, a fist caught him on the side of the face, crumpling him to the ground. Worth followed with a headlock and drove Hume's bleeding face into the gravel. A sizeable crowd gathered, with Hume and Worth on the ground in a frenzied entanglement of body and limbs.

"Stop it! Stop it now," Ellen screamed.

The principle's arrival parted the crowd.

"Get up you two! Now! Worth, let go of him! Now! Worth!"

Worth released his grip. Hume stood and brushed the grit from his face and pants.

"Hume, I thought I told you to *leave*. This is what I was talking about. You're trouble waiting to happen. Now get in your truck and get off school property before I call the Sheriff's Department!"

"But I..." Hume attempted.

"But *nothing*, Hume. Leave now!"

"Mr. Scott," Ellen interceded. "Hume did not start this fight. *Worth* started it. Hume didn't even have a chance to defend himself!"

The principle slid his glasses down to the end of his nose, looked at Ellen and offered, "Ellen, Hume attempted to crash the dance earlier tonight, saying he was your date. Whether he was or not is not my concern, but I don't think Mr. Reston would have approved if he *had* of been your date. Shall I tell him of tonight's events? I don't think you would like that, now would you?"

Ellen turned to Hume, her back to the principle, removed a handkerchief from her purse and wiped the blood from Hume's lips.

"You may tell my father if you please, Principle Scott. I *am*, but for a few more days, finished here at Monticello High School and will not need further guidance from you. I can, and will, make my own decisions in the future, including my personal matters."

With that said, she and Hume left the Monticello High School crowd in the darkness. After putting sufficient distance between them and the unpleasantness that had just transpired, Hume pulled off onto a sandy lane they had frequented before on happier evenings, stopped the car and massaged his swollen jaw.

"You think it might be broken, Ellen?"

"I can't see it very well in the dark, but it certainly looks swollen," she comforted as she gently rubbed his jaw. "That animal! I can't *stand* Worth Baker."

"Well it sure didn't look like you couldn't stand him when y'all were twirling around the dance floor."

"You *saw* that? It was only one dance and he insisted on that. He followed me around all night until I relented for that one dance. I'm sorry you saw that. You didn't deserve what happened tonight."

"Maybe I *do*, Ellen."

"What do you mean by that?"

"Worth Baker was right. My family is a stable of no-count losers. My daddy, uncles and granddaddy lost all that land back to the bank. From Reedy Fork to the Rockingham County line. How the hell do you *do* that? All he ended up with was that hardscrabble plot of land that he somehow farmed and eked out a living on."

"Well, something called The Depression certainly helped."

"That was just the final straw, Ellen. My family's decline started before that."

"Hume you're not like them. You are a good person. You have nothing in common with your father, except a last name."

"You're right, Ellen. I'm not like my father. Least that is what I tell myself before I go to bed every night. And I can tell you this. I plan to be a tobacco farmer myself. It's all I know, and since I don't own a high school diploma, that's probably all I can do anyway. I'm not going to go to work in a cotton mill. I'm gonna farm, but I'm not gonna fail. I swear to God, I'm gonna bring this family back. People will say the Rankin name with respect again, someday."

"I don't doubt you, Hume."

"Really, Ellen?"

"Of course I don't. If I did I wouldn't be sitting here with you now." Ellen turned Hume's head toward her and said, "They don't know you yet, Hume. I do. And they will."

And so was the relationship between the two men—one that was honed and nurtured on their dislike for each other, which accompanied them into manhood. Even though Hume eventually took Ellen for his wife, he never took Worth Baker lightly... as though the contest was over and he had won. He knew Baker's nature, and that nature played to the end. It never gave up.

Chapter 5

Spring 1958

Spring looked as if it would break early. An early spring never ceased to give Hume a feeling of optimism, which was usually backed up by what he had read in *The Farmer's Almanac*, as well as the signs he observed in the woods over the winter. He paid special attention to how the critters in the forest behaved, as well as the traits of the insects making their winter homes in the tree bark or under the carpet of decaying leaves on the forest floor.

"Come on, ole boy," Hume muttered, playfully patting Rhody on the hind end as he walked around to the side of his mule, tethered in the stall. "You and me've been through this a time or two before."

Through the years, Hume had taken notice that over the dark season, both he and his mule built up restlessness inside them. The creature endured the monotonous daily hunt out in the pasture for whatever grass nubs he could scrounge. Come the evening, when the mule was brought into the warmth of the barn, the four walls of the stall probably closed in on his nature. Hume felt a kinship. His relationships with his mules were intimate friendships. Same with most farmers. The death of a mule was never taken lightly. It was like the passing of an old friend that had shared and understood the hard life of tobacco farming. The farmer endured a period of mourning with each mule's passing.

From the tack room, he brought the same type of bit and the exact same harness he had used on his mules for the past sixteen years. He didn't hold much for curved bits. He preferred the straight ones. Some farmers swore by the curved bits, saying they reined in the mules and made them behave better in the field. Hume didn't cotton to that method. It seemed to him, a little cruel on the mule's mouth.

"Come now, open wide," he directed as the mule conformed.

There was a good reason why folks used the phrase "stubborn as a mule" to describe a hard head's affliction. But Hume's mules always seemed to have a willing disposition, all the way back to Lady, the white mule that was his first purchase as a young man. He had named it Lady out of the smartness of youth—mules are neither lady-like nor man-like—the poor creatures aren't either gender. Hume loved to see the look on city folk's faces when they first learned that a mule couldn't beget a mule—took a horse and a donkey to do that.

Must have something to do with the straight bit, Hume thought as he slipped the bridle over Rhody's large head, while simultaneously setting the bit in its opened mouth.

Seeing as how it had been a while since his mule had a bit in its mouth, Hume gave it a few minutes to sit. He gently stroked the animal under its massive jawbone. As soon as it appeared his mule remembered, he calmly placed the leather harness over its broad back. Rhody stood fifteen hands high, causing Hume, who was not a tall man, to have to go to his toes to complete the task. Finally, he ran the leather reins, now worn to an almost blondish color, along both sides of the mule, through the brass ringlets that held and guided the reins along the mule's withers to the rear.

Hume backed the big mule out of the stall, across the open dirt floor of the barn. He tugged on the left rein to turn Rhody out into the barnyard. He remembered how he used to hoist a young Alford up onto the animal's back and led the happy, giggling boy, straddled across the mule's broad back, out into the yard. Years since, he'd intended on bringing the younger boys out to continue the tradition as a rite of spring. But Ellen worried for young Alford's safety, perched atop such a tall mule. She had scolded Hume for his recklessness, so he thought better of it.

Once clear of the barn, he buttoned up his cotton twill jacket, pulled down his wide-brimmed hat and looked up at a turbulent March sky. Thick, gray-knotted clouds, back-dropped by a slate-blue sky, sent a cold wind across the still-barren landscape.

"We'll have days like this," Hume muttered more for himself than for his mule. "But the change ain't far off. The warming is near. Still, ain't no reason a man can't use a day like today to his advantage. Let's us go and wake up the land."

That said, both man and mule turned north, out of the barn's domain, and entered a path that cut into the thick woods that lined the backyard of the barn. The old trail wound through the woods, finding the way to the tobacco field. At one point along the path, another of Hume's smaller, older tobacco fields opened up on the right.

Ellen and the older children would set the this year's vegetable garden there. Then the path descended sharply, as the landscape broke away and fell downward to meet the creek below. Sure-footed mules had no problem negotiating that type of trail.

Part of the reason they were put on this earth, he mused. *Other part being they worked harder'n any man, and they didn't make a man feel guilty about the children needing new clothes when the old ones wore just fine.*

Hume's black 1945 Ford pickup was another story. Twice a year, spring and then fall, the old truck would make the precarious trek down and then back up the ravine. Hume and his brothers, Mose and Sanders, had built an old wooden bridge, standing just before the bend in the creek, allowing the Ford and all other wayfarers to cross without fear of being washed downstream when the creek swelled up. In the spring, Hume navigated the pickup down the path, stopping as he arrived at the top of the ravine to contemplate the downward negotiation. The winter's snow and rain always changed the features of the switch-backs—so much so that the trail took on a totally different look and feel each spring, demanding total attention and white knuckles as he inched the old truck down.

During the spring planting season, Hume used the truck to make runs to the creek to fill up two fifty-five gallon wooden barrels, which he kept in the truck bed to fill the tobacco setters which were used to inject the young plant into the soil. The plants were dropped into the setter's V-shaped chamber, and at the desired place along the row, the farmer would jam the tip of the cone, by hand, into the soil and pull a trigger releasing a flume of water that was contained in a separate chamber. This allowed him to set and water the young plant in the soil in one motion, where it would remain and grow under the summer sun. The young-uns made a game of running alongside the old pickup, jumping on the sideboards and hanging on as the truck bounced its way down to the creek. Hume filled the barrels, while they played on the sandy beach in the bend of the creek. Eventually, one of them bravely entered the chilly, springtime water, and soon, all would be dancing along on the river rocks that collected in the bottom of the creek bed, looking for crawfish hiding in the cool recesses.

On this day in late March, Hume leaned across the railing on the near side of the pickup truck's bed and admonished his daughters.

"Y'all be mindful now and take care not to wet your dresses. Ain't got time this morning to run any of you back to the house for a dry change."

He pulled out the double-bladed Old Timer pocketknife his daddy had given him on his twelfth birthday, and he pared off a thick slice of his favorite chew, Days Work plug tobacco. Using his right index finger as a base, he eased the knife blade through the brown rectangular shaped plug and placed the cutting in his lower right jaw, all the while gazing at his young-uns playing in the creek bed. His attention settled on Mary Ellen, his wife's namesake and the fifth oldest. He always felt his wife held partial to Mary Ellen, seeing as how she was the meekest of the females in the Rankin brood. Ellen always said that she "Loved seeing Mary Ellen coming," mainly because she didn't always try to control Ellen, or tell her what to do or not to do, like Fredericka and the others.

A lot like Ellen herself, Hume mused, smiling to himself as he recalled the look on Mary Ellen's face when, as a younger child, she had pleaded for a taste of the "chocolate brownie" he always carried in his trouser pocket. He finally relented once and cut her a small plug for her curious consumption. The initial look of glee soon turned to one of unexpected disgust. After sucking the juice from the plug, she expelled both brown broth and the malicious chunk of tobacco plug.

"Why did you do that?" she yelled at her father between gags.

"Cause you been asking for a taste since you were knee-high to a June bug," came Hume's brown stained, grinning response.

"Well you coulda just *told* me how awful it would be!" she retorted.

But again, just like her mother, the girl didn't forget, but did forgive him for the prank that only he saw the humor in.

Hume's thoughts came back to the present, to his five daughters playing on the river rock, splashing droplets of water up into the mid-morning sunlight that filtered down through the slatted openings in the thick forest roof above the creek. He likened the droplets to hundreds of sparkling diamonds, falling from the swaying limbs that hung over the rushing water.

If those were precious stones falling from the limbs hanging over the creek bed, there was not a doubt as to which of the five girls would gather up the most, filling both front pockets of her shift and then slipping a few more out of some of the other less suspecting sisters' pockets as well. *No doubt that one would be the eldest, Fredericka,* Hume thought to himself.

Walt Neal and his son Sam appeared on the far side of the bridge. "Morning Mista Hume," Walt hollered through cupped hands, as the creek was up and the girls' commotion in the stream made conversing somewhat difficult from this distance. The two closed the distance and Hume observed a nasty looking cut under Sam's right eye. The girls all shied from Walt. They had heard enough about his dark, rough world. All kept their distance, except Mary Ellen.

"Mista Hume, Alford said you wanted to talk to us about them plants," Walt said.

"Yeah, I gotta feeling things... What the *hell* happened to your eye, Sam?" Hume asked, turning his attention to Sam, in mid-sentence.

Sam stood looking off to the side, ignoring Hume's question.

"When we gonna start pulling them from the beds?" Walt asked, deflecting Hume's question.

Not satisfied with the answer to his question, Hume looked at Walt, then Sam, then back at Walt before he answered.

"I figure this morning seems to be about right. The weatherman said it looks as if it's gonna be mild the rest of this month and into April, same as the *Almanac.* How about you and Sam fill up those two barrels on the back of the truck and then we'll head on in. We'll pull some of the plants, enough to get started and then let the girls work on the rest. Alford will be here by then and we'll get started."

Walt and Sam pulled both barrels to the end of the truck where they would fill them with creek water from a pair of buckets. Fifty gallons of water was not a feat that two or three men could lift back up into a pickup's bed.

"Here," Walt said as he handed one of the buckets to Sam. "You start and I... I'll be right back." Sam knew, this morning, not to quarrel with his father.

Walt walked back up stream towards where the girls were playing, but he stopped short. Mary Ellen was downstream away from the others, squatting, facing the riverbank. Her lips moved in unintelligible words, her hands moving as if describing something in excitement.

"You see him up in there, child?" Walt said in a low voice.

"Yes, Uncle Walt," Mary Ellen said, not looking up. "He hasn't told me his name yet, but I believe he's the one Daisy told me about. This is the first time I've seen him, but I've talked to him before. He usually stays back up in the brush. But today he was out sunning himself on the rocks. He ran back up into the weeds when you walked up."

"What does he tell you?"

"He was telling me that they are paying attention to daddy, that this is his season. He said they would stay close, once they are called on. What do you think he means by that, Uncle Walt?"

"Lawd, child," Walt said through a toothless grin. "The world works in ways that's sometimes over my head. Daisy may know. But for now, I'd say to just stay where you are with your eyes open. Pay attention and listen. Daisy goes on sometimes about the little people in the middle world. Sounds like you just may have latched on to one there."

Mary Ellen looked up and smiled, "Think so, Uncle Walt?"

"It sure be sounding like it."

Chapter 6

Fall 1958

Hume met with C.E. Tenser, Vice President of North Carolina National Bank in the fall, to discuss his outstanding loans with the bank. Tenser had sent him a letter concerning the next year's tobacco crop and the balance owed from two years previous. Prior to that meeting, Hume had never met the new loan officer, but he understood Tenser had moved from Pittsburgh and had been in the Greensboro area less than a year.

Upon arrival, Hume reached for the bank's door handle, just as it was being opened from the other side. Awkward, he stumbled forward, like an old man chasing a hat being blown along the ground by a wayward wind. He stopped teetering when the top of his head met the chest of the person who'd opened the door from the other side, causing his wide-brimmed hat to fall to the floor, coming to rest on booted toes. Reaching down, he retrieved it and settled it back on his head. He rose slowly, muttering his apologies, only to meet Worth Baker's large, snickering face. Both men held a cold, empty stare for several seconds, until Baker finally broke the awkward moment by offering a slightest acknowledgement.

"Hume."

Rankin responded grudgingly with, "Worth."

"Planning on putting in a new crop next spring?" Baker asked through his smirk.

"Reckon so," Hume responded. "Springtime's still planting time, ain't it? Unless somebody's changed that without bothering to tell me."

"Never know, Hume," Baker replied tartly. "Just like seasons, things change."

"Meaning?"

"Admit it, Rankin. You've been struggling with that patch of land for some time now. Barely making ends meet each year. Maybe farming just ain't for you. Maybe you want to think about giving it up and going to work in the cotton mills. Steady pay, although on the low end. But you'd have a company providing you a guaranteed income and a mill house to provide for those nine young'uns.

Besides, I'd bet Ellen wouldn't mind moving back to town. Back to where her family came from."

"Where'd you come up with that mis-information, Baker? Things are fine over my way."

Again, both men's eyes locked in a silent stare until Baker broke the stalemate, stepping to the side in a mocking manner, ushering Hume into the bank lobby with a wave of his right arm, slightly bending at the waist.

"Might wanna think about it. Oh, and be sure and tell Ellen hello for me," Baker added. "Still think her stewed apples are the best in the county. Tell her that for me. Will you?"

Hume acted as if he did not hear Baker's last taunt. But without a doubt, he had.

Gathering himself, he entered the bank and looked around to see if anyone had observed his encounter with Baker. It appeared no one had, as everyone was busy and preoccupied. Scanning the lobby, Hume sensed a different atmosphere, a change from the last time he was here. He couldn't rightly put his finger on it. But something definitely had changed. Like the air just before winter's first snowfall. You just smelled it.

In the least, Hume expected more of a greeting than what he got on that day. Not one of the employees looked up and offered smiles or acknowledgements as he entered. All three tellers remained with their heads down, performing whatever task they were supposed to be doing, looking solemn as well. To the right sat Helen Watson, the bank's longtime receptionist. Hume angled over to her desk, took off his wide-brim hat, the one he kept clean for just such occasions, clutching it in his right hand and trailing it around his back to where it met the left hand.

"Good day, Ms. Watson. I trust you've had a nice summer and put away plenty for the winter," Hume offered.

"Good day, Mr. Rankin. Please be seated. Mr. Tenser will be with you shortly," Ms. Watson said curtly, ignoring his attempt to break the ice as she, too, went back to whatever she was doing before Hume walked in.

Feeling estranged, Hume edged over to the worn, brown leather couch and delicately slid up both pant legs so as not to wrinkle the freshly-creased khaki pants that Ellen had pressed for him that morning. He eased down onto the couch. Nervous, he fingered a dog-eared Saturday Evening Post magazine as he waited for the bank officer.

A fidgety twenty minutes or so passed before the door finally opened and Hume glanced at the figure of a man of slight height and build, bespectacled, with round-rimmed glasses that sat at the end of a sharp, pointed nose. The man was dressed in a conservative manner, in a freshly pressed brown suit with matching vest, completed with a hand-tied green-stripped bow tie.

"Mr. Rankin?" Tenser uttered in a flat, nasal tone.

"Yes sir," Hume responded, standing.

"Come into my office."

Hesitant, Hume entered and took a seat in the wooden, spindle-backed chair that faced Tenser's large wooden desk.

Chair's bout as uncomfortable as it looks, he thought to himself as Tenser walked around the desk to his chair.

Hume glanced around the office. Unlike the previous vice president's lavish decor, the walls were bare. Tenser, or somebody, had stripped the office of all vestiges of the previous occupant, or any occupant for that matter. Before, landscape paintings adorned the walls. The previous desk had been scattered with photographs of children and grandchildren. Lamps had warmed the corners of the room. Tenser's desk was stark, except for the neatly-stacked manila file folders to the right of his elbow. He obviously preferred the more direct, overhead lighting emitted from the white opaque glass fixture hanging from the ceiling in the middle of the room.

When Tenser sat down, the expanse of the desk, combined with his somewhat small stature, accentuated the distance between the two men.

Tenser put Hume on hold while he riffled through a manila file folder. He moved his pointed face up and down as he scanned the pages of the file, all the while making a high-pitched utterance that to Hume sounded somewhat gleeful. The file, Hume presumed, was his.

After several tense moments, Tenser spoke.

"Ahh... Mr. Rankin. It appears you have made a habit of being in arrears... Ahh, that is... being constantly behind on your balance to my bank. As far as our records go back, there have been periods of delinquencies... Ahh... you were behind in your payment to us. And, I see here that several years ago, we offered to lend you five thousand dollars for the purchase of a tractor and perhaps retire that old mule of yours. But you refused to change."

Hume attempted to explain.

"Well, Mr. Tenser, that's the way we've done it here for years, during my years of farming as well as my daddy's. North Carolina National Bank has known us and understood our plight as farmers, but they have always known us to be good on our word and knew we'd pay what we owed soon as the next good crop comes in. And we all got families..."

"Mr. Rankin," Tenser interjected, "that was yesterday, a time that I do not hold in appreciation. This is today, which means I loan you a specific amount of money to put your crops in, for a specific amount of time. If, at that assigned time, you do not pay me back what you owe me, plus interest, I will be forced to initiate 'Due Process.' And that, Mr. Rankin, is a remedy available to me by law. You do understand that we currently have a lien on your land and equipment? From here forward, each year's loan will be paid in full by the end of that year, that being at tobacco auction time. Are we now clear on this?" came the high-pitched screech from the vice president.

Sitting uneasy in his uncomfortable chair, Hume shifted positions by moving forward, as if starting to stand. Feeling threatened, Tenser responded by bringing both hands up, as if to cover his face. Upon seeing that Hume was simply changing his position in his chair and meant no harm to him, Tenser attempted to restore some of his lost dignity by adopting somewhat of a conciliatory attitude.

"You do understand we have rules that we must strictly follow, don't you, Mr. Rankin? We must if North Carolina National Bank is to continue its splendid growth pattern, which entails more preferred services for its customer base. I'm sure you understand growth, what with being a farmer and all. You *do* wish for growth each season in your tobacco stalks, now don't you, Mr. Rankin? Growth, which is derived from the rain that hopefully falls on your stalks in a timely manner? Just as we depend on your timely payments, so as to grow *our* stalks, if you will."

Feeling talked down to, Hume gave it back as good as he got.

"I *do* get your point, Mr. Tenser, and I can appreciate what you're saying. I *do* depend on the rain and sunshine to grow my crops. You're dead right there. But if I look back at history, there ain't been a season yet that the rain ain't finally come through. May have been late and caused me worry. May have been more sparse one year and caused the yield to be less. But in the end, it all evens out. One year may be lean, but I more than make up for it the next year or the year after. And this bank ain't never took a loss on account of me. Or from my daddy, either."

At that, Tenser came unglued. Standing up behind his large desk, an act that made him look all the more diminutive, he looked like a skinny bird trying to take off, waving its scrawny wings as he screeched across the expanse.

"Mr. Rankin! Do *you* see your daddy in here? I don't! He and his time have gone! They are just a memory now. And our records indicate that he and his brothers sold a considerable amount of their land back to the bank to avoid foreclosure. So I don't want to hear about your daddy and the way he conducted business again. Do we understand each other?"

Hume then understood that this man, this Tenser, did not know or appreciate the ways of the South. A man was a gentleman and was treated as such until proven otherwise. *If you've got business with someone, you take it up with him, but you never insult a man's family in the process.* Tenser's manner was brusque, bullying. It was apparent he looked down on the small farmers and wanted little to do with them. He had just made it clear to Hume that all balances, including the current 1958 balance would be paid off in full by at the end of the coming year's tobacco auction."

Hume could no longer hold his tongue.

"I may be a man of the land and with that, as people like you understand us to be, somewhat uneducated, but I fully understand your intent, Mr. Tenser. However, I would like to ask you just one question," Hume's jaw muscles knotted as he spoke through clinched teeth. "Just what is it that is in people like you that make you to wanna come down here and not only change mules in the middle of the row, but feel the need to insult a man while looking down at him as you mount that new mule?"

"You people think..." Tenser uttered.

Hume cut him off.

"Mr. Tenser, this is the first time I ever met you, and to my knowledge, I ain't never crossed you or cut across your path. I just come in today, at your request, to account for my fall bill. I've been doing that for years, just like my daddy done. But in your world, it looks as if a man's word don't account for much. You've laid out the new rules clear. And I got to admit, it looks as if the reins are in your hands for now. But take my word, Tenser—I don't know what it's like where you come from, but down here, taking a man's land is a very serious thing. And it ain't done without a fight. And that's what you can expect, Mr. Tenser, if you're intent on riding this mule you've mounted—a fight. The good Lord willing, and the creek don't rise, you'll have your money paid back by the end of next year's harvest. Good day, Mr. Tenser."

As he stomped through the bank lobby, the pounding in his head and the shade of crimson he was seeing through dimmed his vision and obscured any knowledge of whether or not any of the bank employees had attempted to acknowledge him as he left.

Hume reached the black pick-up and in one quick motion, ratcheted the door handle open, slid under the steering wheel and slammed the door shut. After turning the ignition, he simultaneously smashed the accelerator to the floor, causing the old black truck to cough in response. In no time, he reached the city limits, gladly leaving city people behind. Hume had one thing on his mind, and that was to get back to his land and simmer over what had just happened.

He bypassed his home, as he elected to leave the hard surface road on which it stood and take an old logging road instead. The road eventually connected with the trail behind his livestock barn. Moments later, Hume found himself at the precipice above the creek, overlooking his beloved fourteen acres of cleared farmland. To the rear of the field stood the barn his daddy had erected. Hume paused and observed the landscape under a fading October sky. The hardwoods, which were mixed in among the pines, were well into the season's change. Oranges, reds, and yellows of all shades dotted the tree-lined canvas, with evergreen being the primary background color. Splashes of purple and gold were thrown across the sky, adding to the warm, mellow hue of the landscape.

The scene momentarily froze Hume. God, how he loved this time of day! It didn't matter whether it was spring, summer or fall. Being washed in this moment gave him a feeling that filled him.

He eased the old Ford down the switchbacks and reached the creek, which presently flowed full. Crossing the wooden bridge, Hume stopped his truck and listened to the sound of the water as it bounced its way over the smooth river rock. At times, Hume swore he could hear voices in that creek. On occasions, it was a crowd of voices in a cacophony of chatter. Other times, usually when the creek was low and meandering, it was just a few lone utterances in a slow drawl.

On this day, there were many voices present.

He drifted as he listened, mesmerized, as the waters passed below the wooden bridge and flowed past the bend. Able to take only so much of it, he shook his head to clear himself from total immersion of these soul-voices in the creek. Mary Ellen had a name for the little fairy-like people who, she said, lived along the creek bank. She told Hume she had seen them, little people she likened to elves. Only Mary Ellen had another name for them. She called them "woodland fairies," or "elfins," or something as such.

Sure enough, at times when Hume found himself coming under the spell of the river voices, he felt a sudden chill and for a silly moment, swore to himself that he saw movement up on the bank, and back in the trees of the forest that lined the creek bank. Mary Ellen's imagination was contagious. But even a momentary entertainment of such an idea was silly for a grown man—too silly a subject to ever broach with another living being.

Moving quickly across the bridge and following the path up to the barn, he pulled the truck up under the overhang. In late summer's priming time, the overhang was full of family and hired help, some of whom emptied the sleds and handed the tobacco leaves in bundles of three to the stringer. The stringer would tie the stalks on each side of the stick until it was full and then holler out, "Stick off!"

Next, one of the older handers would lift the stick from the wooden frame, (called a "horse," that horizontally held the loaded tobacco stick) and laid it on the ground at the end of the overhang. When the men came in at the end of the day, they would climb up into the barn, and the loaded sticks would be passed up to others who were positioned up in the barn's rafters.

The sticks, swollen with sticky tobacco leaves, would be placed on the rafters, where they would remain for curing. Hume always likened that part of the barn to a front porch, or a social hall. It was where people congregated, shared news, and swapped lies as they worked or waited for a fresh sled full of tobacco, drawn in from the field by the sweat-lathered, high-stepping mule, with Hume at the reins, perched on the sled's runners.

Hume cut the truck engine. He eased himself from under the steering wheel and walked aimlessly into the field. Just about midway in, he stopped. Feeling a need, he dropped to his hind side, down onto the sandy soil. Then, he did something totally contrary for a man who removes his boots only for a bath, or just before ending his day. Hume found himself untying his bootlaces.

He then removed his boots and pulled off his white, cotton socks, while watching the October sky change in shape and color above him. Leaning back to watch the astral show, he set both palms down onto the soil, while extending his painfully white bare feet out in front of him. What happened next, he couldn't explain. Without a conscious understanding, the farmer began clawing and digging his fingers and his toes into the ground, moving each digit back and forth, digging deeper and deeper into the cool October soil, until both feet and hands were buried in the loamy earth. He didn't know why he found himself suddenly buried up to his wrists and ankles in field-dirt. He just felt a need.

Chapter 7

Ellen sat at the table in the dimly-lit kitchen. The children had all been fed, their dishes cleaned and put away. The two eldest girls, Fredericka and Emmaline, made sure the younger siblings bathed before putting them in bed. It was past dark and time for the lights to go out in the upstairs bedrooms.

Across the table from Ellen sat Hume's supper. The fried chicken, turnip greens, fried fatback and cornbread lay cold on his plate. She knew he had an appointment at the bank that afternoon, but she had not heard from him since he left, and he had not shown up for dinner. She'd asked Alford if he would walk out and about the farm to see if he saw any signs of his father or his black truck, but Alford, in his curt way, suggested that doing so would be a foolish waste of his time, and Alford's time was not to be wasted.

As was Mary Ellen's nurturing nature, she sensed her mother's worried silence at dinner and came back downstairs, sitting beside her at the long, empty table.

"Don't worry Momma. Daddy will be all right."

"Oh I know, Mary Ellen," she replied. "But still, I wish I could be as sure of that as you sound," she added under her breath.

"I *am* sure, Momma."

"And what makes you so sure?" Ellen inquired, somewhat hopefully.

"Cause the wee people are out tonight. You know—pixies, the elfins. They're all out tonight, working late under the harvest moon. I saw them at twilight tonight, just before you made us come in. And Jebeddo told me, even though he's been acting up, they would take care of Daddy and let no harm come to him tonight."

"And just who in the world is Jebeddo," Ellen asked?

"Jebeddo is the elder farm pixie and lives in the rafters of Rhody's barn. His cousin, Roondar is a forest pixie. Jebeddo told me he and Roondar had decided to let no harm come to Daddy tonight."

"Lord, Mary Ellen... I don't know. Any living being—no matter what their brain size—who would *choose* to live in the rafters of that dirty ol barn, has been breathing too much mouse dust! I just don't know if I could put much faith in whatever they said," Ellen teased.

Standing silently in the hallway with her back against the wall, listening to the conversation between Mary Ellen and her mother, Fredericka bristled with resentment. How in the world Mary Ellen could carry on such nonsense with their mother, who was responding in kind, was completely outside Fredericka's circle of understanding.

Mary Ellen's sweetness and innocence appalled Fredericka.

Bursting through the doorway into the kitchen, Fredericka, a sneer across her face, startled Ellen and Mary Ellen in mid-sentence. Both mother and daughter knew the look all too well. When enraged, Fredericka's upper lip would quiver and a little white line would dissect the middle of it.

"What is this molasses you're spreading about good fairies that are gonna protect Daddy from any harm or evil will? You don't believe that stuff any more'n I do, Mary Ellen. You're just trying to sugar coat the fact that he didn't come home and that he don't care *who* he hurts!"

"Now, Fredericka..." Ellen started.

"Now nothing, Momma," Fredericka bellowed. "When are you gonna stop protecting her and make her grow up! She's thirteen-years-old! She can't go through this world, skipping along, thinking everybody and everything is just peachy. Cause everybody and everything *isn't*."

Having tolerated Fredericka's tongue-lashings before, Mary Ellen stood and excused herself from the table, understanding that to be the best recourse to save herself and her mother from further abuse. She hated when Fredericka erupted, and she felt guilty for causing her sister's venom to be directed at her gentle mother.

Fredericka had her eye on Mary Ellen, much more so than the other sisters. Mary Ellen was well aware of her sister's scrutiny and thought it was because the other sisters had tougher exteriors. They could deflect Fredericka's arrows back at her in a give and take manner. That, and the fact Mary Ellen was the one most like their mother and was her namesake. She understood it was the cause of Fredericka's aggression and tried to avoid conflict with her older sister, or conflict with the others, for that matter. Her sisters,

Mirabelle and Emmaline, constantly chastised her for her meekness.

"Why don't you stand up to her and set her in her place?" Mirabelle would scold. "It's just gonna keep getting worse if you don't stand up for yourself."

Emmaline was more direct.

"You are such a weakling. You are scared to death of Fredericka. You'll never amount to anything because people are going to walk all over you all your life."

If Mary Ellen fought back, it was with a simple, "No I'm not."

She didn't see the need. Fredericka was just something she had accepted as being a condition of her life. She never saw the need to tell her sisters that Fredericka's best friend was secretly wearing their mother's pendant with the initials, M. E. R. It had disappeared the day after Fredericka heard their mother tell Mary Ellen that since the locket bore her initials, it would one day be hers.

The full moon strained hard against its celestial restraints, seeming to swell, so as to shed more of its light on the black speck in the field below. It appeared to slowly distend itself closer to earth to better illuminate the curious figure below. The moon detected a faint glimmer, as if a reflection of its own moonlight was being sent back toward it. Coming more into focus, the moon was able to make out the figure of a man, sprawled on his back in the field below. The left arm hung lazily from the side of the body; the right arm was splayed out, above the head. The reflection came from a shining object, held at the end of the right arm. Moving ever closer, the moon was just barely able to make out the letters:

S-o-u-t-h-e-r-n C-o-m-f-o-r-t

Chapter 8

Spring 1959

Fall melded into winter, which in turn, yielded to spring. Hume and Alford rose, as usual, well before first light. Earlier Ellen quietly slipped out of the warm, damp sheets, and draped her thin, cotton housecoat over her shoulders before easing down the staircase. She cooked breakfast, which would be consumed by Hume and Alford, mostly in silence. After the men were fed, she would turn her attention to preparing the morning meal for the rest of the family.

She awakened the children soon as Hume and Alford took leave of the house, independently of each other, heading for the fields, where they would be met by Walt and his son, Sam. Walt was shirtless, his faded blue bib-overalls exposing long, black, leathery arms, which led up to bare, bony shoulders. He wore a pair of old, worn brogans to protect the thinning soles of his feet. Sam, much younger, still sported thick, tough skin on the bottoms of his feet, enabling him walk across rocks and stones without flinching. He worked barefoot in the sandy soil.

The spring of 1959 came earlier than usual. The seeds were set in early February, and Hume and Walt performed the daily, monotonous chore of weeding the new plant beds. That year, Hume and Rhody finished turning the land in mid-March, as opposed to the usual April opening. He and Alford had included preparing the New Ground for planting that year, as Tenser's new rules deemed it necessary.

The early thawing of the ground allowed him such an advantage, and he was going to have to make use of all the breaks in order to meet Tenser's demands. In April, again beating the usual mid-May setting of the plants, Walt, Sam, Hume and Alford began the task of pulling the plants out of the plant bed by hand, one by one. They then gently placed the plants in wooden crates, to be transported to the field for setting. During this early stage of the cultivation, Hume walked along one side of a row with the tobacco transplanter, while Alford walked beside him on the other side of the row, with the plants, dropping them in the setter's chamber, one at a time.

Across the field, Walt, transplanter in hand, worked with Sam on the other side of the row, both appearing in the sunlight as shadowy images of Hume and Alford. After all was said and done, the men set approximately 6,000-7,000 plants per acre. After long grueling days spent under the spring sky, the four men would finally meet in the middle of the field, signaling the end of that phase of the planting cycle.

And so it was, on that much anticipated day in April 1959, upon completion of the setting of the tobacco plants, Hume leaned against his transplanter, mopped his dripping brow, looked up into the afternoon sky, and saw storm clouds, brewing in the east.

Chapter 9

Summer 1959

The cultivation process kept Hume, Walt, Sam, and Alford bent over nearly all of June. The sun burned bright and hot in a cloudless, Carolina-blue sky—with such blueness that the sunlight took on a surreal light, illuminated in a silvery hue.

Thus far, the sun seemed to have its way, except for an occasional afternoon tease of benign thunderheads. Hume scanned the June skies, daily at first, then more often than not—hourly, as dry June days blended into the next. Historically, June produced most of the summer rain, but now, well into mid-June, there hadn't been as much as an afternoon shower.

"What's your take on this, Walt?"

"Take on what, Mista Hume?"

"This lack of rain. Think it's a sign of things to come?"

"Don't rightly know, Mista Hume. Been studyin on that myself. Ain't quite right to go this far into summer, and the ground be dry as a hound's chewed-up bone."

"Kinda concerns me, Walt. The Almanac don't specify this being a lean month for rain."

"Sho nuff. Might wanna see what Daisy says about the signs. She always be dabblin in the haint world, ya know."

"Naw. I don't know, Walt. What do you mean, *dabblin in the haint world?*"

"You know, Mista Hume, the dark world on the other side—in that place where haints be. Daisy calls on them sometime, when things get bad. Some people go to church and ask the good Lord for help—some call on the dark side. That be Daisy."

"Didn't know she was *that* superstitious, Walt."

But then again, lots of colored folk, women especially, dabbled in the world of signs, hexes, spells and all, Hume thought.

"I don't reckon it could hurt, Walt. Yeah... go ahead and see what she says."

Hume glanced up, taking another reading of the sky. Shielding his eyes, he gazed to the south, over the top of the hill on the other side of the creek, where the switch-backs began, leading down to the wooden bridge at the creek.

As he scanned the expanse, he caught sight of something at the top of the precipice, appearing as the dark shape of a figure up on the top of the rise. Pulling his hat down closer to his eyebrows, Hume squinted and peered at the figure, which again appeared to be the dark shape of a man standing motionless, as if observing them from the summit. The form, in some unexplainable way, had a familiarity to it.

"Alford," Hume called, summoning his son, "Your eyes are better'n mine. Take a look up to the top of the hill and tell me if you see someone up there."

Alford leaned against his hoe and cast his eyes in the direction his father indicated, his flattened hand pressed against his brow, shielding his eyes from the bright sunlight. He too, glimpsed the dark outline of a figure, perched atop the hill. The person seemed to be studying the four farmers.

"Yep," Alford reported. "Looks like we're being watched."

"Can you tell who it is?"

"Naw, Daddy. Not from here, especially with the sun at his back."

Whoever was up there, had to come across Hume's land at the home place to arrive at the perch above them. Hume didn't like that. He dropped his hoe and started across the field, clearing two rows at a time, cupping both hands and hollering up at the figure.

"Hey you! What are you doing on my land? You hold it right there!"

The figure made its first movement, sideways, and disappeared into the stand of apple trees that crowned the peak.

"Alford... come with me. Walt, you and Sam keep working your side of the field," Hume instructed before entering the darkness of the woods to cross the creek on the wooden bridge.

Just as Hume's feet found the far side of the bridge, Alford entered the shaded canopy of the forest and hollered out to his father.

"What's your hurry! Probably just Mose or Sanders."

"Naw, it ain't," Hume muttered to himself, as he started up the switch-backs with Alford close behind.

Arriving at the top of the precipice, both were panting from the run and stopped momentarily, bending over with hands on knees to recover from the exertion.

Hume was the first to stand and walk into the small grove of trees. Alford followed a moment later and found his father, kneeling on the ground, holding a twig in his right hand. He stirred the ground.

"Had time to smoke himself a few," Hume surmised. He used the twig as a wand, circling an area in front of him, about two feet in circumference. Then he pointed to three "Lucky Strike" butts that had been freshly stubbed out in the soil.

"Being that most folks don't chain smoke three of these coffin nails in a row, I reckon he'd been up here eyeing us for a while," he concluded.

Although tobacco was their product, most tobacco farmers who Hume knew *chewed* tobacco, but did not smoke it. He didn't rightly know *why* that was. Only thing Hume could relate to was himself, and he just never cottoned to firing up. But he sure loved a good chew. However, there was one man standing out in his mind who *did* light-up. Only, Hume was not certain of his *brand*. He made a mental note to find that out.

"Whadaya figure he was looking at?"

"Don't rightly know, Alford. Reckon we'd better be mindful and keep our eyes open in the future. Ain't a big thing. Not right now. But still, be mindful. Why don't you go on back down and work Walt and Sam until quitting time. Send them home early if ya like. I'll leave that up to you."

"Daddy, don't you want to spread out and take a look around?"

"Naw. You take care of things down in the field for me. I'll scout around up here some, and then head on back to the house."

He watched his son disappear down the path and into the woods before returning his attention to the three cigarette butts.

Probably making a mountain out of a molehill, he thought to himself.

Still, with what had transpired at the bank last fall, something in his gut told him different.

Hume pushed himself from his squatting position with both hands, letting out a soft grunt. Standing up to recreate the view the figure had observed, he surmised that the intent was not to learn something or gain some type of information, as there was not much to be gained from that vantage point. The spot was more of a thinking, contemplating perspective, as if the figure enjoyed simply mulling and pondering over the scene below.

Hume put the butts in his pocket—not so much as to preserve the evidence, but owing more to the fact that he couldn't stand the thought of an intruder littering his land with discarded cigarette butts. Looking down on the field below, he observed Walt and Sam, glistening in the sun as they worked, a pair of ninety-degree angles, cultivating the rows of tobacco stalks. Momentarily, Alford entered the field from the forest below and approached the two black men.

As Hume observed the three men in conversation he felt a sense of family and loyalty. Alford was his boy. He was wayward at times, but he worked hard when he wanted to. And even though Hume and Alford had words often enough, he still felt his son's allegiance.

And there was Walt and his son, Sam, who had been with Hume for right near fifteen years. Sam had been out in the fields since he was old enough to stuff bundles of tobacco under each arm. Both were steady workers and faithful friends, even though the relationship had its boundaries. *A man knows who he can count on. And those who can be counted on can be counted as family or friend, I reckon*, Hume thought. *Even if the friend's skin is a shade darker than mine, it don't matter none.*

Hume held his gaze for a few moments more before taking a cursory walk around the top of the knoll. Finding nothing more of interest, he turned and headed south, through the woods for the house.

Hume arrived at the screen door, entered the back porch and started for the wash sink. Since he had cut the day short, he decided the customary wash off was not warranted, and he entered the kitchen without one.

His arrival startled Ellen.

"Lord, Hume! You frightened me. I wasn't expecting you home this hour," she blurted, spinning around.

"Yeah, well I just thought I'd call it early today."

Somewhat taken back, Ellen replied, a mite hopeful.

"Well Hume... that's nice. Anything you had in *mind* for your afternoon off?"

"Yeah... I reckon I'll pour me a glass of sweet tea and go sit under the shade tree out front and read the almanac. You got some, ain't ya?"

Looking toward Ellen, and then around her, he spotted a container of stewed apples on the counter behind her. It appeared to Hume as if she was trying to hide the container by moving to her right, so as to cut off his view. The last time he'd given any thought to Ellen's apples was the day he had the run-in with Worth Baker at the bank.

"What's them *apples* out for?" Hume demanded.

"What? Oh *those*?" Ellen nervously flitted, waving her right hand in the air as she moved back and forth in front of the counter. She finally landed to the left, exposing the container.

"Those are for supper. I'm fixing your favorite tonight... tomatoes, cucumbers, black-eyed peas, corn on the cob and stewed apples. I took them out of the icebox to let them come to temperature," she offered.

"You took them out of the icebox to come to temperature *this* early? What? We starting to eat supper at four o'clock now days?" Hume questioned Ellen, his head cocked at an angle, both eyebrows raised.

"No Hume. I just thought about them as I walked by the icebox and decided to..."

Head still cocked, but eyebrows now lowered to cover narrow, squinting eyes, he inquired, suspiciously.

"Worth Baker been round here today?"

"Worth Ba...who...why would he..." she stammered.

"Dammit woman, don't you lie to me! You damn well better tell me the truth, so help me!" he thundered, grabbing Ellen by her right shoulder with his left hand. He raised his right hand, which ended in an ugly ball.

Ellen's ashen face framed panicked-filled eyes. Her look of bewildered horror was captured in a freeze-frame image in Hume's mind just as Mary Ellen entered the kitchen from the hallway.

"Daddy!" Mary Ellen screamed. "What are you *doing*?"

Hume's head rotated between his daughter and his wife, who he presently held in an unfamiliar embrace.

"Gotdammit!" Hume bellowed. "I don't *need* this! Not from the two of you! Not from *anybody*! But I will say this and I *mean* it! If Worth Baker *ever* comes on my property again, I'll kill him!"

Releasing Ellen's shoulder, his right arm dropped limply to his side, the menacing club now reduced to a bewildered appendage with no place to go.

He turned and stomped out of the kitchen onto the back porch, yanked open the screen door and came face to face with Earlene Wyrick. She was the neighborhood gossip, who had been at the back screen door, frozen in place with her knuckles tucked, preparing to knock as Hume made his exit.

"What the hell do you want, you ol busy-body," Hume shouted as he made his way past the stunned woman and into the backyard. On the way, he kicked at the family's black and tan coon hound, Dixie, who had made the mistake of taking a nap under an oak tree, directly in Hume's path of retreat.

Arriving at the chicken coop in the back of the yard, it came to Hume's fragmented attention that the chickens were in a state—running about, flapping their wings, with not a fox in sight. He recalled that Walt's wife, Daisy, used to spout about an old wives tale, allowing that when chickens behaved in this manner, a storm was rite nigh. It was at that moment, when something else caught his attention. There, at the edge of the coop, was an empty, crumpled-up cigarette pack. Bending down to retrieve it, he stood up and slowly unfolded it, revealing the stark black brand name against a red, circular bull's-eye background: *LUCKY STRIKE*.

"Well! I can see I came to call at a bad time. I'll get back to you another time, Ellen," Earlene Wyrick responded in her normal, sanctimonious manner.

"Yes, Earlene. I think that might be a good idea," Ellen shot back. "And in the future, my phone works just fine. From now on, you may want to call before you come peeking through my back door."

"Well, I've *never*!" the neighbor exclaimed in a huff, as she turned and made her way across the backyard.

Feeling weak and somewhat nauseous, Ellen staggered to the kitchen table and slid into a high-backed chair. Mary Ellen, ever observant, ran over to the Kelvinator and pulled out the half-gallon glass container of ice water. She filled a tall glass and set it in front of her mother.

"Momma, you look peaked. Here, *drink* this," she pleaded, pointing to the sweating glass of water.

Ellen pulled out the white lace handkerchief, which she kept tucked in her bra, and wiped at the perspiration dotting her forehead and cheeks.

"Thank you, dear."

"What happened, Momma?"

"I don't know, Mary Ellen. I just don't know what's got into that man. Meanness has just overcome him lately. He isn't the same man I married. And his drinking's gotten so... Oh, what am I doing talking to *you* about such ugly, grown-up things?"

"It's okay, Momma. Maybe I know more than you think I should."

Wiping the moisture from the corners of her eyes, Ellen looked at her daughter through a distant gaze.

"It's got something to do with men. I don't understand all of it, but Jebeddo told me Daddy is gonna have a chance to get it all right—to learn something that men have to learn. Jebeddo had a name for it. Called it 'straightening in the fire'... or 'straightening by fire'... something like that. But he said this is Daddy's time to learn. And if he does, he's gonna be all right. Jebeddo said he's a good man, deep inside, and the little people are gonna do what they can to help him along, because daddy needs to find that goodness again."

Ellen's stare cleared as she looked into Mary Ellen's soft, brown eyes.

"Hon, not now. I can't clutter my mind with anything else right now. I've got thinking to do. How about checking on the children?"

Mary Ellen returned the intense gaze.

"Okay, Momma. I understand. They told me older folks' minds have a harder time believing. Like you, right now. Your mind's too busy to see."

"Believing in what? See what?" Ellen asked, somewhat impatiently.

"In *their* world—*the in-between world*," Mary Ellen said over her shoulder as she took her leave of the room.

Chapter 10

Ellen sat at the table, mulling over what had happened. She couldn't understand what brought Hume home so early, or how he knew about Worth Baker's visit. Worth had been standing on the back steps, holding the screen door open as he conversed with Ellen about the children and her stewed apples.

Worth hadn't said where he was headed, but she figured he was bound for the tobacco fields, given the direction he was going when he left. To be sure, Ellen felt an unexpected stirring, somewhere in her being, as she stood there, talking innocently enough, to the ruggedly-handsome man. She found herself looking down into his face after answering the unexpected knock at the back door.

"Miss Ellen," Worth Baker had said to Ellen as he stood on the top back step. "I haven't had the opportunity to speak with you in some time now. Seems I never make it to church anymore—always something going on at the farm—but I was in the area and just wanted to stop by and see how you and the children are doing? I haven't seen them, or you, for that matter, in a while. I bet them young-uns are growing like weeds."

"That they are, Worth. Alford just graduated high school, but just isn't sure what he wants to do. He's shown an interest in attending State College to study agriculture or animal husbandry or something along those lines."

"He ain't interested in staying *here* and taking over the farm someday?"

"No, not at all. He says he feels trapped here and wants no part of tobacco farming to be in his future. I guess I understand. Young folks are different from us old fogies," she shrugged, smiling off into the distance. "They want to broaden their horizons, I guess."

"Graduated from high school, did he? Seems like just yesterday that you and me crossed that stage. You and he make the second generation to graduate from Monticello, doesn't it?"

"Well, yes... I guess if you look at it that way..."

"I can understand Alford not wanting to work with his daddy, as ornery as he can be at times, and all," Worth suggested.

"Well, no—I don't really think *that's* it..."

"By the way, you still make those stewed apples? Like the ones that won you first prize at the fair?"

"Well, yes...yes I do, Worth, and thank you for remembering that. My... that was so long ago."

"Well, some memories settle into a man's head that he can't get rid of, no matter how hard he tries."

"I'm touched that you remember all that, Worth. Would you like for me to pull a container from the Kelvinator for you?"

"I tell you what, Ellen. You *do* that! I'll pick them up on my way back through."

"Well, Worth, maybe you better take them now. I don't ..."

"Thank you Ellen. I sure do appreciate that. I'll be back through here in a little while to pick them up," he said over his shoulder as he left the backyard.

He hadn't stopped back by to pick up the apples like he said he would. She shook her head and started out the back door, as she needed to think. Striding off the back porch and into the yard, she suddenly felt she wasn't in a place where she needed or wanted to be. After all, it was the same yard that both Worth and Hume had just appeared from and then disappeared into. The backyard contained too much recent unpleasantness for the moment.

She walked to the front of the house and settled herself in one of the two metal spring-back chairs under the big maples—chairs she and Hume sat in during the cool of the evenings, discussing, or not discussing, whichever felt natural.

Ellen's mind wandered back to the beginning of her relationship with Hume. Ellen's daddy's folks, the Reston's, came to the Piedmont from Walnut Cove, a quaint town in the foothills of Stokes County, when Ellen was in her early teens. The Reston's of Stokes County were numerous and somewhat prominent folks, especially before the Civil War.

Ellen's granddaddy and great uncle were businessmen who made respectable livings, owning a tannery and a railroad-tie business, respectively. Ellen's family name was highly regarded. Her great uncle, Seneca Reston, was a lieutenant colonel in the Confederate Army who was killed leading the second charge at the Battle of First Manassas in Virginia. Folks said the colonel was a man who knew no fear (though perhaps *just a tad might have been prudent*, seeing as to the outcome, Hume always countered).

Ellen first met Hume right after she had turned sixteen, the summer before her sophomore year at Monticello High School. It was at a "covered dish supper" at Lee's Chapel Methodist Church on a warm Wednesday night in June. Since her people were Episcopalian, she did not tell her parents that she was going to a Methodist church with friends. Episcopalians thought of Methodists in the same way that Methodists thought of Baptists, so attending a Methodist function was "beneath" the fine Episcopal descendants of English lineage.

Sitting under the spread of a hundred-year-old oak tree with a group of friends while eating fried chicken, Ellen first laid eyes on Hume, who was eating a tomato sandwich just across the churchyard. She was staring at the attractive stranger when, at that very moment she glanced over, a more than generous slather of mayonnaise ran from a corner of the sandwich and onto his chin.

As he went to wipe his chin with the back of his hand, Hume's eyes caught Ellen's. Frozen in place, and thinking the better of it, he slowly reached around and pulled a freshly folded handkerchief from his back pocket and made himself presentable again. The shy smile that recomposed his tanned face endeared Ellen instantly. The dark-haired boy had a bashfulness about him, yet there was also an air of confidence, that enabled him to recover from a potentially embarrassing social situation with just a smile.

She and Hume were properly introduced that evening, and both experienced an immediate attraction. Throughout the rest of that summer, the two renewed their acquaintance at church socials, Brunswick stews, and hay-rides, each eyeing the other with bashful side-glances, until one or the other overcame the awkwardness of the moment by having the gumption to break the ice.

With each meeting and renewal, the acquaintance seemed to pick up right where they left it the last time. Not long into conversation, friends could hear their laughter and giggles threading through the exchange. She would occasionally touch Hume's forearm, patting it ever so gently in appreciation for making her laugh.

On the first day of their sophomore year, Hume and Ellen experienced the giddiness of being assigned to the same class. Hume saw her first as she stood on the other side of the room, in front of a large, paned window. The sunlight, streaming across her dark hair, made it appear as if fine silver threads were woven through it. Hume let the moment run as he folded his arms and leaned against the blackboard, observing her beauty from a distance.

Ellen was in animated conversation with another student who Hume did not recognize, flaunting her right arm back and forth in describing the subject at hand. In the middle of her deliberation, she suddenly glanced to her left and spotted Hume across the room, her arm pausing in mid-motion. His smile disengaged her thought process, causing her to stop in mid-sentence and gaze excitedly at the face of her newfound classmate.

The two became a couple. Schoolmates speculated Hume and Ellen would probably marry as soon as their senior year was over. However, unbeknownst to them, and without forewarning, circumstances forced Hume to suddenly leave school in order to take care of his family's farming business, due to his father taking ill. It was an act of selflessness for which his father never expressed gratitude. Ellen felt his having to leave school was such a deep blow to Hume's "manly" feelings.

He had been a good student and excelled at math. Having to quit high school, he was never to be able to obtain his degree, while Ellen remained and got hers. The sacrifice created a deep hurt in Hume that would always remain. It was that, and the fact Worth Baker sat behind Ellen in class during their senior year and followed her across the stage when they received their diplomas at graduation. The memory of that curtailed any high school reminiscing between the two past the eleventh grade. For Hume, it was as if senior year never happened.

The Rankins were land people. Hume's daddy and his three brothers and his grandfather started buying land in the Brown Summit area, and at one time, well before the Great Depression, the Rankins owned all the land, stretching from Reedy Fork Ranch to the Rockingham County line—several thousand acres, it was told. They were tough, crusty, rural folks.

Hume's daddy was a hard cuss, who never backed down from any man. And he dealt with Hume, his youngest son, with the same iron fist he used to mete out justice to others. His will was as hard as his fists, which made for a bad combination when raising a boy, especially when that boy could never do anything right in his father's eyes. Hume's two older brothers were able to escape their daddy's wrath by marrying and leaving home early, while Hume remained behind to bear the father's brunt.

Ellen's folks, on the other hand, were sophisticated people of English descent, who lived in the well-to-do neighborhood of Fisher Park. Her father, a merchant who brought *his* daddy's tannery business, from Walnut Cove to the south end of Main Street in downtown Greensboro, settled the family in the fashionable downtown district for a few years before moving to the country. He bought the restored pre-Civil War home that was owned by the Reston family before the South fell. It was never kept a secret by Ellen's daddy that he felt Hume, by way of his family's caste, was not the man for his daughter. He insisted she had married down when she married into the Rankin clan. Prideful, yet feeling, at times, unworthy of her, Hume carried his seeping inadequacy tucked inside him.

Not so with Ellen. She put Hume on a pedestal and admired him with glowing warmth. In the years that ensued, she often remarked that looking into Hume's face was like "coming home," and that their relationship, from the start, felt as natural and comfortable as an old shoe. After Ellen's graduation, followed by a two-year courtship, she and Hume were married in the old, whitewashed Episcopalian Church that she had grown up in back in Walnut Cove.

Built in 1893, many of the church's stained glass windows bore (inscribed at the bottom in gold lettering) the names of various Restons, who found it necessary to secure their salvation, and perhaps their name in the community, by donating numerous stained-glass windows to the church. All the names were placed in the east wall of the sanctuary, with the exception of a larger window, directly behind the pulpit. The eastern placement of those windows conveniently allowed the Creator's morning sun to pour its golden light through the multicolored glass, illuminating the inscribed Reston names glowing at the bottom of the windows.

Their marriage and relationship remained comfortable and close through the subsequent years. Ellen adored Hume, and he— her. Both loved to laugh, and each was endowed with a sharp wit. The Rankin house was always full of banter and laughter. The two were in love, and all who entered their world were immersed in that love. Friends joked of the continuous brigade of children, understanding their intoxicating love to be the culprit.

Their marriage remained as such for the most part, until the latter years, when Ellen noticed a change. Hume had always carried a complex nature in him, but he had developed a brooding nature. It was as if something bigger was beginning to bother him— something way down deep, where Ellen was not allowed to follow.

Chapter 11

Hume climbed the ladder to the upper level of the barn and swung himself onto the barn's loft, sitting his rear on the edge so both his legs dangled over into the soft, dusty light. The back wall was stacked with leftover bales of hay Hume had bought from his brother, Mose, stored there for Rhody's winter use. Hume sat for a moment, immersed in the contradiction of anger and humiliation that now battled inside him.

It seemed to him that anger might be getting the better part of it, but he didn't care at the moment. He stood and brushed the barn dust from his soiled, khaki pants as he looked around in the dim light, like he was to remember something. When the thought was answered, he walked back to the hay bales, reached in and retrieved the brown bottle his thoughts had just embraced.

Walking back to the edge of the loft, he resumed his previous position beside the ladder. He stared down at the bottle that both hands now cradled in his lap.

Why! What the hell have I done to deserve this? he wondered aloud. *First it's Tenser and his ultimatum. Then it's Baker. Hell! That ain't changed. He's been waiting for me to slip all my life. Sombitch come to my house while I ain't there and managed to turn Ellen against me! And Mary Ellen as well! That sombitch, Baker! He's the one responsible for that problem! And I'm gonna put a stop to it this very day!"*

With that said, Hume peeled the seal from the bottle with his dirty index finger and took a long draw of Southern Comfort. The welcomed numbness settled in as he closed his eyes and tilted his head backward, giving free rein for the intoxicating potion to do its work.

After partaking more of the libation, he returned to the moment and brought his head up straight and slowly opened his eyes. Just as they were about half-open, a sudden flash, a quick movement, down in the lower corner of the barn floor, startled him.

"What the hell was *that*?" Hume cursed as he pushed himself back from the edge of the loft.

The blur had appeared as something akin to a little man—somewhere between ankle and calf high, with a long, white beard—darting across the barn floor and into the darkness of one of the empty stalls. Hume sat motionless in the late-afternoon light that filtered through the cracks of the old barn, hearing only the silence hanging in the golden sunlight.

"On top of all else, I'm losing my damn *mind!*" he fumed. "I gotta get outta here!"

He swung back onto the wooden ladder and, in one fluid motion, shimmied down its outer wooden rails, worn smooth from years of use. His boots landed in a dusty thud on the barn floor.

Entering the dimming sunlight outside the barn, he had to pause for his eyes to adjust to the sudden change. The alcohol left him with a dry palate that required another slug of the brown liquid. Hume stood for a moment, gathering his sedated thoughts. Putting his hand in his right front pocket and feeling the crumpled cigarette pack along with the three butts, brought him back to his previous intent.

Think I'll pay Mr. Baker a visit.

Standing on a little rise overlooking his largest tobacco field, Worth Baker yelled through cupped hands at the three dark and two skinny white figures in the end of his field.

"You boys need to move them rows along and quit dawdling. I'm gonna need this damn crop to make it to market sometime before Christmas!"

Gotdammit! he rumbled to himself, *Leave them boys for one hour, and they think it's a damn holiday. By God, they'll stay in the field tonight till dark sets in. I swear by God if they won't!*

Worth Baker, the youngest in the Baker family, had two older brothers and two older sisters. It was always the consensus of the family and community that Worth, the youngest, was rendered spoiled from early on—a trait that traveled with him into his adult life. Even though the single women blushed whenever they found themselves in the tall man's presence, he never found it in him to marry. Folks wondered why he never took himself a bride. Family members, and those closest to him, surmised there were possibly two answers to that question.

One, *Worth Baker used up those who were allowed into his inner sanctum.* Women were flowers to be picked, enjoyed for the intoxicating aroma while it lasted, only to be cast into the weeds when the sweet fragrance started to wane. The second reason was that *Worth Baker was too selfish to part with any of his world and share it with another.* He was a conqueror, and that which he conquered and did not consume, he hoarded.

True to Worth's word, it was dark when he allowed the help to come in out of the field. Seeing as how it was getting on toward evening, Worth's two older brothers, Mason and Cyrus, had stopped by the barn earlier to see if Worth needed any help shutting things down for the night. Upon seeing the tired, bedraggled workers amble into the soft light emitted from a lantern hanging from the rafters, Cyrus commented to Worth, joking.

"Think them boys will have anything *left* for tomorrow? They're pretty beat-up looking."

At that, Worth cut his older brother a look that told him, without a word being spoken, that his workers were none of his business. Looking over his shoulder as the disheveled group passed out of the lantern light into darkness, Worth admonished them.

"And you boys *better* stay out of the damn liquor tonight! I want you here tomorrow at first light. It's gonna be a long, hot day!"

Cyrus, who didn't fear his younger brother, but tended to give him plenty of room, advised. "Brother, you can't work your help like that! They'll bolt for another field to look for work, and *you'll* be the one to pay in the end."

Just as Worth opened his mouth in retort, a commotion arose from the far, dimly-lit corner of the barn porch. The bundles of tobacco sticks stacked up against the corner of the right front wall suddenly came scattering into the lantern light, covering the dirt floor.

"What the hell!" Worth yelled, startled.

Just as the three brothers turned in unison to confront the commotion, a lone figure tumbled out from the darkness into the lantern light, and fell onto the hard-packed, earthen floor.

"Rankin!" Baker exploded. "What in the hell you doing snooping round here?"

Stunned by the screaming and the light, Hume looked up at the three men before finally pushing himself to a standing, although somewhat staggering position. Dusting himself off, he attempted to make eye contact with Baker. Ignoring the brothers standing on either side of him, Hume challenged the man.

"Naw, Baker—the question is, what the hell were *you* doing snooping round *my* place this afternoon? *That's* the damn question!"

A sly grin slowly spread across Baker's lips. Feeling superior and having the upper hand, he spoke in an exaggerated drawl.

"Now Hume... ain't you being un-neighborly-like? You mean, I wouldn't be *welcome* over at your place? Well, I don't know who or what you're talking about. But in the event whoever you're referring to was me—which it weren't—at least I didn't come slithering around after nightfall, in the dark like you just done." He smiled. "Sounds to me like whoever you're referring to was man enough to make his presence on your property during day light, unlike you."

"You lyin *sombitch*!" Hume snarled. "I know it was you! You spied on us from the perch, smoked yourself a few Lucky's and then had the damn gumption to pay my wife a visit while I wasn't there! Hell Worth, I've known you all my life. You been wanting what I have ever since high school. And you been eyeing my bottom land ever since your daddy gave you this patch of red clay!"

"The *hell* you say, Rankin? If there was anything you had that *I* wanted, it'd be mine already! Maybe I just ain't been quite ready to take what you got! But then again, maybe *now* I am," Baker grinned.

Enraged, Hume drew back his right hand, rounded his fingers into a ball and with all his drunken might, swung into the space occupied by Baker's face. Seeing the birth of that clumsy movement, Baker made a quick movement to his left, and all Rankin's fist felt was empty air just before his face and chest, once again, met the hard-packed ground.

Baker, not one to forego an obvious opportunity, took one step back and slowly arched his booted right leg, then slammed it forward, like a pendulum, into Hume's face with a sickening thud. The blunt end of his dusty work boot met the flesh and bone just under Hume's right eye and was followed by a sickening moan.

Reacting to the outburst from their younger brother, Cyrus grabbed Worth, pinning both his arms around his brother's back while moving him away from the man lying on the ground. Mason went for Hume, rolling him over to observe the damage his brother had inflicted. A nasty gash had been opened under the eye at the cheekbone. Hume's scarlet blood ran down his cheek, mixing with and staining the ground in dirty crimson. Mason gave him a few moments to recover before helping him to his feet.

His arms still pinned behind his back, Worth sneered at Hume, swearing.

"You ever set foot on my land again, and you'll have hell to pay!"

With cold, but intense clear eyes, Hume looked back, deep into Baker's face, and answered the threat.

"You ever come on my land or call on my wife again, I'll kill ya."

With that, Worth looked at his two older brothers and spoke, through a sneering smile.

"You boys *heard* that, didn't you?"

Mason broke the standoff.

"Come on Hume. You need to get on home."

Mason led Hume to the edge of the barn's light and released his wounded neighbor, stumbling out into the darkness.

Chapter 12

Ellen stood in front of the sink, looking out the kitchen window into the vast darkness of the backyard. Earlier, she watched her husband disappear past the chicken coop, headed in the direction of the barn. Hours before, she sent Alford to look for his father, but when the young man returned, he had no news for her. She stayed at the window into the night, softly weeping.

Stirring in the dark woods, Hume woke with an aching head. It was not the dull throb he had experienced on numerous other awakenings. No, this one was different. He hadn't felt a headache this bad—ever. When he rubbed the right side of his face, his hand came away with a sticky substance that he was unable to identify.

What the hell? *Had Rhody finally gotten lucky and landed one?* he contemplated groggily.

At the completion of the thought, something caught his attention in the woods next to him. It appeared to be an iridescent light, gradually sputtering and coming to life a short distance away. He also detected a circular movement of shapes around the flickering light, accompanied by soft music.

Rolling his pounding head to the left, he tried focusing on the light, but his eyes wouldn't cooperate. He turned his head away and stared straight up into the night canopy. Then he took several deep breaths before again, laying his head to the left. Summoning all he had in him, he strained to see through the wavy haze that clouded his eyes.

Lifting his head ever so slightly, he peered into what seemed to be a gathering of little folks, gaily dancing around a small fire. The music had changed to a chant. Closing his eyes, he concentrated on the cadence. It was in a language he did not understand, but the strange hymn permeated his being, as a thought or memory that hung just out on the edge of his consciousness, one that he couldn't seem to pull it back in.

He wasn't certain how long the apparition held him, but just as gradually as it appeared, the firelight sputtered and faded into darkness again. Hume closed his eyes and succumbed once more to the pounding in his head, recalling his mother's distant warning.

You be mindful of the wee folk when you're out in the field or in the woods, Hume. Take special care when you're by yourself. They like to come out and work their mischief, especially at night. It's been said, given the chance, they won't hesitate to snatch-up people and turn them into changelings.

He recalled her words as everything went dark.

Sunlight eased through the forest canopy, finding him lying on the forest floor. Hume opened his left eye, and he held the one-eyed gaze as he remembered the incident at Baker's barn. He remained on his back, motionless, recounting the events of the night before, hoping he had not done anything more serious than he realized in his unfolding memory. Then the pain hit him at once, like a dull bull's horn. Placing his hand on his right eye, he attempted to survey the damage.

He moved his hand over and around it and discerned that the eye was swollen shut. It felt strange, as though it was not part of his face—as if he was examining the surface of a foreign object. Below the eye, just on the cheekbone, he fingered torn flesh, caked with what felt like dried blood.

Now we both know where each other stands. It's out in the open now. This ain't over yet, Baker, he thought.

The mental recitation of the name Baker and its association bridged his thoughts to Ellen.

She must be worried sick, he realized. A pang of hurt and sympathy moved over him before he caught himself and defended his actions.

It's her damn fault, siding up to Baker like she did yesterday and turning Mary Ellen against me. She'll not get an apology from me on this one. It's me that ought to get an apology and she'll do it too, or else I'll move into Mose's spare bedroom!

Rankin pushed himself up and surveyed the landscape with one eye. The dry-cotton feel in his mouth caused him to gag a time or two as he ambled off to the house to confront what waited.

As she stood at the sink washing the morning dishes, Ellen first saw him as he broke through the tree line beyond the chicken coop. The rush of relief was quickly followed by anger. She watched as he made his way up past the coop and stepped into the backyard.

When he was about midway to the house, she noticed something was frighteningly wrong with the right side of his face.

As he closed the distance to the back porch, Ellen's hand flew to her lips as the disfigurement to the right side of his face became more evident. Dropping the drying rag in the sink, she bounded out the back door and met Hume just as his foot reached the bottom step.

"Lord, Hume! What in the world happened?"

He stared at Ellen through his good eye, while the rounded, bruised mound of his right eye seemed uninterested, separated from the conversation. Hume smelled of stale whiskey. A bloodshot spider-web pattern embellished his one opened eye.

"Hume! Tell me what happened to you," Ellen demanded.

He held the imperfect stare for several seconds before answering.

"Me and Baker had a run-in last night."

Throwing in, as a possible excuse for his obviously receiving the short end of the stick, Hume continued.

"Weren't exactly fair though. His two older brothers happened to be there when I made my call."

Completely missing his intent, Ellen looked down at her husband, unsympathetically.

"You went *there* and got into it with him and his brothers? What's *wrong* with you? That was a pretty dumb thing to do!"

Hume remained, his one good eye staring up at her on the steps. The two stood motionless until Ellen finally broke the silence.

"Come on in and let me tend to that wound," she said, shaking her head.

Hume followed her up the steps and into the kitchen. He sat at the table, while Ellen walked over to a cabinet on the side of the sink and pulled out a clean cloth from the drawer of old wash rags. Then she crossed the kitchen and opened the door to the pantry, taking out alcohol, mercurochrome, and bandages.

"Now tilt your head back so I can see."

Standing over him, she washed the wound with the alcohol.

"How bad is it?" Hume asked.

"It's deep, but a pretty even cut. I don't think it's going need to be stitched. I'll pull it taut enough to mend."

Ellen gazed down at the top of Hume's s head, where his salt-and-pepper hairline met his tanned forehead, presently soiled with dirt and dried blood. She recalled the dark, wavy mane of his younger years.

"What's happening, Hume? Where have you gone?" she asked, while moving his hair aside.

Somewhat taken back by the question, he looked up into Ellen's moist eyes.

"What do you mean, Ellen? I'm sitting right here, nursing a busted cheek, courtesy of your *friend*, Worth Baker!"

"See what I mean, Hume? Exactly what I'm talking about! No, you haven't been here in some *time*. And I don't know how much longer I can put up with your ways."

"Well I'll tell ya what, Ellen. *You've* changed, too. Here I am, sitting with a hole in my face, and you're threatening to *leave* me? And this, after you and Baker been in cahoots in my own backyard."

"Since when is it *your* own backyard, Hume? Seeing as how you and I raised nine children here. Now it's *your* backyard? I suppose the house goes with that, right? And furthermore, I was not in cahoots with Worth Baker. If I was so inclined as to fall in cahoots with someone, it certainly wouldn't be him."

"Don't you be talking to me with disrespect, Ellen. I won't stand for that," Hume snarled.

"Then you stop disrespecting *me*! Worth Baker just happened to *drop* by. It isn't my fault. I looked out the back door and there he was. I sure enough didn't invite him over here for lunch!"

"Didn't *need* to invite him for lunch, didn't look like. Looked to me like you were fixing to send him on his way *with* lunch, with them stewed apples he likes so much."

"Hume! I *mean* it! Are you going to keep persisting in this manner? I can't go on with much *more* like this! If you aim to keep this up, you can just leave. You can go take up with your brother, and the two of you can just drink yourselves into early graves! But you'll do it by yourself. You won't have me there to testify to your ruination!"

Staring up at Ellen, he saw the steel in her resolve. Feeling as though he had been backed into a corner with no direction left to run, the truth escaped from his lips.

"I'm scared," he admitted, almost inaudibly.

Hearing the quiet desperation in her husband's voice, Ellen softened a bit.

"What do you mean, Hume? Scared of what?"

Fearful of relinquishing more of his manhood, he turned from her to hide what ran down the cheek from his good eye. Yet a slight sniff betrayed him.

Ellen's strong hands slid up his back, continuing over the knotted muscles in his shoulders and came together, clasped in a protective shield over his breast.

"Tell me, Hume? What's *in* here that's causing you such pain?"

"I don't rightly know, Ellen. It's just an overall feeling I have—like I'm lost and forgot my way home. I know things are happening out in the world, for a fact. But for the most part, I just have a feeling inside me that I don't like."

"What do you mean, *things are happening out in the world*?"

"Things! Ellen—things are changing, and I don't know if I have any control over them anymore."

"Like what things?"

"Like the damn *lien* that bank has on our land!"

"Well, that's always been the case, Hume. The bank hasn't taken our land as yet."

"Yeah! As *yet*! But that ain't no guarantee for the future."

"Hume! What?"

"This lack of rain's got me worried, plenty. Last fall, I had a meeting with the bank's new vice president... fella from up north-bout the rudest man I ever met. Anyway, he's changing the rules. It's gonna be his way or no way. If the crops don't come in so as to pay off the loans in full, he's gonna foreclose on me. No more carrying over debts from one year to the next. It's year by year now. What's more, I got me a sinking feeling Worth Baker's somehow got wind of my predicament, and he's preening his feathers like a vulture, just waiting on a meal. And that meal is our land."

"Hume! Why didn't you *tell* me about this? You can't carry a burden like that all bottled up inside you!"

"Ellen, what kinda man is *that*? A man takes care of his family and don't go sniveling bout his troubles. He just takes *care* of things!"

"Hume, I'm..."

Cutting his wife off in mid-sentence, he whirled around and glared at her through his damp, good eye.

"I can't take losing my manhood, Ellen! And what is a man without his land?"

At that, he stood and walked back out the door. Ellen didn't follow.

Chapter 13

The sun peeked up over the landscape, hot and ornery—unusually so for a June that was no longer young. In the past, Hume always enjoyed his early morning walks through his woods on his way to the tobacco field.

June mornings were typically still fresh with a coolness, intensified by the wetness of morning dew. The walk allowed a man time to think as he strolled with both hands in his pockets, making his way to the day's work. This morning, however, was unlike past June mornings.

Spring into early summer had not deviated from the dry course it maintained. He had seen early dry seasons before, but this one seemed to be persistent and more selfish about letting go of the rain. Arriving at a clearing in the woods, he looked up through the open tree branches at a deep blue sky.

Don't look as to be breaking today either, he thought.

At the precipice, he stopped and pulled a plug of Day's Work from his back pocket and carved himself out a smooth slice. Inserting it between his gum and cheek to let it soften, he spanned the landscape below, gazing at young tobacco stalks, motionless in the still, morning light.

"Crop don't look half bad, considering," he muttered to himself as he drug the back of his hand across his jaw, which sported yesterday's stubble.

"Still early. The rains bound to come. Always has."

He continued down the switch-backs to the creek. Standing at the center of the bridge, he stopped again, this time to savor the early morning coolness of the forest and the swift-moving creek below him. The glistening water made him aware of the dryness in his mouth and throat, again from his over-indulgence the night before.

It's a funny thing how spirits creeps up on a man, he thought.

He had told himself after the last blowout that he would put a cuff on his drinking. A few social drinks at night were considered acceptable by anybody's standard. Damn though, once again, he'd drained the entire bottle before bedtime.

Stepping off the bridge onto the sandy bank, he crouched down to a place where the water smoothed out and took a few turns in an eddy before heading back into the flow downstream. Cupping his hands to gather water for his parched throat, he paused and gazed into the pool, enclosed in his hands.

Although familiar in likeness, the image frightened him. Peering down at the face he held in his palms, he saw an angry, older man staring back up at him. Weathered, wrinkled skin canvassed hollow eyes that were set in a sunken face. But the face emitted another, subtler, emotion. Although anger appeared to be the frame in which the face was set, a deep sadness seemed to seep its colorless tint into the picture as well. He held the sad, angry face in his hands for an indefinite moment before forcing himself to break the spell by throwing the figure back into the stream from where it came. The motion caused him to fall back on his haunches. Sitting on his backside in the sand, he heard a commotion behind him.

Turning, he looked up the bank and into the brush, catching the blur of something vanishing into the undergrowth, followed by the movement of limbs swaying back and forth.

"Who's *in* there?" he attempted to yell, but his throat was clamped in the grip of fear. The utterance came out much less threatening than he intended.

Recovering some of his bravado, he whirled and stood, facing the now-still brush.

"I said, who the hell is *in* there? I ain't playing now, Gotdammit!"

Silence followed his demand, framed by the babbling brook. Such silence in a forest was unnerving. It felt as if the forest was harboring things that could not be seen... a *presence* that could only be felt.

Hume broke from the creek bank, dusting off his hind-side, as he scrambled back up onto the bridge. Running, he crossed the bridge and stopped at the other side, just at the edge of the forest. He turned and looked back into the dark woods and saw only the familiar setting of the wooden bridge, water, and trail leading up the switch-backs. He felt embarrassed. Yet he was not certain he could dismiss what he had just experienced as childish imagination. He turned back and followed the sandy roadbed, which skirted the eastern edge of his tobacco field, making its way by Walt Neal's place, before eventually ending at the tobacco barn.

I gotta do something bout my drinking! he swore to himself.

Sitting under the span of a spreading oak tree in what served as their sandy, grass-less front yard, Walt Neal fanned himself with a cardboard church fan, affixed to a wooden handle, while Daisy knitted. Both took occasional sips from Mason jars of water they kept stored in a gallon jug. The cool water was freshly drawn that morning from the outside well that Rankin had dug and cased long before Walt and his family arrived at the Farm.

Seeing Hume crest the hill in the roadway, Walt rose from one of the two metal-framed chairs that he and Daisy kept out under the tree.

"Mornin, Mista Hume!" Walt shouted as he waved his boney arm. "Come up and sit a spell and pour yourself a cool glass of water. Just drawed it from the well a little while ago."

Hume stepped into the yard as Walt's two curious baying Plott hounds circled him, sniffing. Pushing his wide brim back and wiping the sweat from his forehead with the back of his hand, he answered the offer.

"Think I'll take you up on that, Walt. Hot enough already and the day ain't hardly begun."

"Yessa, Mista Hume. I knows what ya mean. Up early this morning myself from the heat. Me and Daisy came out to catch a breeze. Ain't much of that goin round either."

Hume dipped a ladle into the glass jug and took a long cool drink of the well water, straight from the utensil.

"Yeah, it's pretty still. Need to stir things up, somehow. You ever mention anything to Daisy bout what you and me talked about?"

"What's that, Mista Hume?"

"Bout working up some kind of a spell to put on this here weather, to see if she could bring about some rain."

Walt's grin slid into a pucker as his cheeks sucked into the spaces his molars once occupied. In a serious mode, he replied.

"Yessa, I did. But it's risky bidness."

Looking over at his wife, he followed.

"You wanna tell him bout it, Daisy?"

Working her hands faster as she sightlessly felt her way along the two wooden knitting needles, Daisy held silent.

Hume looked curiously toward Walt and whispered.

"Did she *hear* ya, Walt?"

Daisy's voice interrupted.

"Yessa, I heard ya, Mista Hume."

"Well Daisy, what with this dry spring into summer, me and Walt, we was talking the other day and he told me you sometimes dabble in haints and hexes and I asked him..."

"I do, sometimes—call on the other side, but I don't call it haints or hexes. I know some folks do, but I calls it working with the other side, in the spirit world. But it can be a tricky thing. They be having their own understanding of right and wrong, and that sword has two sides."

"I'm not sure I'm following you, Daisy," Hume responded.

Daisy emitted a low chuckle.

"Well, how the spell is done is—I draws a circle in the sand, and I builds the fire for my alter. Then I mix the potions—jasmine, mistletoe, foxglove and a few others I ain't supposed to tell—and I set them in the fire and let the smoke rise. Has to be on the right night, with the right moon... an Esbat—that be Midsummer's Night—that be the most potent time. And that's when I done worked your spell. And then I just wait on one of em to come. They come in theys own time, but come they do. Yours ain't come to me yet. But I be expectin them any time now. And depending on which one comes, depend on how the wish be answered. I just do the asking. They know bettern me."

"I'm not sure I understand. Who knows *what* better than you?"

"Thems over there—the ones in the middle world. I just don't know how they decide which one comes. Cause some be happy, some be sad, some be mad. I don't know which one be showin up. Be it a undine, a salamander, a sylph or a gnome. Now, the gnomes be called pixies or nature fairies, too. But it don't matter none which they be called—cause they still the same spirit."

She took a swallow from the Mason jar.

"But it won't be the salamander—they be about fire. Most likely though, it be a undine, seein as how they's all about water, and that what you be askin somethin to be done about. But *could* be a sylph! They be all out in the air, and the water you be askin for is stuck somewhere up there in the sky.

She sat back, shaking her head.

"Then again, *could* be a gnome or pixie—cause they be all about the earth. And I guess that take in both air *and* water."

The word pixie fell hard on his ears. He'd heard Mary Ellen use that name for what she called nature fairies, or nature elfins. Hell, he wasn't sure.

"Daisy, that there last one you mentioned? Gnomes—tell me about them."

"All I knows, Mista Hume, is what I seen, and the little they done told me bout theyselves. That, and what my momma told me. But they be wee people—dwarf-like. Stand oh, bout six inches to a foot high. Strange-lookin, little things, that live out in the forest and fields. Some take up in barns. The married ones, they make theys homes in the forest, under old oak trees, down between the roots. All the ones I done told ya bout, they be called the Four Spirits. But you asked me about the gnomes, and so I'll tell ya. Theys purpose is magical spells. Especially healin spells. But you gotta watch out, cause they love to dance and create mischief. They can be a bunch of ruffians, if they take a mind to."

"And the part about knowing better'n you?"

"Like I done said, they knows *how* and *if* they gonna answer the wish. And if they do, the outcome be up to them."

Glancing over at Walt, a worried look furrowed Hume's brow.

"Don't reckon I bargained for all *that*. I didn't *know*," Hume insisted, troubled.

Thinking the better of it, he laughed it off.

"But hell, it's just old-timey superstition anyway. A person really *believing* in all this would be another thing!"

Both men cast wary glances in her direction but the still, milky eyes did not join in concert with the knowing smile that creased Daisy's lips.

Chapter 14

Three weeks had passed since that evening in the yard with Daisy and Walt. Hume first heard it in the wee hours of the morning, just as it began to fall on the tin roof of their upstairs bedroom. At first he thought he was dreaming. But as he lay there, the dream became reality and as the reality took hold—he understood that it was actually raining!

He eased out of the bed, so as not to awaken Ellen, and he crossed the wooden floor to the window on the far side of the bedroom. Pulling back the shades, he saw rivulets of water as they paused and then raced, snaking their way down the outside of the windowpane.

Looking past the immediate and into the gray darkness, he was able to make out the shimmer of wetness on the ground below. Placing both hands out against the window frame, he leaned in, head-bowed, and steadied himself. He felt as if a heavy weight had just slid off his back, causing him to feel light headed. As he peered into the glistening darkness, he felt the gentle placement of a hand on his shoulder.

"Think this is the end of it?" Ellen asked.

"I don't know. Sure is a start, though!"

Turning, he faced Ellen and smiled, pulling her to him, enveloping her in his arms as he whispered.

"How bout you making Daisy and Walt a pie with some of your stewed apples?"

Pulling back, Ellen looked at him with a curious smile.

"I don't know," he explained. "I just thought that sometimes we don't show those two how much we appreciate them. Couldn't hardly make it through a season without them."

Staring into her eyes, he proposed an idea.

"It's several hours till daylight. And if this rain keeps up, it's bound to be a day off. Why don't we go back to bed?"

Sliding back under the covers, they snuggled into the cotton mattress and embraced with a passion neither had experienced in some time.

Rising before Hume, Ellen draped her cotton housecoat over her shoulders. Gray daylight did its best to illuminate the room as she paused a moment to stare down at her sleeping husband. His breathing was deep and even. The covers pulled up tight around his neck, his repose was soft and peaceful. Ellen lingered a few moments before taking the vision with her downstairs to start breakfast for the children, who would soon be stirring.

Hume came downstairs later in the morning, after the children had been fed, to a quiet kitchen. He poured himself a cup of black coffee and gazed out the window behind the sink. A steady rain saturated the ground. Puddles now stood in places where patchy, cracked earth had been the day before. He pictured his field and the rows of tobacco stalks, their leaves washed and glistening in the morning rain.

What joy must be taking place in the field this morning! he thought.

Hume took a seat at the table just as little John came bounding into the kitchen for another biscuit from the batch Ellen kept in the breadbox. Several days' worth of biscuits amassed with each morning's leftovers. The children were most fond of the days-old biscuits, which would harden such that the first bite would be followed by a shattering of crumbs across the kitchen floor.

Standing on tiptoes to reach the bread-box, John timidly spoke to his father.

"Is the rain gonna save our crops and make you happy, Daddy?"

"What makes you think I've been unhappy?"

"Momma said you've been mad lately, cause you been worried bout it not raining, and the tobacco needs *rain*. She said for us to stay out of your way."

A wounded smile forced its way across his lips.

"She said that? Well, you just come over here and sit on my lap. I'll show you how *mad* I am."

John's face melted in a smile as he ran across the kitchen floor and into the open arms of his father.

"Johnny—sometimes I might not act like it, what with the chore of putting in crops and depending on nature to cooperate— but it ain't never been the day that I don't love you, your mother, your sisters, and your brothers. The farm and this family is all that matters to me. And someday, I hope it'll be yours or Jackie's. Don't seem like Thomas has much interest for such things, and Alford says he wants to look for work in town. I want you to always remember that now, you here?"

Bouncing on his father's knee, John looked up into his father's face.

"I'll *try*, Daddy. I'll try."

The remainder of June and July saw healthy amounts of rainfall, mostly in the form of afternoon showers, enough so that the parched ground was replenished to a healthy state, finally settling the dust. The entire family now worked the field daily, walking the rows, pulling the ever-present nuisance sucker leaves and the big, fat, green tobacco worms that dined on the tobacco leaves.

The younger children played as they worked their way down the row. Jackie and Johnny fought off make-believe robbers and kidnappers, shooting with tobacco stick rifles as the villains popped their imaginary heads in and out of the tobacco rows.

Of utmost importance for the three, was saving their sisters from being snatched up by one of the evil kidnappers. According to the boys, children had been known to suddenly vanish in the fields, even with their parents close by, at the hands of these villains who roamed tobacco fields. Emmaline and Mirabelle played being the victims, squealing and running from the imaginary bandits, only to be saved by their younger brothers' sure-shot mastery of the stick rifle.

Mary Ellen and Etta knew the *real* reason children sometimes suddenly disappeared in the field. Mary Ellen once explained to Etta that her friends, the farm and forest elfins, told her about an ill breed of wee people who, in order to save their dwindling race, would steal human children and leave in their place—sickly, undernourished elfin children. Thus, "being an actual changeling" was the reason some children failed to be healthy. The unsuspecting family never knew that the soul of the sickly elfin now inhabited their household in the form of their own child.

Both girls often held conversations with the wee people under the summer sun, while in the field. But Etta mostly stood back, as it was Mary Ellen who was regarded in highest esteem by the little people. However, seeing that her heart was pure, they often allowed

Etta into their realm to observe Mary Ellen as she conversed with them in their in-between world.

Fredericka sneered at her younger siblings' childishness as she worked her way down the rows, vigilantly pulling suckers and popping the stubby heads off the tobacco worms.

The weather cooperated through July and into the beginning of August. Spirits were high. Hume had put the New Ground in tobacco and it looked as if, with the additional crop and the good fortune of the change in the weather, he would be able to comply with the bank's demands.

A certain degree of suspicion remained in him, though. Running into Worth Baker that day at the bank, just before his meeting with Tenser—the day when the banker advised him that the way of doing business had changed. And then there was Baker, spying on him from the top of the hill just before, or after, paying his wife a visit. Something didn't feel right. It was a gut feeling, that told him the banker and Worth Baker were in cahoots. Couldn't rightly say how or why, though.

Shielding their eyes against the August sun that hung low in the sky, Hume and Walt stood without speaking, both looking admiringly over the tobacco, whose leaves had now turned a yellowish green.

Walt broke the silence.

"When you think we be ready to prime, Mista Hume?"

"Looking like a week, week and a half, if this hot weather holds."

"This here year, it *won't* be soon enough."

"Sure started off bad enough, didn't it? Reckon I need to thank Daisy, seeing as how all that changed," Hume replied with a chuckle.

"Best to let that lie. Less spoke of those things, the better, Mista Hume. Least that's Daisy's thoughts on it."

"Not that I subscribe to any of that, Walt. But it sure is a coincidence that the weather changed soon after the summer solstice, ain't it?"

"Coincidence? Maybe, maybe not."

"Well, in any event, we need to be thinking about getting the tobacco into the barn in about a week or so."

"Reckon we do, Mista Hume. Can't say as I won't be ready."

"Me neither, Walt. Me neither."

Chapter 15

The grainy black-and-white screen cast a glow into the dark living room. The Channel 2 weatherman had just climbed to the top of his simulated weather tower for his nightly newscast. It was obvious the tower was a prop in the television studio, but when he rose, as if coming from a ladder below the tower, he had the children's attention. They would sometimes ask if he was cold, or if he was afraid to climb up that tall ladder into the weather tower.

Walter Lucas was the Shell Weatherman, and he wore what appeared to be a gas station attendant's uniform. His outfit included a shiny-billed officer's hat—similar to what policemen wore—a bow tie and a khaki-colored shirt. He always began his nightly broadcast with a broad smile, accompanied by a salute and a familiar greeting.

"Walter Lucas, with the weather!"

The salute fit right in with the shinny-billed officer's hat.

But on this night, something was different. Lucas forgot to salute. The smile appeared to be forced. The drama was not completely lost on Hume, seated in his rocker, nor on Ellen, Alford, and Fredericka, all tucked-in on the living room couch. The younger children, seated on the floor, immediately asked about the salute, only to be stifled by Fredericka..

"Shhhh! We're *listening* to this!"

The elders had heard talk about a big, nasty storm that might be bearing down on the Carolina coast. It was the beginning of hurricane season, and just the right path could mean rain, and possibly lots of it inland. A good soaking would be beneficial at that time of year, right before priming time.

"Good evening," Lucas began. "We have a storm in the Atlantic that has now reached hurricane strength. The Associated Press says this storm has already been named and its name is Hazel. Although this is preliminary and it's still too early to tell, the weather bureau advises that this hurricane has great potential. Perhaps it's as big a storm as the east coast has ever experienced.

"At this point, we are unable to offer much information as to the possible time and place of landfall. However, if it continues on its present course, that would take it somewhere between Wilmington, North Carolina and Little River, South Carolina.

"There is some early thought that this storm, if it continues to grow and makes landfall in the area currently considered—could bring possible heavy winds and torrential, damaging rain inland as far as Raleigh, Wilson and Greenville. Areas further inland, such as Greensboro and Winston Salem might also feel the effects. Currently, the storm is over the southeastern Bahaman Islands, and it appears it will be some time before it poses any threat to us, if any at all."

Through the darkness, Hume and Alford exchanged worried looks. Ellen cast her glance over toward Hume. Alford finally broke the silence.

"A good day of rain would be a nice boost just before priming time. But any more'n that, we don't need."

"Yeah. If they're talking about a day or two of downpour, or anything of that nature, I don't wanna see it. That creek is prone to flood its banks in spring and fall. But in August, I ain't never seen it happen. It runs awfully close to what we planted down in the bottom. And a heavy surge through there, especially on down at the New Ground, where it narrows and makes that sharp right bend, could put all of that underwater."

"Well, it's a tad too early to start worrying about something that isn't set in stone yet," Ellen soothed. "I'll start to worry when that happens—not when somebody says it could or might happen. Anyway, *The Almanac* never made mention of any of this."

Staring at the grainy tube, the light from the television cast a glow on Hume's worried face.

"Yeah, but Daisy mentioned it's a double-edged sword..."

"What? Daisy said *what* could be a double-edged sword?" Ellen asked.

"Oh nothing. Just some nonsense she was spouting about one day back in June. Think I'll turn in. Got a lot to do in the coming days to get this crop in the barn. Night."

"You children need to get on upstairs yourself," Ellen said. "Wash up and get your pajamas on. I'll be up directly. Fredericka— you go up and get them started. I'll be up in a minute."

As soon as the young Rankin exodus was complete, Ellen and Alford sat alone in the darkness, watching the rest of the newscast.

Ellen's blank face reflected back the black and white movement that was being emitted from the TV.

They sat in silence, until Ellen said, to no one in particular,

"I sure don't relish seeing that worried look on that man's face again. Last couple months—he's been almost *tolerable*."

"Me neither. I can't take any more of his moodiness. If so, I'll go work for Mose and Sanders, or I'll find work in the city. I *swear* it!"

"Alford—you shouldn't swear."

"Well, I *do*, and I *mean* it!"

Ellen's voice softened.

"Alford, can you find it in your heart to show a *little* tolerance for your daddy? Perhaps we don't know all he's been wrestling with."

"I *know* what he's wrestling with! Him! *Him* and his impatient ways. Smallest thing don't go right makes him ill as a hornet! I can't stand to be around him most times now!"

"I know. He seems to stay in an angry state. I used to expect it this time of year. Getting the crop in, curing it and taking it to market and all. But of late, it's been pretty much constant."

"And they say *males* don't go through the change of life!" she added, in an undertone,

"What'd you say, Mother?" Alford asked. "Males don't what?"

"Oh, nothing Alford. Just thinking out loud. I need to go up and see to the young ones. Don't fall asleep down here with that TV on and use up all that electricity. Good night."

"I won't. I want to watch a little of the Ed Sullivan Show.

"Oh? Is that replacing *Toast of the Town*?"

"No. It's just changing names. Tonight's the first night."

"Ed Sullivan's too stiff. I like *The Milton Berle Show* better. He's funny."

Hume rose from a fitful sleep. He had dreams that made him toss and turn and recalled one specific dream that had to do with a problem he needed to use math to solve. He hated to do math in his dreams. He could never come up with the answer, because the answer kept changing. It was elusive, as were the figures, which kept slipping from under his control.

Dressing in the dark, he put on his usual sleeveless T-shirt under a khaki shirt that tucked into khaki pants. He sat in the spindle-back chair across the room to put on his white, cotton socks, so as not to wake Ellen.

Downstairs, he decided to forgo the coffee, so he poured himself a glass of buttermilk and ate one of the hard biscuits from the breadbox. He didn't have much of an appetite. Stepping onto the back porch, he bent and laced up his leather work boots.

As he opened the back screen door, he paused and observed the first light of morning, breaking in the east. Taking note of the peculiar redness of the sky, he stepped off the back steps and walked out to the chicken coop to gather the morning eggs—more out of restlessness than the actual need to perform the task. Ellen or one of the young-uns usually gathered those.

That morning, he just felt a need to meander some, to take his time and remember something—he wasn't sure what. Maybe it was the simple joy he again experienced when reaching under the hens and finding the still-warm egg, with perhaps a feather or two stuck to the shell. Maybe it was the satisfaction of being the first to find the eggs. Maybe it was simply "the finding," that drew him to the chicken coop early on that August morning.

Later that morning, as he made his way to the field, a strong breeze picked up, blowing out of the southeast. It was a warm wind that had an almost tropical feel to it. Looking up at the hardwoods, he observed the wind whipping around in such a manner that the pale green underbellies of the leaves were turned up. His daddy always said when the wind inverted the leaves on the maple tree, a thunderstorm was comin on, which usually proved true. But the skies were clear, and there was no sign in the distance of anything brewing.

As usual, Walt and Sam were waiting for Hume on the far side of the bridge when he arrived at the creek.

"Morning," Hume muttered as he passed.

The two men fell in line behind him and responded, "morning," almost simultaneously, and then they followed in silence to the barn, where the three men waited for Alford under the shade of the barn's overhang.

"I'm planning to start priming bout mid-week, and I'll want Daisy to string again this year. I don't know how she does it, but she can tie faster'n any two sighted people. Ellen and Fredericka can share *stringing* on the other frame. I may want to have your girls *handing up*—depends on who and how many of mine I put in the field and who stays at the barn."

"Ought to be enough to cover it," Walt said.

A few silent moments passed as Hume's irritation grew at Alford's late arrival.

"Let's get started," he finally directed. "The day ain't getting any younger. Can't wait all day on him."

The three men disappeared into the rows of green.

Chapter 16

Wednesday night vesper services at Lee's Chapel Methodist Church was a hit-or-miss affair for the Rankin family, especially during summer. Ellen enjoyed the service and encouraged the family's attendance whenever the farming life allowed. With the priming several days away, things had slowed a bit, and Ellen thought it would be nice for the family to attend the service. As usual, Hume balked, suggesting the rest of the family should go on without him. Ellen, however, was persistent.

"Hume, don't you think it might be appropriate, seeing as how we're so depending on a good harvest this year, to give our thanks to the Lord in advance?"

"Naw, you go on and take the children. Besides, I wanna hear the weather forecast bout that hurricane."

With a penetrating look, Ellen responded.

"Hume, you know how important the harvest is. Especially this year, *don't* you?"

Rethinking his decision, he answered.

"Well, I don't guess it could hurt none."

On that Wednesday night in the middle of August, Reverend Hiram Ward, a short, circular man, whose distended belly pushed the limits of his vestment, met the Rankins at the church steps. His white mane circled the back and side of his bald head and curled around his ears, adding to the merry charm of the man. The Methodist church moved its ministers every four to five years. But the congregation so loved this kindly parson that they petitioned the Methodist conference to extend his appointment for an additional two years.

"So good to see the Rankin family again for Wednesday night vespers! I *know* it's difficult for a farming family, especially this time of year. Y'all come on in. Ellen—the organist will start any minute. I know how much you love the music."

"Thank you for remembering, Reverend. The music really does add so much to our services," Ellen approved.

"Well, we're fortunate to have such a talented music director. And you are *so* right—his music adds greatly to the service. Hume, how's your *stand* looking this year?"

"About as pretty as I've seen it in recent years, Preacher Ward. Real pretty."

"Good. Good. I'm glad to hear it. Been hearing that from a lot of our farmers—thanks to the late rain. The Lord works in mysterious ways, but works, he always does."

As soon as the congregation was seated and the organist finished the prelude, the reverend stood from his leather seat behind the podium and addressed his flock.

"It's heartwarming to see such a good crowd for Wednesday night vespers. I know we're all busy, especially during this time of summer. It's just truly a blessing, seeing all of you here tonight. Now let us stand and open our hymnals to page 123," he said as he lifted both his arms upward, motioning for the congregation to stand. The force of people standing caused the old wooden pews to creak in unison, as if a prelude to the congregation singing.

> *Sowing in the sunshine, sowing in the shadows,*
> *Fearing neither clouds nor winter's chilling breeze;*
> *By and by the harvest and the labor ended,*
> *We shall come rejoicing, bringing in the sheaves.*
> *Bringing in the sheaves, bringing in the sheaves,*
> *We will come rejoicing, bringing in the sheaves*
> *Bringing in the sheaves, bringing in the sheaves,*
> *We will come rejoicing, bringing in the sheaves.*
> *Going forth with weeping, sowing for the Master,*
> *Tho the loss sustained our spirit often grieves;*
> *When our weeping's over, he will bid us welcome,*
> *We shall come rejoicing, bringing in the sheaves.*

Though Hume knew this old standard well and had sung it since childhood, the words, on this night, brought moisture to his eyes and blurred the stanzas.

The Rankins arrived at home well after the local news broadcast. Hume called his brother, Mose, to see if he had caught the news. He knew Sanders wouldn't know, because he didn't own a TV, and he seldom listened to the radio.

"Awlllright?"

No one quite knew why, but the Rankin brothers always answered the telephone with a statement.

Phrased as a single word, the emphasis on the first syllable. Thus, the greeting sounded like "AWLLLright?"

"Mose, we went to vespers tonight. I missed the weather. Hear anything bout that hurricane?"

"Naw, I missed it myself, but Bill Latham said he heard on the radio that it had come on like gang-busters, moving 30 miles an hour toward the coast, and then stalled just off shore. Don't look like it's gonna mount to much for us. If it does come ashore, they're saying it might be tomorrow or tomorrow night."

"Well, that's good news a-plenty. The rain would have been nice, but we don't need no high winds and flooding rain right now."

"You got *that* right! We don't need no toad strangler right now. When you gonna start pulling?"

"Day after tomorrow, or the next. How bout you?"

"Probably the same. But I could start tomorrow up on the ridge. Those leaves look ready."

"Well, all right then. Mmph."

"Mmph."

As with the beginning of their phone conversations, the ending made about as much sense, as nothing was said. There was no "goodbye,"—just an utterance from each, that sounded something like someone trying to swallow a mouthful of peanut butter— simply an "mmph" sound, a sound that signified to both that the conversation had come to its end and it was time to hang up.

Standing by his dresser, looking out the window as he got ready for bed, Hume noticed that the wind, which had blown gently but steadily all day, seemed to have picked up. The big maple tree's limbs, which stood just outside the window, were swaying back and forth in a graceful dance. He looked past the tree to see if there were any clouds out, but all he saw was a starry night.

"Wonder if that hurricane's changed its mind again and is coming on in. These winds could be a forerunner of what's to come."

Ellen, already in bed reading a *Life* magazine, answered.

"You think a hurricane can move that fast? We're two hundred miles from the coast."

"I don't know. Mose said Latham heard it was moving thirty miles an hour before it stalled offshore. I don't know much about hurricanes."

"Well, we'll see. Tomorrow is a new day," she replied.

Chapter 17

An ear-splitting crack was the sound that ushered him into the new day. Hume had fallen into a deep sleep the night before, and he slept soundly until the ruckus outside brought his body straight up, into a sitting position. The ensuing earth-and-house-shaking cannonade, as the large maple tree hit the ground, brought a scream from Ellen's lips.

"My God! Hume! What *was* that?"

The sound of wind and rain crescendoed outside the window.

"It must be the hurricane! Damn thing must have moved in overnight!"

Hume tore back the covers and was at the window in one movement, where he saw the wind blowing in roiling gusts. It was not a steady wind as he had imagined. The trees in the yard bent back and forth like boxers, weaving and bobbing against the ropes, doing their best to maintain and not topple over. The rain came down at an angle.

"This must be the beginning. Except for the maple, everything else looks to be riding it out—at least for now. Maybe we better wake the kids and take them downstairs, away from the outside bedrooms and down to the interior of the house... just in case another tree goes."

Ellen pulled on her housecoat and went down the hall, knocking on bedroom doors and calling out the names of the older children.

"Alford, Fredericka, Mary Ellen, Mirabelle! Wake up! We all need to get downstairs. *Now!* Get all the children and take them downstairs to the hallway!"

Doors opened and children appeared, some wiping sleep from their eyes, asking what was happening.

Not wanting to alarm the young ones, their mother answered.

"We're in the middle of a bad thunderstorm, and if branches start falling from the trees, we will all be better protected in the hallway downstairs. Now come along. Hurry!"

Alford stood in the rear of the group. Overhearing her reply to their questions, he telegraphed his own concern back at her through a confused expression. Ellen responded with worried eyes. Nothing more needed to be said.

"Come on, kids. Like Mother just said—downstairs. Now!"

The children moved down the stairs in thundering unison and herded up in a bunch at the bottom. The older children took seats on the steps, and the younger ones were on the floor with their backs to their older siblings, using their knees as seatbacks.

"Now we're going to stay here until this storm passes," Ellen explained to the children. "The wind and rain may get a little loud, but it will pass in time."

After securing all the upstairs windows, Hume bounded down the steps and joined the group, taking a seat on the step behind them. The look on his face was that of a worried man, of a man with absolutely nothing to do but take a seat and wait for whatever was to come.

The family had not been settled in the hallway long when the conditions worsened. The wind and rain increased, producing a sickening howl. The beast was outside, moaning its own insane misery, and that beast wanted in. Hume rose from his perch and ran back up the stairs to the bedroom. Parting the curtains, he was not prepared for what he was about to see. The rain was coming down sideways in torrents. A sheet of water on the outside of the pane distorted the view, making it impossible to observe the damage outside. The continuous sound of wood cracking told him what he could not see. The wind rattled the windowpanes, so he backed away, certain they were going to shatter at any moment. He attempted to comprehend what was happening, but his mind could not grasp the onslaught that was taking place outside his window. The rain and wind became deafening.

Standing in the middle of his bedroom with both arms up around his head, covering his ears, Hume turned round and round in circles, praying to a God he'd really never known.

Downstairs, the children began a mourning song of their own. Some whimpered, some cried softly and others moaned. Ellen and Alford did their best to comfort them, encircling them with steady arms, attempting to provide some sense of security.

Fredericka did not join in, preferring to sit away from the others. She felt more secure depending on herself for salvation. She knew, by instinct, how to survive.

"Hume! Are you all right? Get down here with the rest of the family," Ellen yelled out over the bellowing intruder. "There is nothing you can do up there! We need you down here!"

He appeared at the landing at the top of the stairs, trembling and ashen, and walked down the stairs to join the others, where he sank down beside Ellen. She reached out for his hand, taking it in her own, as they sat quietly for what seemed the entire morning, amid the competing choruses outside.

Chapter 18

Just as suddenly as the rage started, it stopped. An eerie silence permeated the house. Gray light filtered its way through the curtained windows. Heads that had been lying on laps or bent over knees slowly rose at the unexpected change.

"What happened, Daddy?" Jackie asked his father. "How come it ended, just like that?"

"I don't know, son," Hume answered. "I've never seen a storm end so suddenly."

Stepping off the bottom stair and weaving his way through the huddled children on the floor, Hume made his way to the living room window, intent on seeing what was on the other side of the curtain.

Parting the drapes, he surveyed the mangled front yard and observed heaps of limbs, resembling twisted appendages. Trees had been uprooted and, if not parallel to the ground, were tilted at skewed angles. Some of the hardwoods made it through the storm, but many of the pines, with their shallow root system, did not withstand the brunt of the wind.

Beyond the casualty of trees, Hume noticed what looked like a river, running through the ditch that separated the yard and the road. It crested well beyond its banks, ushering brown water into the roadway, submerging one lane completely.

Then the thought came rushing, just as rapidly as the dirty water Hume observed in the ditch, and he remembered.

"The New Ground!"

He bounded across the living room floor, grabbing his yellow rain slicker, headed for the back door.

"Where are you going?" Ellen demanded, running to catch him.

"The creek by the New Ground! I've got to check on the tobacco!"

Grabbing the arm of his raincoat, Ellen whirled him around.

"Why don't you just wait and see what this thing is gonna do. I've heard something about hurricanes having an eye, a calm in the center of the storm? You going down there isn't gonna change anything, Hume. Either the low area is flooded, or it's not. If it's done, it's done!"

He twisted his raincoat from her grip.

"I can't just sit here in this house and do *nothing*! I'm about out of patience. Alford! You stay here and watch over everyone. And don't let nobody go outside! Them trees out there are uncertain. One of the young-uns could get hurt."

With that, he exited the backyard and made his way to the woods, through the entanglement, to his tobacco field. Twisted limbs and brush in places obstructed the trail. At times, the thick trunks of hardwoods blocked the way, forcing him to crawl under them on his belly or to climb over and through the tree's broken, yet still-attached, extremities. His face and arms became covered with bloody scratches and cuts from his effort.

Heart pounding, he arrived at the precipice and took in the power of the storm. The once meandering creek had emerged from its hiding place in the woods and had become a fast flowing river. It was horribly swollen out of its banks and invaded the low land. The area where tobacco once stood looked like a brown lake.

The dryness in his mouth caused by his exertion became exacerbated to the point that his throat felt paralyzed. He could not swallow. He hacked and hacked, tying to bring up sputum, in an attempt to liquefy his parched throat. His hacking turned into gagging, which brought up the acidic fluid from his stomach. The farmer, nauseous and regurgitating, fell to his knees, then to his belly, and lay prone in the soaking mud.

The pelting on his shoulders brought him back around. From his lowly perch on the soggy ground, he turned his head to the side and looked through a mask of wet mud and leaves. As he did so, he thought he envisioned an image of little figurines, just like the one he had seen in the barn. But this time, there was more than one. There were several—all carrying wooden staves, disappearing into the grove of apple trees. He maneuvered himself into a sitting position and looked around. Although the sky had built itself back into thick brownish-gray clouds, it dawned on him it was not raining. He thought it was the rain pelting on his back that had awakened him, but he was not certain.

He sat on his backside, knees drawn up into his arms, and was contemplating the re-occurring vision of the little people with their little wooden staves, when suddenly the storm was reborn in all its fury. The wind, which had been coming out of the south earlier, now howled directly from the north, across the field, into his face.

Back too, was the rain, coming sideways, riding in with the wind, blowing across the field below and working its way up the knoll where he stood. Backing away from the coming onslaught, he surveyed one last time his drowned crop in the bottomland below and felt a nauseating kinship with its plight.

By the time he found his way to the backyard, the storm seemed to be abating. He had no idea how long he had been away. Walking up the back steps, putting one foot in front of the other took all his strength. Arriving at the back porch, he paused before opening the door. He entered the kitchen, without emerging from his work boots, and allowed the rain slicker to fall to the floor in a wet heap around his ankles. He started across the kitchen just as Ellen entered from the hall.

Their eyes met, and without a word, his face told her the bottomland was lost.

Chapter 19

It took seven days for the land to dry enough for him to get back into the field to harvest what remained of his crop. The sky cleared, as was always the case after a storm of any size, and presented days of the most brilliant blue. In different times, the endless blue horizon would have filled Hume with a sense of joy. But the bright sky now only highlighted the darkness that resided within him.

"Step it up now! We gotta get this in the barn sometime today," Hume declared to all present in the field.

Directing his attention to his son Thomas, who was struggling in the row several steps ahead, both arms chocked full of gummy tobacco leaves, he bellowed.

"Boy! You're dropping more'n you're carrying! Pick up that leaf you just let go there by your heel and tuck it up under your arm! Then put what you've got in the sled."

Because he had so many children, at times he took to calling them out simply by gender. It didn't require any thinking and got to the point quicker.

The priming procedure started with the first prime. That was all that needed to be said, because everyone knew the first prime meant the backbreaking process of pulling the bottom leaves and working the way up the stalk as the priming proceeded in the days to come. A day in the field, spent bent over from the waist down, was bound to cause short tempers in some already ornery men—especially when all just might have been lost anyway, thus rendering the brutal days in the sun useless.

Mornings in the field didn't last long. The pleasant, early coolness, with the damp tobacco leaves wiping against the shoulders of each who passed down the row, turned into a lie by mid-morning, as the sun climbed in the sky and turned their brown necks browner.

It was at these times that Alford allowed his mind to slip away from the drudgery to escape and revisit the week-long vacation he'd taken at Carolina Beach the summer after his high school graduation. With the cool waves of the Atlantic washing over his shoulders, taking him far away from the hot tobacco fields of his homeland, he would dive deep beneath the oncoming wave, arching down to the sandy bottom and remain there, letting the cool blue waters wash the upland soil from the pores of his body.

It had taken extensive persuasion, along with the aid of his mother, to make his daddy see the light and realize it would do no harm to let the boy take the well-deserved trip to the coast. Hume was able to make do without Alford for a week in early June.

Besides, Hume recalled enjoying his own infrequent trips to Carolina Beach. He remembered how he enjoyed strolling in the late afternoon surf, his khaki pants rolled up to his knees, wind blowing straight in off the Atlantic, as he walked along, gazing mindlessly into the clear, shallow water. He thought of the frothing waves that came racing in, cascading up his calf and wetting the rolled cuff of his pant legs. And he revisited the thoughtless peace and joy that simple ritual brought him, so that he found himself slipping his son five silver dollars as he shook his boy's hand good-bye that sunny June morning at the Greyhound bus station in downtown Greensboro.

Alford was still deep beneath the waves when Hume's voice intruded on his daydream.

"You gonna sit there, crouched between the rows on your haunches all day long, or can I bother you for some work? Time is getting short, boy. And just now, I need your help."

Alford came up out of his squat and instantly whirled around, meeting his father's glaring face with his own.

"There's ways to *talk* to people, you know! You don't just walk up behind someone and yell out in their ears! Damn if you don't talk to that mule better'n you do the *rest* of us!"

"Gotdammit, boy! Now ain't the time for this..."

"Boy! The *boy* left several years ago. My name is Alford!"

Uncertain of the next step, Hume moved forward, fists clenched at his side, and fixed his stare directly into Alford's determined eyes.

"I told you, this ain't the time."

Taking a half-step back, Alford looked down to see his father's clinched fists and returned the threat.

"You aiming to do something about it? Cause I ain't backing up any further."

Seeing the escalating situation, Thomas came running down the row and stepped between the father and son.

"Y'all stop it! Ya hear, now? We got work to do, and *this* ain't getting it done!"

By that time, Walt had ambled over and took up a position behind Alford. Looking away, but directing his voice toward the back of Alford's head, he spoke in a low voice.

"Now Mista Alford, you know I can't be just standing by on this one. Why don't you back off, and let's get this crop put up."

Turning, Alford looked at the weathered face and knew, what with the current mood everybody was in, if he pushed it much further, he would have a fight on his hands, and someone would be hurting before the morning was over. Walt and Sam had been jawing at each other as well, so Walt was not in the best of moods. Even at his age, Walt Neal was not a man Alford wanted to test. He decided to listen to the older man to avoid any further risk to himself.

"I reckon I've had my say. Let's get to work," he relented.

The men went back to work and pulled leaves in quiet. Fortunately, conversation was held to a minimal until, with a full sled, Hume stood upon the rear runners and took the reins in his hands.

"Y'all take a break. I'll be back with an empty sled directly."

He spoke to the mule.

"Come up, Rhody!" giving the beast a pop on its withers.

The creature responded and picked up a prance that took both man and animal out of the row, heading for the barn with the first load of tobacco to be tied and put up to cure.

Feeling the deep percussion of the mule's heavy dance and hearing the sled turn the sandy corner as it came out of the lower end of the field, Ellen and Fredericka yelled-out the warning cry, "SLED IN!"

The children, who played riding stick horses out in front of the barn while waiting for a full sled to arrive, instinctively scattered, scampering out of the path the mule would be taking up to the barn.

"Y'all get here under the eve of the barn! That mule don't stop for nothing till it gets up here to the tie horse," Fredericka admonished.

The pounding of hooves and the ching-chang of the metal hitch and chains that attached the sled and mule preceded the mule's appearance as it rounded the corner, white saliva foaming in the corner of its mouth, its breast heaving, glistening dark with sweat in the morning sunlight.

"Whoa, mule! Hold up!" Hume hollered as he leaned back on the runners of the sled and pulled up on the reigns, bringing his mule to a stop in front of the tie horse. Stepping off the runners, the farmer let the reins drop on the full load that was now even with the top of the sled, admonishing the young-uns.

"Now y'all stay put under there until I get this sled unloaded. Don't be getting in front of that mule."

The next to youngest of the children stood back in the shadow of the barn's protective overhang and watched the lathered beast snort and alternately stomp its hind hooves, swishing its tail back and forth, shooing the black horse flies that were so big their bites sometimes drew blood on human flesh.

Jack, caught up in the mule's apparent discomfort, spoke out, more to himself than for any other reason.

"That poor mule! He's so miserable! Can't somebody do something about those horseflies?"

Standing next to him, Walt's oldest daughter, Bessie, responded.

"Naw, child. That animal so dumb, he ain't got no feelins!"

"You're wrong, Bessie! All God's creature's got feelings. You just don't know nothing about that, cause y'all don't go to church. Oak Grove won't let y'all... I heard they wouldn't let y'all attend cause of your daddy..."

"Jack! You hold your tongue *right* there, young man! Don't you say another word," Ellen admonished.

"Well, it's true. Y'all said at supper, once..."

Daisy, sitting in a wooden chair, waiting for the tobacco to be unloaded while twiddling with a ball of string, responded.

"Honey, the Lord don't say all his children have to worship up under a roof. He let some worship by just preciatin being alive under his beautiful blue sky. Or under a black night, spread clear across with endless twinkling stars, and his moon hung in one corner.

"I can't see that picture with my eyes, but I knows it's still up there, and I remember it clear. Just that now—it's all inside me. But I still sees it, just as when I had sight. So he *do* make exceptions."

An uneasy quiet settled in the barn. Hume, just within hearing distance, looked up and observed the idleness.

"What y'all doing in there? Listening to her go on about such stuff? Wish to the Lord I'd never paid any attention to some of her nonsense! Come out from under that shade and help me get this tobacco out of this sled and on the table. They gonna be napping in the field by the time I get back!"

Ellen shot Hume a look of disdain, while Daisy continued twiddling with the ball of twine, as if she didn't hear.

Unlike his brothers and some of the other farmers in this part of the county, Hume did not have a change of sleds. The driver, with help from the stringers and handers, had to unload his sled and stack it on a wooden table, located behind the tying horse, before he could return to the field.

Timing was important in getting the tobacco from the field to the barn. The person tying had to keep up a steady pace, so that by the time a sled arrived, they were caught up and ready for the new load. If all went well, the stringers and the handers would have time to rest and pass the ladle that hung in the water bucket, before the next sled-full arrived. If not, the wrath of the driver made sure the next sled was handed-up and tied with less talk.

Mary Ellen extended herself on her tiptoes and leaned over into the sled as far as she could. Grabbing an armload, she turned, and before placing the bundle on the table, she buried her nose and inhaled the sweet, musty fragrance of the plant. The familiar odor took her to past Augusts—to memories that were happy, to times when the whole family was together.

In a strange way, even though the work was hard and the men's tempers were often short, she thought of it as family time, of sorts. The impending end was a happy time. That part of the work was coming to a close, and after the priming, all that was left was taking the tobacco down from the barn, putting it in the pack-house, and then carrying it to market for sale.

Her daddy was a different person after the market. He laughed more. Her parent's love seemed to rekindle. She hoped it would be like that this year, but she just didn't know.

"Mary Ellen, quit your daydreaming and start handing! You've been holding nothing but air between those three fingers. How about putting some green stalks in there so I can finish up this stick?"

Fredericka's voice caused her to jump.

"Okay. Sorry. I was just thinking..."

"Thinking about your little *friends*? Maybe you can talk some of them into helping us hand up this tobacco. Or better yet—maybe they could put a spell on it, and *poof!* The tobacco will be tied and put up, and it will all be done."

Opening both hands from the ring finger to the index finger, Mary Ellen bundled three leaves in each of the spaces between her fingers and held them out to her sister.

"You shouldn't say things like that about them," Mary Ellen warned.

Fredericka responded with a look that told her younger sister the conversation was over.

Come noontime, when the August sun was directly overhead, all the workers in the field returned to the barn for lunch. Ellen usually made tomato sandwiches with cucumbers, salt, pepper and mayonnaise. If not tomato, she would more than likely make her homemade pimento cheese sandwiches—the ones where she'd slice off the bread crust and cut the sandwiches into triangular shapes. And there would always be plenty of sweetened iced tea with lemon, poured from a gallon jug into individual Dixie cups. Walt and his family usually took their fare to the house and ate, after first washing up, using the fifty-gallon barrel kept at the barn just for that purpose.

On that exceptionally hot day in August, no breeze could be found stirring the tops of the pines that fronted the north side of the structure. The field hands came to the barn with an apparent sense of mission. The jovial banter that normally accompanied them from the field was lacking. The atmosphere was charged, and they all felt it.

The field workers had not been at the barn long enough for everyone to complete the task of washing the morning's tobacco juice from their hands and arms with a scrubbing of *Twenty Mule Team Borax* and water. Those waiting on a turn to clean up milled around at the water barrel in an aimless wait.

Frederica and Daisy were just finishing tying up their last sticks before lunch. Little John had wandered to the far end of the barn and was standing behind Walt, staring at the lathered mule, tethered to a large oak tree that shaded it from the merciless sun. It shivered its hide so as to shoo away the horseflies before they had a chance to set up for a bite.

"John—come on over and get in line to wash up," Ellen called.

Turning, he had barely taken a step, when Walt and Sam, who had been standing just behind John, suddenly erupted into unintelligible sounds, obviously aimed at each other, accompanied by quick, violent movement.

The crack of wood against flesh followed as Ellen's attention turned in the direction of the commotion, just in time to see Sam come down mightily with a tobacco stick onto Walt's bent arm, thrust upward so as to shield his face. She saw half of the tobacco stick go flying over Walt's right shoulder as a spear, narrowly missing implanting itself in John's face.

"Ya sonofabitch!" Walt growled at his boy. "Now I'm gonna kill ya!"

"Walt! Sam! What the hell?" Hume yelled in a useless attempt to intercede.

Just as he voiced his objection, Sam bolted from the barn and ducked into the tree line, disappearing into the forest.

"You *betta* run, boy!" Walt thundered as he left the barn and headed in the opposite direction down the sandy road to his house.

"That boy been lippin off all morning, and he ain't gonna do it no more! I aim to put a stop to it right now!"

Still fiddling with the ball of string while sitting in the wooden backed chair, Daisy moaned.

"Oh Lawd! Sam's gone forever now. He ain't coming back. This commotion is bad. This ain't a good sign."

Anticipating her father's violent nature, Nettie ran into the field, hidden by the first two tobacco rows, and made her way to the family's cabin, just moments ahead of Walt. Inside the dark house, Nettie frantically searched the door-less closet that indented the wall at the foot of her parent's bed, in the three-by five-foot cubicle.

Her frenzied hands searched the dark corners and found the cold, impartial steel, right as she heard the front screen open with the familiar creak. Grabbing what she came for, Nettie escaped out the back door just as her father entered the front room. Hearing her exit, he hastily followed.

Suspecting an intruder, he backed his way along the outside wall until he reached the back corner of his house. He stopped and peered around the edge in time to see his youngest daughter running back up the sandy road, already halfway to the barn, with his twelve-gauge double barrel in tow. Such insolence by his daughter added to the burning rage inside him.

Nettie entered the shade of the overhang with the menacing shotgun in hand.

Standing in place with knees and legs moving back and forth, as if walking in place, she pleaded in compromised fear.

"What do I do with it now?"

Bessie, her older sister, responded by snatching the weapon from her. She ran around the barn and into the field, where she hid the gun.

Everyone stared in frozen suspense as moments later, the angry man arrived and walked through the barn's overhang to confront his youngest daughter.

Staring into her soul with steely, bloodshot eyes, he demanded.

"What'd you do with my damn gun, girl?"

Without responding, Nettie inserted her index finger into her dry, cracked lips and stared down at the narrow span of ground that separated them.

"Damn you girl! I ain't asking you twice! You best tell me now!"

Several tense seconds passed before Walt started a slow turn to his right. A sense of relief began to rise in the little crowd under the overhang, when Walt suddenly backtracked his movement, whirled toward his daughter and slammed the boney apex of his elbow into her shift-covered belly.

Nettie moaned and crumpled in a heap at his feet.

"Stop it! Stop it now!" Bessie shouted at her father.

Turning to his eldest daughter, he lifted the back of his hand and snarled.

"You be just like your brother!" bringing his knuckles across his daughter's face.

The blood formed immediately in the bottom of her lower lip, spraying a red mist in his face as she screamed.

"You damn fool! She's *pregnant!*"

Chapter 20

Early September 1959

The morning broke with the farmer awake. He had not slept much the night before, bouncing from side to side, fidgeting and trying to find a comfortable niche in the bed. At the same time, he fought the nervous twitch in his left leg. He hated the nervous leg, a malady that took up in him occasionally at night, ever since childhood. There was nothing that could be done when it made its nocturnal visit. He was forced to just lie there, kicking at nothing until sleep, finally, mercifully, interceded. He heard that drinking soda water helped, but it always was that none could ever be found in the house during the wee hours when the condition came calling.

The rooster had crowed its last time when Hume rose from the bed. One way or another, the day had to be faced. The outcome would be what it was going to be. The hurricane had done its damage, and there was no going back and changing any of that.

"Are you gonna ask Alford to go to the auction with you?" Ellen asked.

"Naw, I don't reckon I will. That boy has a way—if he's a mind—to make a bad situation worse," Hume responded.

"It might do both of you good. He can see first-hand what the outcome is. And you need to put more trust in him. He's not a boy anymore. I think he needs that from you."

"It would just be easier *without* him. I don't want to be answering a lot of questions at a time like this. My nerves just can't take it. Not today, Ellen."

"Well then soon, Hume. Take time and share some things with him. Not just farm talk. Tell him your thoughts and problems. He'll be doing for himself someday, and he needs to know the world doesn't spin evenly at times."

"We'll see, Ellen," Hume muttered as he disappeared into the hallway.

Smothers' Tobacco Warehouse in Burlington was loaded with pallets of cured tobacco by the time Hume arrived with his first load, the bed of his truck full, his work bulging out at the sides under the tarp secured to the truck-bed's four corners. The auctioneer was already droning on in his staccato cadence with the buyers from R.J. Reynolds, Williamson, and Leggett and Brown following behind, making their subtle gestures, raising or declining the bids.

"Morning, Hume."

Howard Lambeth greeted him amid the auctioneer's prattle, as he walked through the sliding wooden double-doors from the bright sunlight into the dim, cavernous light of the warehouse.

"You look a little peaked this morning, a little green around the gills. You didn't do a little pre-auction celebrating last night, did you?" Howard grinned.

"Naw. I always get a little unsettled at auction," Hume replied.

"Well, I don't figure you got much to worry about. It's the same song and dance every year. Nobody's getting rich, but most are able to put bread and butter on the table. All in all, it's a good life, I suppose."

"Reckon so," Hume answered as he stepped in the din.

Walking the center runway, he spotted George Faucette, the warehouse manager.

"George. Where on the floor do you want me to put mine?"

"You fellows from Brown Summit got a space on the far aisle, up by the front of the warehouse. You'll see them bout, all the way up on the right."

Hume preferred the Burlington market to the Reidsville market, though he didn't know exactly why. It just felt better. The folks in Reidsville seemed to be more Virginian then Carolinian. Most had that slight Virginia brogue, but he didn't think that had any effect on his liking Burlington better. Maybe it was all in the journey. To get to Reidsville, he had to travel the Old Reidsville Road to Highway 29 into Reidsville, where it ran right by the warehouse. It was *a rather boring, uninspiring drive*, he always thought.

Though a bit longer, the way to Burlington headed through the country on N.C. 150, past Ossipee and Altamahaw, where he picked up U.S. 70 into Burlington. He liked the ride to Burlington better. He thought that might be it—saw more of the old home places, with their rolling pastureland, occupied by herds of milk cows and horses. These folks were farmers, but more dairy and horse farmers—whereas Brown Summit and Monticello farmers got their fingernails dirty in the *soil*, raising the green leaf.

In any event, most of the local farmers went to Reidsville, including Worth Baker. And Hume liked to keep his business as much to himself as he could.

Walking up the aisle, he looked for familiar faces, so as to know where to unload. Approaching what he thought to be the area, he heard, above the loud conversations of the other farmers, a familiar voice that caused his stomach to tighten, his insides tensing into a nervous jitter."

"Yeah, fellas—I'm expecting one of my better yields this year. Hazel did nothing but help me."

At that moment, Hume's eyes settled on the one person he did not expect, or want to see at auction, or anytime for that matter. Worth Baker had always sold at the Reidsville market. Always, except for this year. Baker already had a cocky smile on his face and was positioned where it would be the first thing Hume saw when he broke through the crowd. It was as if Baker had scanned the crowd and was prepared, waiting for him. Hume stopped and looked around for a friendly face in an attempt to put off the inevitable.

Baker's loud voice went silent, giving Hume a sense of relief. The respite was short-lived, however, because when Hume looked up, he saw the congregation Baker had been preaching to as it parted into a V-shaped pattern, all looking back at him with knowing, smiling faces. The tall, sneering Worth Baker was at the apex of the V.

"Well, well, Rankin—fancy seeing you here on this fine morning. I believe your space is back over there," he said, pointing his thumb over his back, toward a small, open spot on the floor.

"I don't think you'll need any more space than that, do you? If so, I think we can move over and give you a bit more. Now, can't we, boys?"

Suddenly, Hume felt out of control. His breathing accelerated into staccato gasps. The room full of people started to spin, and he felt he was going to pass out. He needed space, light.

"No. I think that'll probably do it," he recalled responding, in a metallic, distant voice, as if someone else inhabited his body and was answering in his stead. As the panic consumed him, he turned and hurried back in the direction where he'd entered, the laughter walling in behind him.

Sunlight streamed in ahead as he neared the big wooden doors. Mercifully, he arrived at the opening and sidestepped to the right side of the building, leaning his back against the outer wall. He lifted his face, searching the blue sky, panting short, erratic breaths as he tried to regain control of himself and his world.

My God! What is going on? Am I going crazy? Hume! This is you! Get a hold of yourself!

Hume wondered, just then, if it was too late. He wondered if he had he allowed the circumstances in his world to become larger and larger, until they grew a life of their own, consuming that which was once his.

Just as subtly as it came on, the panic began to wane. He was aware of his "self," slowly returning to his body. Whatever had just come over and taken hold of him seemed to be leaving.

Though his body felt racked and weak, his senses re-gathered when Howard Lambeth made his presence known again while passing Hume, who was still leaning against the outer wall of the warehouse.

"You *sure* you okay, Rankin? Can I get you a drink of water?"

"No, Howard. I'm fine now. Just needed a little air. It was a little tight in there. I don't know what hit me just now. I haven't ever *felt* like that. Hope I never do again."

"Well now, you just slow down and take it easy, Hume. That family of yours needs you around for a few more years, at least. You don't make it or break it today. There's always tomorrow, next week, next year."

"Yeah, I suppose," Hume replied.

But you really just don't know how wrong you are about that, Howard, he thought to himself.

"Reckon I need to get on back in there and get on with selling what I came with. Thanks for your kind words."

"Sure Hume. But I meant it, now."

"I know you did, and I preciate it, Howard. I really do."

———————

"Forty-eight, forty-eight, forty-eight. Who'll give me forty-nine, forty-nine," the auctioneer sang out in a monotone cadence as the buyers trailed him.

Their eyes followed his animated movement up the aisle. Hume followed behind the buyers, in his assigned place, since it was his tobacco being sold. Behind him trailed a clump of farmers, eyeing the proceedings with various degrees of interest. One in the group however, exhibited a more than usual interest in what these particular pallets were selling for.

Hume and Ellen had figured with pencil and pad the night before, what they thought their storm-reduced crop needed to fetch so as to call off Tenser. Figuring the amount due on the two previous year's balances with the bank, plus this year's crop, his figures indicated that nothing less than a miracle was needed to clear his debt and keep his land—a miracle on the order of a lightning bolt, sent from the heavens, to strike Mr. Tenser, thus putting an end to his uncompromising position.

That, or maybe, as Ellen said, "perhaps Tenser didn't mean what he said. Maybe, with his being new to the south, he was just trying to establish himself and his ways."

And sure enough, he was going to be a tough man to deal with, but surely he was not so hard-hearted so as to take a man's land and his livelihood, and with that, any ability for the bank to recoup its investment. That just didn't make any sense.

But taking away the two possibilities, the number that appeared on the pad looked to loom somewhere close to sixty-seven cents a pound, a considerable amount more than the average of fifty-nine cents a pound in previous years.

"Forty-nine, I got forty-nine. Now who'll give me fifty, who'll give me fifty?"

Hume saw four hands signify they would see that price. Four out of six buyers still looked promising.

The two others could still be in it, just waiting for the bid to get in the price range they had in mind. Some played the game like that—choosing not to ride the ladder up, and climb up the rung ahead of time, waiting for the price to come to them. It was usually the older, more seasoned buyers who bought that way. The younger ones seemed to enjoy the process, relishing the importance their bids had in affecting the price of tobacco. It was free enterprise, and they were brokers in the game of buying and selling.

Things changed in short order. Two out of six buyers remained and it didn't look promising. Four buyers looked disinterested. It looked to be about over, done with his pallets of tobacco. The price had not climbed above fifty-five cents a pound.

Hume, breathing deeply, felt a sense of relief that it was over. But the sickness in his stomach overcame the relief he momentarily felt.

Chapter 21

Hume was scheduled to meet with Tenser on Monday morning, October 2, 1959, at ten o'clock. Postponing the inevitable only made him more miserable. In the past, such situations usually resulted in his reacting in one of two ways— he would either run away from the problem. Or he would blindly confront whatever was in front of him. Hume felt the former emotion had won out most times in his life, usually resulting in him waking up drunk, passed out in the bushes, with his family looking for him.

This time he chose the latter. Not sure why, he just knew there was nowhere to run to, and the bushes weren't an option.

Ellen wanted to go with him.

"It just might give him reason to pause before taking a family's land," she argued.

Looking down into the pale, drawn face that framed her pleading eyes, Hume answered.

"No, Ellen. This is between me and him."

"It is not just between you and him, Hume! It's between him and me as *well*. It's between him and me and my *children*! Because if he goes through with this, he's taking the spoon away from me, making it so I can't feed my children. And that makes it between you and him and *me*!"

"What you're saying may be true... *is* true, Ellen. But I can't allow that. This is a man's business and it's between him and me. I'm sorry. That's just me, and that's the way I was raised," he insisted as he walked out the door.

Ellen heard the old Ford truck come to life and back out of the dirt and gravel driveway. She was now beyond anger. She was tired... with a tiredness that rest could not console.

———————

"I told you not to marry the man. I told you he and his family were beneath you and that one day, you would regret marrying him. Nothing comes from nothing! I told you all along—Worth Baker was the man for you. If you'd a married him, you wouldn't be in this predicament right now."

108

"Daddy, I know what you think of Hume. You've made that very clear all along. But you have never seen or understood the man I fell in love with—the gentle, caring man that he was before all this. He was different from all the other farmers."

"A barren soil produces no fruit."

"Bears no fruit? What about your nine grandchildren?"

"You would bring *that* up."

"It's just that you never gave Hume credit for the good man that he was. Granted, right now he is lost, but he wanted to be different from his daddy. He wanted to bring respect back to his family's name."

Though Ellen's composure broke, she struggled not to become emotional.

"It's... it's just... it's all about the damn *land*! If, somehow, he could salvage that— I think he could salvage himself and possibly this marriage. If not, then all may be lost. I still love Hume, but our life hasn't turned out the way I thought it would."

Sensing his daughter's desperation, the old man softened.

"Ellen, what can I do to help you?"

"Oh Daddy! If I could ask just one favor of you..."

Hume took a seat in the same old worn leather couch he had occupied in the bank lobby on his last visit. The atmosphere hadn't changed, except that Mrs. Watson no longer occupied the receptionist's desk. Seemed to Hume the tellers knew why he was there, as they avoided his eyes while they robotically discharged their duties.

Hume sat motionless, feeling exposed, like a wounded rabbit, waiting for the owl to swoop down out of the forest roof and snare him in its talons. He had waited for what seemed to be half the morning when the door to Tenser's office opened and was half-filled by the diminutive, bespectacled man.

"Good morning, Mr. Rankin."

Tenser's greeting seemed uncharacteristically friendly.

"Sorry to have kept you waiting. Will you come in?"

The cheerful greeting birthed a small flicker of hope in Hume. Maybe Ellen was right. Maybe it was all tough talk by a man who was not from these parts, trying to establish himself in a strange land. Hume felt an unwanted tinge of sympathy.

"Have a seat Mr. Rankin. Can I get you something to drink? Coffee? A glass of water?"

"No thanks. I had my fill of coffee at home this morning. Anymore and I'll have to conduct my end of the business from the john."

The attempt to lighten the moment went unappreciated.

"Fine. Fine then."

Turning in his leather swivel chair to the credenza behind him, the banker muttered aloud.

"Now, let's see—where is your file? I was just looking at it a few moments... Oh, *here* it is."

Turning back in his chair, he opened the manila folder and took a few moments to review its contents. *A senseless thing to do, seeing as how he said he was just looking at it a few minutes ago,* Hume thought to himself. Hume waited, feeling like a schoolboy, remanded to his seat while the principle reviewed his transgressions.

"Now, Mr. Rankin, I believe we spoke last fall. And at that time, I advised you that North Carolina National Bank would no longer carry balances from year to year, and that each year ended the contractual obligation of NCNB, as well as all previous outstanding loan balances upon completion of this year's harvest. Now I trust you had a successful yield and are here to fulfill your obligation to my bank?" Tenser posed, a seeming threat underlying the question.

He rested his elbows on his desk, hands clasped under his chin, supporting his bony head while flashing a malignant smile across the expanse.

"Mr. Tenser," Hume began, his opening suspended in a moment of wordless silence.

Taking a deep breath, he began again.

"Mr. Tenser, no. I did not have a good year due to elements beyond my control. And I want to tell you before I begin that I did take our earlier talk to heart. This year I put my New Ground in crop and increased my acreage in an attempt to meet your demands. However, that was before I suffered the misfortune of Hurricane Hazel, putting a small lake in the lower..."

"Excuse me for interrupting," Tenser interrupted. "But in my business, I hear some of the most *creative* excuses, or reasons, why people—mostly through their own doings, or as in your case, nature's—can't fulfill what they promised and know they owe. Sometimes, I think if they put as much time in working to fulfill their obligation as they do in creating these well-crafted excuses, they just might have fulfilled their obligation."

Undaunted, Hume proceeded with his prepared speech.

"Mr. Tenser, let me get to why I came in today. As you well know, I make my living from the land. And my toiling of that land enables my wife to put food on our table and feed our children, of which, you may or may not know, there are nine. Now if you take my land, then you will, for all practical purposes, be taking the spoon from my wife's hand, and she will no longer be able to feed my children. What's more, if you take the land and sell it off, you would be eliminating the only way possible I have to pay off what I rightly owe."

"Mr. Rankin, I don't..."

"Mr. Tenser. Please, let me finish."

Pulling a white envelope from the inside pocket of his jacket, he laid it on the table and slid it across to Tenser.

"Now I brought enough money with me today to pay you just over three fourths of what I owe you. That would pay off the old loans and apply the rest to this year's loan. I know it would just about be a wash, but at least I won't be going backward any. We'll be exactly where we ended last year, and it would give me a chance next year, by putting the New Ground back in crop again, to catch up. And that, Mr. Tenser, is all I ask for—a fair chance to get caught up."

Tenser sat unchanged, his hands still clasped under his chin. He stared across his desk, cold and emotionless.

"Mr. Rankin. I have someone waiting and I can't drag this meeting out any further. The only question I have for you today is whether or not you're going to do what any responsible man could and should do. And from what I have just heard, it sounds to me that you have, once again, reneged on your obligation to my bank. So, with that in mind, I have heard all I need to hear. Good day, Mr. Rankin. You'll be hearing from our attorneys promptly, I suspect,"

Tenser indicated as he gathered the envelope in his bony hand and tossed it back in the direction from which it came.

"I won't take your money now, Mr. Rankin. It's too late. Your loan is in default."

Staring at the crumpled envelope, Hume searched his brain for something to say that could change what was about to happen. But with the noise from the train that was now rumbling through his head, nothing came to mind. And, even if the words were there, the parched void in his mouth would have stopped him from being able to articulate in a manner that would have changed anything.

That being said, he stood and turned, tucking the meager envelope back inside his jacket. He dreaded returning home to Ellen to tell her he could not stop Tenser from taking their land. Truth be told, he was not *man enough* to protect her and the children from this outsider—taking what was theirs by birthright.

Hume pulled into the driveway and eased his truck into the backyard. He cut the engine and sat motionless, in a state of numbed confusion, his hands remaining on the steering wheel. He was uncertain how long he had been there when the sound of Ellen, knocking at the half-rolled down window, broke the spell.

"Hume," Ellen's voice floated through the opening, "You don't have to tell me. I can sense what happened. I won't make you go through that again. But I just want to tell you, now don't be mad at what I'm about to say, just hear me out. Just in case Tenser did not agree to your offer, I went to see Daddy, Hume."

Turning and glancing up at her, incredulous, he paused and spoke.

"You did *what*?"

"I know how you feel and what you've said about involving him, but I didn't know anything else to do. So I went to see him and *told* him. Hume, I can't do this by myself anymore, being left out. I had to go to someone."

Staring through the front windshield he closed his eyes and asked.

"What'd he say?"

"He said he would *loan* us the balance we owe the bank. He will want a second mortgage on the farm. But just like the bank, the loan would exclude the house—and unlike the bank, none of the farm equipment. He said he has no use for Rhody," she added, a slight smile creasing her face.

"The *whole* amount?" Hume asked, still looking straight ahead over the rusted ornament on the hood of his truck.

"The *whole* amount. Here's a check made out to North Carolina National Bank," she said as she slid it out of her apron pocket and placed it into her husband's hand.

He studied the check his wife gave him for several seconds before looking up at her waiting face.

"You did good, Ellen. Thank you. I just hope it's not too late. Tenser said he wouldn't accept my money. That is was too late. He said we had defaulted on the loan."

"Hume, for all that my Daddy is not, he *is* a businessman. He may not know farming, but he does know business. He said Tenser is a businessman and that businessmen have one common understanding. And that is money."

"Maybe he's right, Ellen. I reckon I could give it one more shot. Maybe he'll still be there and I can settle this thing with him. I'll think about that common understanding all the way to the bank. Maybe that will keep me focused and in the middle of the road so I won't run off and kill myself or somebody else."

A slight smile parted his lips as he looked up at this wife and patted her hand while cranking the old truck back to life one more time before making his way to back to town.

It was a little past five. The tellers had just closed their windows and were balancing the day's transactions when the door to Tenser's office opened. A gentleman in a dark blue suit, holding a briefcase, exited.

"I'll begin the proceedings in the morning. It's a clear violation, and I don't see any problems," the man said to Tenser as both men shook hands in some apparent agreement.

"My understanding, exactly," Tenser followed. "Get back to me sometime tomorrow with some idea of a timetable. I'm anxious to move on this."

Looking past the man, Tenser spotted Hume and pulled back his suit sleeve, looking at his watch.

"What is it now, Mr. Rankin?"

Hume stood with hat in hand.

"Mr. Tenser, could I have five minutes with you? I apologize, but just five minutes?"

Returning his gaze to this wristwatch, Tenser answered as he stood sideways, holding the door to his office open.

"You have exactly five minutes Rankin, and not one minute more."

The farmer entered and started to take the seat he had occupied in his earlier visit, but suddenly thought the better of it, he shuffled sideways and took the seat next to it.

Tenser walked around his desk and remained there, standing, causing Hume to have to look up at him in a manner that was not to his liking.

"Please, have a seat Mr. Tenser. I really don't cotton having to look up at a man when talking to him about business. Seems to put one of us at a disadvantage, right off."

Remaining standing, Tenser placed both his hands on his desk, his voice irritated.

"*What* is it you wanted to say, Mr. Rankin? Your time is running."

"All right, I'll get on with it then. I have some news that I think is going to please you, Mr. Tenser."

"And what might *that* be, Mr. Rankin?"

"Well things *happen*, unbeknownst to us all at times, for whatever reason. And when they happen to offer up remedies that were previously unknown, that is simply a blessing, Mr. Tenser."

"What *is* it, Mr. Rankin? Stop your gibberish and just tell me what it is you're trying to say."

"Well, okay. Mr. Tenser, I will."

Pulling the check from the inside pocket of his jacket, he laid it on the table.

"This is what I was trying to say. This makes everything even again. This brings my account current. And that is a blessing for you and for me. My father-in-law is a businessman, just like you. Earlier today, while you and I were meeting—getting nothing accomplished—my wife took it upon *herself* to get something accomplished. I was too stubborn and proud to consider it. But she went to her father and told him the whole story—about the bind we were in and all—and evidently he had enough confidence in me to loan me the balance I owed you. So, the amount written in on this check makes us all square."

He stood and offered the check with one hand and extended the other to shake the banker's hand, but Tenser met the gesture by folding his arms under his armpits.

"Mr. Rankin, let me *explain* how all this works. You say your father-in-law *loaned* you the money?"

"Yes sir," Hume proudly replied.

"Well, that really does nothing for your position, now does it?"

Confused, Hume was slow to reply.

"I'm not sure I follow you."

"Well, you may not owe *me*, but you still owe *somebody*. So, in essence, the debt is not paid. And I don't like the position I'm in, having another creditor holding an interest in your land and equipment. In short, I just don't think you're a good future risk, Mr. Rankin."

"But you have your money now. We're flush. And that's better'n taking my land and trying to recoup your money by having it auctioned on the courthouse steps. You take my land, and I ain't got no way of paying you back. It just don't make sense to me."

"What makes sense or does not make sense to *you*, Mr. Rankin, is of no concern to me. However, some things may not always appear or make themselves known to the less-informed."

Sitting again in his chair, Hume looked into the face across the desk with a dawning sense of awareness.

"Am I hearing what I *think* you're saying? That you won't accept this payment and you're still gonna take my land? But you aren't going to risk selling it at auction, are you, Mr. Tenser? You got something already in mind, don't you?"

Supporting his skinny upper torso on his balled fists resting on the tabletop, Tenser leaned across the table to close the distance between them and smiled.

"Good day, Mr. Rankin. I believe that just about finishes all the business there is between us."

Chapter 22

"Ma'am, can you tell me where the stacks are? This is my first semester, and I've got a paper to do. My professor said I could find my area of research in the library stacks," the student asked a middle-aged woman who was bent over a book cart.

"Oh, yes," she said rising, "I'm new here, too. But I believe if you take the stairway behind you, go to the third floor, turn right and go all the way back, you'll find the stacks. They're the tall shelves, in the very rear."

"Thank you, ma'am."

"You're very welcome," Ellen Rankin returned, watching the young woman, who appeared to be just a few years older than Fredericka, ascend the stairwell.

She felt fortunate of her relationship with Tom Spence, dean of the anthropology department and a Reston family friend. The Restons and Spences lived, for a while, on the same street in the College Hill neighborhood, located near the university.

The family friendship had proved useful in her obtaining employment at the college. Albeit as a library assistant, the job allowed her the opportunity to work daily in the inspiring world of academia. It was a world that, even though observed from a distance, gave her a renewed sense of worth. And after what had recently transpired in her life, she was grateful for that.

Making her way back through the maze of shelves, she placed books from her cart into the dark slivers where each belonged. Normally, she did not read the titles—just their categorizing Dewey decimal numbers—so she could replace the books at a faster pace. She was thankful for the employment and wanted to extend her gratitude by doing a good job.

Reaching for the next book on her tray, she gripped an ample spine that was too wide for small hands that were more used to handling dishes, pots and pans and stalks of tobacco. She lost her grip and the book fell to the floor with a loud thud. As she bent to retrieve it, she looked around to make certain no one saw she had dropped it, only to find that she was alone in the dark recess.

She stood and started to slide the book back into its proper spot, when the image on the cover of the book caught her eye and stopped her hand in mid-motion. The figure was that of a smallish man, with a chubby face and elongated ears that ended in a point at his temple. She stared at the little man on the cover, who appeared to be looking back at her. The half-smile embedded in his full, white beard hinted that he smiled from the inside, and a knowing look in his eye seemed to suggest he had been waiting for her.

On the front cover of the book, written in beautiful cursive longhand, above the figure was the title, *Gnomes*, by Wil Huygen and Rien Poortvliet. Her right hand was shaking as she opened the book and thumbed through the opening pages. The beautiful diagrams depicted little human-like creatures with merry, cherub faces. The male figures wore white beards that flowed to their chests. The females were solid build, with large breasts that rested on thick torsos.

Ellen turned deeper into the book, where she found several pages that diagramed a typical Gnome underground abode, beneath the roots of an oak tree. Reading further, the authors explained that the little people usually came out late and performed their chores under the cover of night—although if needed, they would surface during daylight hours.

Could it be that Mary Ellen's stories were more than her imagination? There it was, a book in a college library that spoke of such an existence. *In a college library!* she thought, recalling Mary Ellen's tales.

Hearing footsteps on the stairwell, Ellen quickly closed the book and replaced it in its berth. Straightening her dress and composing herself, she thought of Tom Spence. *Gnomes and Fairies must fall somewhere in the neighborhood of anthropology.* She wasn't sure how she would approach her friend with such a childish matter, but she knew she had to do it. It was important.

The tobacco warehouse in Burlington was not so busy a place after the auction, and a broom in his hand was not a tool he was used to. But he had no choice. Hume was grateful enough for the work. The pay was minimal, but thankfully, the house and truck were paid for.

Since the farm would soon be sold at auction, it was no longer a financial burden that needed to be tended to.

Putting food on the table and warm clothes on the children for the upcoming winter is all I can concern myself with now, he told himself.

But it wasn't. Hume had an ache inside him that seemed to take up residence, permanently. It was there when he woke and stayed with him until he went to bed. It even sat with him on the side of the bed in the dark, wee hours of the night.

He'd never felt like that. The feelings that roamed in him ranged from anger and rage at times, to a heavy, burdening sense of sadness and hopelessness that cloaked him in his presently gray world. To wake and not work his day on the land was foreign to him. The strange place he was in made the world feel off-center. There was a wobbly-ness to everything. And then the rage would set in again.

"Hume," a farmer acknowledged, his eyes averted to the floor as he passed.

"Johnson," Hume returned, as he continued sweeping, not looking up.

It was mostly that way since he started working at the warehouse. The farmers who came by didn't look Hume in the eye, and in a sense, he was grateful for that, as he did not want inquisitive eyes surveying him.

George Faucette had reached out to him when he heard about the loss of his farmland, and Hume was much obliged for the sensitivity of the man, who acted as if Hume had some decision in it and he had not been forced to give up farming because his land was taken from him.

"I hear you've decided to quit farming, Hume," he had said. "I need a good, experienced man in the warehouse. Not much to do these days but keep up with maintenance and some house cleaning. And it don't pay much, but it might help keep you going until you find your direction. Come next September though, things really get going around here. But *you* know that."

Hume accepted the offer without consulting his wife. She had been first to find a job. The unspoken implication of her having to go to work added to the humiliation of his predicament. That, and taking into account that Ellen's mother would be watching the young-uns after school, didn't do a whole lot for his self-esteem.

Ellen's daddy had made it clear he didn't hold much for the fact Hume was unable to work out a settlement with Tenser, especially given the fact that his daughter had put the balance owed in his son-in-law's hand, and he still lost the land. He told Hume he just didn't understand a man who could go under and lose it all, given that advantageous circumstance.

Hume never fought back, because he was at a loss as well, as to exactly what happened and why Tenser did not accept the offer. He felt the answer might be found in the simple dislike of two men for each other—men who were very different and from entirely different worlds.

Yet again, he felt there might be something more convoluted going on—something he had no proof of—only a gut feeling. But Hume knew that type of subjective reasoning would not sit well with his father-in-law, a man who demanded yes or no answers, not unfounded theories. So he just let it simmer, along with all the other past indignities.

Ellen phoned Tom Spence's office the following day. He was not in, but his secretary took the message and promised she would tell him as soon as he returned. The return call came to the library's front desk late the following afternoon. She was nervous over the fact he had not returned the call, and she was fearful she was over-stepping their friendship. But when he finally did call, he made it clear that such was not the case and he would be more than happy to see her.

Ellen ascended the granite steps at the front of the library. The late October sun sat low over the red brick buildings on west campus. The early fall chill prompted her to pull the felt collar of her car coat up around her exposed neck. She had recently cut her slightly graying hair shorter, in a style similar to many of the female students. The change had caused a stir between her and Hume, who accused her of trying to be one of the co-eds.

"What are you trying to do?" he asked. *Attract some young male student, or one of those stuffy, egghead college professors, who saw no shame in going after pert, young college students? Male or female—didn't matter to those socialists.*

At times, she felt ashamed and regretted cutting her hair. Then she would realize that the insecurities were his, not hers, and she would shake her hair back in a defiant salute to her independence.

The sidewalk leading from the library's front steps ended at Main Campus Drive. There, she turned right and briskly covered the distance to the three-story Brownstone that faced Spring Garden Street, where Tom Spence's office was located. Although he'd previously told her during their phone conversation that his office was number 23, and was located on the second floor, she stopped in the lobby anyway and looked his name up on the roster. Finding it, she gazed upon the name and the title that followed, savoring a sense of privilege, in that the head of a college department would take the time for her. She wished the subject she had to discuss with him was different—something of intellectual importance, such as the cause of the diminishing numbers in a pigmy tribe south of the Equator. But no. A tad embarrassing—she was stuck with Mary Ellen's imagination.

After arriving at the top of the landing, she observed the room numbers went up, left and right of the landing, with the even numbers to the right and odd numbers to the left. Turning left, she trailed her hand along the smooth, wooden banister as she walked down the balcony, and she found the number 23 in gold plating on the door.

The numbers stood out proud and looked rich against the backdrop of the dark, mahogany wood. She tapped gently. Receiving no reply, she removed the glove from her right hand and knocked again, this time tucking her fingers into her palm, forming a half fist. This rap was harder and resounded off the walls and wooden floors.

Ellen shrank. She had always been timid about announcing herself from behind closed doors and hated the imagined intrusion it caused on the other side.

"Come in," came a feminine response.

Ellen turned the gold knob and entered the room. A petite woman appearing to be in her sixties, silver hair drawn up into a sophisticated bun, sat behind a blond wooden desk in the center of the room. The name on the desk placard read, *Jane Reed, Secretary.*

"May I help you?" she asked.

"Yes, I believe so. My name is Ellen Rankin."

"Oh yes, Mrs. Rankin. Dr. Spence's *neighbor*?—I believe he said?"

"Well, yes, our families used to live...we're more like family friends, actually."

"Have a seat and I'll tell him you're here."

"Thank you."

She took a seat on a sofa, positioned along the far wall, directly in front of Mrs. Reed's desk. It was covered by a white tick slipcover. Ellen picked up a copy of National Geographic and took a cursory look, thumbing through the first few pages before setting it down on the sofa beside her. She glanced around the office. Framed black-and-white photographs of dark, half-naked natives, with bows and arrows strung around their necks, brought a blush to her face.

Continuing to look around the room, she observed the walls and the light oak floors and sensed a golden glow that embellished the office. It was a warm room, emitting a feeling of security. Her earlier embarrassment had subsided and she felt she could lie down on the couch, draw herself up in a ball, nap in a cocoon and all her troubles would have to wait outside the thick, protective wooden door.

The fuzzy lull ended moments later when the door behind Mrs. Reed opened and Tom Spence filled the space. Walking around Mrs. Reed's desk, he opened his arms and moved toward Ellen, who stood.

"Ellen, so good to see you. Are you enjoying the library?" Tom asked as he embraced her in a hug.

"Oh yes, Tom. I have a lot to learn, but I'm enjoying it so."

"Come into my office, Ellen. Is there anything I can get you? Coffee, a glass of water," he offered.

The nervousness had crept back, abiding in her dry throat.

"Yes, I think I will have some water, if you don't mind."

"Not at all, Ellen."

"I'll get it, Tom," Mrs. Reed said.

The glass of water arrived on Spence's desk, in front of Ellen, almost as soon as she sat.

"So, Ellen—tell me, what brings you here today? Something about one of your daughters and a problem she is having with an inflated imagination? I don't think that is going to fall in my field of expertise, but if I can help you or point you in the right direction, I'll be glad to do what I can."

A sinking feeling crept in.

"I'm not sure where to start, Tom. We... uh... Hume and I have been going through some things of late."

She paused as the welling in her throat competed with her voice before she abruptly exclaimed,

"We lost it, Tom. We lost the farm to foreclosure."

With that, the long-awaited emotional floodgates opened from deep within her as she sobbed, shaking, burying her face in her hands.

He came to her from around the desk and placed his hand on her shoulder.

"Here, Ellen," he said, handing her his handkerchief from the front pocket of his tweed jacket.

She wiped the tears from her face.

"I'm sorry, she said. "That is not the reason I came here today."

"Maybe it *is*, Ellen. You just didn't *know* it until just now. Obviously you and Hume have been going through a lot lately. And that type of stress can put an extraordinary amount of pressure on people's lives."

"Yes, Tom. I guess it has. Please, bear with me."

"Certainly, Ellen. Take all the time you need."

Taking a moment to gather herself, she finally spoke.

"This is all going to sound so silly, but here I go. Tom, I was in the library the day before yesterday, I think it was, putting books back in the stacks when I came across this book, like a child's book. I'm not sure. But the book was about—and here comes the silly part—but the book was about gnomes. Fairies. And this is where Mary Ellen comes in."

She dabbed her eyes, even though the tears were gone.

"Hume must have seen the trouble brewing with the farm long before I had any idea. And he has been hard to live with lately. Not only have we had financial problems, but it has taken a toll on our marriage as well."

"I can understand that, Ellen," Tom comforted, returning to is chair.

"Mary Ellen has been talking about these little creatures she calls 'gnomes, fairies and little people.' She calls them by various names, but she says she can see them and she talks to them. Says they live out in the woods, the fields and even out in the barn. But she has mentioned several times that they are there to help Hume—that his problems have something to do with him 'finding himself' and 'he has to straighten himself in the fire,' or something to that effect."

"*Tapasia*," Tom said, more to himself than for any other reason.

"I'm *sorry*?" Ellen replied.

"Tapasia. *Straightening by fire*—that is an eastern, Hindu phrase, which means "to change...the inner struggle.""

"Go on," he said, leaning forward on his table, his chin cradled in his hands.

"Well, anyway, there have been times that I suspect I'm being watched. And when I turn around, I sense I'm seeing the end of movement—that something is on the end-side of disappearing. I know you think I'm crazy, Tom."

He sat motionless for what seemed like several minutes. She waited, hands in lap, an embarrassed smile on her lips.

"Is there anything more? Why is it *she* can see them and you can't? Does she have anything to say about *that*?"

"Actually she did once, maybe twice. I don't know, exactly. She said they told her most adults are unable to see or hear them because their minds are too busy. 'Too cluttered,' may have been the words she used."

The professor sat back in his chair, hands folded under his chin, elbows on his armrests. His face seemed to show a keen interest.

"Ellen, I have done some study in this area, and although it is more in the area of folklore and mythology, it *does* fall within the realm of anthropology. But from an anthropological perspective, the phenomenon of all this—in the recorded history of all civilization, from the past to the present, there has been a belief in a world unseen where unseen beings dwell. From barbaric tribes to the archbishop of Canterbury, going as far back as possible in human origins, there is some belief in a fairy, or spirit world. And they all had a name for this."

He cleared this throat and continued.

"The ancient civilizations called their inhabitant's gods and demons. Christianity named them saints or angels. And on the other side were demons and the souls of the dead. The uncivilized tribes thought of them as the souls of their ancestors. And the world of the Celts had fairies of many kinds."

He paused, smiling slightly.

"The great thinkers and philosophers of the middle ages in Egypt, Greece and Rome studied this phenomenon and devised a metaphysical theory. They were very scientific in their methods and divided all invisible beings into four classes. And these were, beginning at the top, the angels, and below them were devils, or demons. The third group was the elementals—the native spirits, who were generally regarded as being pygmy-like in stature. And the last was the souls of the dead.

"Now the third group, Ellen, is what you're interested in, I believe. The great thinkers put the elementals in four kinds of spirit classes, based on how they inhabited the four chief elements of nature.

"The ones inhabiting the air were called *sylphs*, resembling the conventional fairies we have seen in books since childhood. The ones who inhabit water are called *undines* and they were said to dwell in fountains, lakes and streams. Those inhabiting fire are called *salamanders*. And the fourth group, which inhabit the earth, are *gnomes*, and *gnomes* are regarded as friendly to man, who generally have man's best interest at heart. It has been said that this group, if sought, could work with mortals in straightening their affairs of the heart—thus the 'straightening by fire,' as Mary Ellen referred to."

Ellen sat, ashen faced, with her hands still folded in her lap.

"What do you make of this, Tom?"

"Well, as a scholar, I'm required to base opinions on study and research. I am not afforded the luxury of thinking from the heart. Yet I am human, and in that context, I too, have had life experiences that would cause one to pause. We all have feared things that go bump in the night, haven't we? And perhaps that remains a lesson from childhood, when we were able to hear and see things that our parents did not."

The color returned to Ellen as her face relaxed and softened.

"Why not listen to what Mary Ellen is saying? She is trying to *tell* you and Hume something. And that *something* is a wonderful, magical story that has been told for the ages, in many different civilizations. And in any event—what can it hurt? Letting her flex her creative muscle can be beneficial. At the worst, she may become a great writer. And that isn't all *bad*, is it?"

"No, I guess not. So your advice is to listen to, and give her rein in this?"

"I think so, Ellen."

Ellen thought for a moment.

"Such a simple solution for what seems a simple problem. Thank you, Tom. You've been such a help," she said, rising from the chair.

"And if you want to pursue this matter with Mary Ellen, what I've relayed to you today can be found in an excellent research book written by a Dr. W.Y. Evans-Wentz. He was a scholarly man who was born and educated in America. He received his doctor of science in comparative religion, from Oxford. The book is an academic study on the anthropologic significance of the phenomena of 'little people' in civilization."

Turning to the bookshelf behind him, he scanned the bookends.

"No, I thought I had a copy of... Well, I *know* I used to. But you can find it in the anthropology section in the library. The name of the book is *The Fairy Faith in the Celtic Countries*."

Reaching into his drawer and extracting paper and pencil, he scribbled.

"Here. I'll write it down for you," before handing the folded piece of paper to Ellen.

"Thank you, again," she gushed. "Seems as if I'm saying that a lot these days. I don't know what I'd do without your help, Tom."

The two friends locked eyes for an uncomfortable length of time before Tom broke the silent moment.

"No, Ellen, thanks is not needed between us. It's my pleasure. I'm just happy to be in a position to be able to offer some assistance. Anytime."

"Well, yes. Thanks," she replied. "Oh listen to me—there I go again!"

"That's better," he replied, looking into her eyes as he enclosed her hand with his soft, smooth hands.

"Give your husband my regards, will you?" the professor said before opening the office door.

"Yes, I will," she answered as she prepared to leave the room.

It was a room that felt good, but still foreign. The difference of texture in the soft hands that had just clasped hers did not go unnoticed. Suddenly, she felt the need to go home to her husband to feel his roughness, a roughness born from a love and connection to the land, from hard, honest work that involved wooden tools and leather reins in calloused palms. It was an external roughness that was not diminished by an inner softness, a goodness that still resided... somewhere in his being.

Chapter 23

Hurrying across the grassy quad, Ellen feared she had overstayed her meeting and risked missing the last run of the "Blue Goose," one of two suburban buses that ran from Greensboro out into the county. One bus served the northern half, while the other the southern half. Cresting a knoll, a wave of relief flushed warm on her insides when she saw the top of the old blue and grey bus idling at the bus stop, its exhaust shimmering silver-blue in the dim glow of the streetlight. Running, she reached the twin glass doors and rapped on the outside before the bus had a chance to pull out on its last evening run.

"Running a little late tonight, huh, Mrs. Rankin?"

"Yes, Charles," she replied to the large man whose overhung belly competed for space with the bottom of the steering wheel. "I'm afraid I am."

"Well, just remember, next time you have too many books and too little time, I make the last run at six o'clock. I can wait a few minutes longer, but I need to get this thing on the road soon after six."

"Thank you. Yes, I will remember that, Charles."

Depositing her nickel in the glass stile beside the driver, she took a seat on the right side of the bus, three rows back. Leaning back on the worn naugahyde bench, Ellen wriggled in, attempting to settle into a more comfortable position. She wanted to mull over what the professor said about the 'little people' and the 'in-between' world Mary Ellen dwelt in.

She was proud of herself and anxious to tell Hume about what she had discovered in her research. She needed to share the information with someone, but the subject was of such a matter that her outlets were limited.

Then she worried how Hume, given his current mood, would take to such a discussion. She couldn't read him of late. He could be at times—an open, intelligent man, inquisitive and willing to accept possibilities. That was the quality that made him different from the others and it was what had drawn her to him in the first place. But in recent years, another side of him had surfaced, sometimes percolating up and filling his nature. That was the negative, doubting side. The cynical side of him, she did not like. It made him like all the other farmers she knew—men who would not allow softer thoughts to enter their minds. Men, unlike Hume. Unlike Hume and Tom Spence.

The sudden, intruding thought took her back. She didn't know why Tom Spence entered her thoughts alongside of her husband. She shuddered at the feelings, stirring inside her.

Absurd! she thought, embarrassed at such a notion.

The dusty, old bus pulled over, and the twin doors opened simultaneously in the dimming twilight.

"Goodnight, Mrs. Rankin. You have a good weekend, now. We'll see you Monday—the good Lord willing and the creek don't rise."

Ellen met the kind bus driver's remark with a sad smile.

"Yes Charles. Let's do pray the creek doesn't rise, *again.*"

The intent of her words wounded him. Wishing he could have caught his words in mid-air and swallowed them before they reached his fare, he fumbled.

"I... I... I'm sorry, Mrs. Rankin. It wasn't meant in that way."

"I know you didn't mean it that way, Charles. You go on now and have a nice weekend yourself. I'll see you Monday."

The exhaust belched from the rear of the bus, covering Ellen as she held her breath, waiting for the foul, grey smoke to clear. Pausing, she looked across the hardtop at her white, two-story, wooden house, the interior lights warming the inside of the abode with a golden glow, reminding her of a Jack-o'-lantern in the cool, late October night.

Looking both ways, she crossed the road and stopped at the mailbox near the ditch at the edge of the yard. Reaching in and extracting its contents, an official brown envelope on top of the heap caught her attention.

"Clerk of Courts, Guilford County, North Carolina" occupied the top left corner of the beige envelope. Her hands trembled as she tore open the end of the sleeve and read.

TO: Humley F. Rankin
    Ellen R. Rankin
    YOU ARE HEREBY NOTIFIED that the Clerk of Superior Court in Guilford County, North Carolina shall conduct a foreclosure sale on the steps of the Guilford County Courthouse on...

Both envelope and sheet of paper fluttered to the ground in the slight breeze as Ellen covered her mouth with her shaking hand. Both she and Hume knew this day was coming, but the official announcement brought reality home in a manner similar to being kicked in the stomach by one of their milk cows, the pain merging with nausea.

Bending down to retrieve the dire announcement, she looked up at her glowing home and felt she would be sick. She placed her hand over her mouth just as she noticed the vehicle in the driveway was not Hume's, but that of her mother's. Steadying herself by holding onto the mailbox, she took deep breaths, attempting to quell the rolling in her stomach.

Where is he? Why isn't he home? Ellen asked herself just before sour liquid spewed from her mouth. After the initial expulsion, the queasiness in her stomach relented and she wiped her mouth with the back of her hand. Then she straightened her dress and stiffened her resolve before encountering her mother.

Ellen's mother was facing the sink, her back to the hallway, cleaning the evening dishes as Ellen stopped there and observed her mother from a silent distance. A dignified woman, her white hair wound on the back of her head in a graceful bun. Ellen idolized her mother's simple elegance and hoped that she was destined to be like her.

"Mother, where is Hume? He's supposed to *relieve* you."

Grace Reston turned and faced her daughter with a questioning sigh, slowly turning her head, indicating that she too, was at a loss concerning his absence.

"I don't know, dear. He's usually home from the warehouse by four, but tonight, he never..."

"Oh mother, I'm so sorry," Ellen said, as she handed her a drying cloth.

"Here, take this and dry your hands and then you go on home. Daddy will be waiting, and I know how ornery he gets when supper is late."

Grace dried her hands before putting on her overcoat. Ellen walked her mother to the door.

Turning, Grace looked into her daughter's eyes.

"Is everything okay between you and Hume? I know you all are going through a lot right now. But are you two okay?"

Ellen paused for a moment, returning a blank stare before she came back to the moment.

"Oh yes, mother. We have to adjust to the circumstances. But, yes, we are okay."

"Well, let me rephrase that. Is *Hume* okay?" Catching herself, Grace blurted, "Oh never mind. I'm sorry, dear. I don't mean to pry."

"It's all right, Mother. You're not prying. Just being your normal, concerned self. I'm sure he will be home directly. Probably something came up at the warehouse."

Grace met her daughter's attempt with a sad smile and patted her on the forearm.

"You take care of yourself now, Ellen. You're under a lot right now."

"I will, Mother. You be careful going home. And don't worry."

Ellen closed the door behind her and leaned back against it with her arms folded across her chest.

"*Now* what? Damn that man!" she muttered to herself before yelling up to her two oldest daughters.

"Fredericka. Emmaline. Will y'all come down here for a minute."

Moments later, Emmaline bounded down the stairs and whirled around the wooden knob at the end of the banister. Fredericka followed in a mope.

"Yes, Mother," Emmaline inquired, standing in front of a brooding Fredericka—obviously put out over the request.

"Do either of you know where your father is?"

"As if you *really* wonder, Mother," Fredericka responded, sarcastically.

"I don't know, Mother," Emmaline offered. "He didn't come home when he usually does, so Mother Reston fixed us supper. Maybe he just got tied up at the warehouse."

"Yeah, he probably had an unusually large amount of trash to sweep out tonight," Fredericka scoffed.

Ellen cut a stare at her oldest daughter.

"Fredericka. I really don't need your smartness just now."

"Okay then. Suit yourself. You've become just *like* him. A mirror image of his sad, frustrated self. You are both pathetic!" she yelled at her mother as she turned and started back up the steps, but not before her mother reached out and grabbed her shoulder, spinning her back around in the direction from which she had just turned. In an instant, Ellen planted the imprint of her five fingers on her daughter's cheek.

"You insolent child! Just *where* did you and that cold heart come from! Go upstairs! *Get* out of my sight! *Now!*" Ellen screamed.

Standing on the front stoop, she tucked her coat collar up around her neck and took a deep breath as she gazed up at the moon. Grace Reston heard screaming coming from behind the walls of her daughter's house—something ugly, foreign and unfamiliar. Uncertain about her decision, she turned and placed her hand on the front door knob, hesitating momentarily before re-entering.

The scene she encountered in the hallway was a surreal freeze-frame. Ellen, her hands on her hips, fronted a frozen-faced Fredericka, who stood motionless with her hand to her cheek.

"Ellen. What in the world is going on in here?" Grace gasped.

Seconds passed in agonizing slowness before Ellen responded.

"Mother, this is none of your business. It doesn't concern you."

"Well, it *does* concern me when my daughter and granddaughter are acting like heathens. And I know why. You can't *hide* it anymore. *He* is the reason for this degrading action tonight. And because of that, I can't help but be involved. "

"Mother, just *leave*! If Daddy hadn't had such a demeaning attitude toward him from the day we were married, maybe Hume wouldn't be acting like this," Ellen pleaded, defending Hume.

Shifting her attention, Grace walked over to Fredericka and removed the hand covering the red hand-print.

"Put a cold compress on that and keep it on it the rest of the night."

Turning back and casting her eyes toward Ellen, she finished.

"Perhaps it won't be noticeable by morning."

"Mother, I can handle this. This is still my family and you don't need to..."

"All right Ellen. I will leave now," Grace interjected. "But you need to do something about your situation. This can't go on. Your father and I are aware of what is going on here, and it's starting to affect the entire family."

With that, Grace let herself out the door.

The full moon crested the horizon and once again, observed the outline of a man sprawled out at the edge of the field below. The prone figure did not move as he dreamed drunken dreams of strange little people, dancing around a fire just inside the tree line. In the dream, he had been walking the edge of the field under a full moon, peering into the dark woods, as if looking for something he had lost. The dream did not reveal what that something was—just something lost or misplaced, something that was very significant, something very important that he find.

The moon's glow caught the hardwoods, bouncing off and scattering a shadowy array of tree trunks and twisted limbs on the forest floor. He was peering into the moonlit areas on the ground for whatever it was he was looking for, when he suddenly detected movement back further in the forest—movement he did not recall from his previous forays into the woods at night. This was not some nocturnal creature that roamed the darkened, sleeping landscape. No, this was different.

Stopping at the edge of the woods, he looked deeper into the forest, around and through the thick trunks of maples, oaks and old pines and he saw a flickering light, about fifty yards in, going off and on in a rhythmic pattern. The hair on his neck tingled with trepidation, but his body moved forward on its own into the woods, as if drawn to the source of light.

Working his way closer through the trees, he heard the faint sound of voices in song. He stopped and peeked around the broad back of an old oak tree to observe a scene that was startling, yet somehow vaguely familiar.

In a clearing in the forest, just ahead of him, were a half-dozen or so little men, dancing around a small fire that to them must have seemed a bonfire. The little folk were shirtless, exposing hairless chests, and they wore furry kilts, bound with thick leather belts, which ended just above exposed knobby little knees. Their legs continued down to shoeless feet on which they danced tip-toed, on stunted, hairy little nubs. Their smooth faces, framed on either side with pointed little ears, were longish and emanated youth.

All were young, except for one, who appeared to be the elder. This one wore a vest that matched his kilt, exposing a hairy chest and arms. His lower face, framed by the same pointed ears, sprouted a white flowing beard, exposing a fuller face with rounded, cherub cheeks, glowing red from the warmth of the fire.

They were dancing around the flame, singing a distantly familiar tune when suddenly, the heaviest and largest of the group, the one who appeared to be the elder or the leader, stopped and slowly turned his head in the farmer's direction. Hume attempted to move back into the dark cover of the tree, but he was too slow. The little man's smiling gaze met the farmer's face, presently exposed and illuminated by the firelight. The glee in the elder's eye did not go unnoticed by the farmer.

The look was warm and inviting, as if to say, *We have been waiting for you.*

At the same moment, above the upward licking flames that illuminated the overhanging limbs came a sound, as if someone calling his name.

Huumm, Huumm, Huumm, came the chilling call as he looked into the fire-lit night in the direction the sound came from.

He scanned the tree line and spotted two big eyes staring down at him from one of the oak trees that lined the circumference of the opening. Squinting through the firelight, he saw an owl, perched on a low limb, looking down at him, and it again, called out, *Huumm, Huumm, Huumm.*

As he looked deep into the nocturnal creatures reflecting red eyes, the circle of firelight began to spin slowly around him, and he heard the owl change its cadence as it seemed to call out,

Huumm, are you ready? Huumm? Huumm, are you ready?

The spinning circle picked up its tempo and spun crazily round and round, flashing the grinning little faces before him in a dizzying, fast forward kaleidoscope of Saturday morning cartoon faces. And that was the last he recalled before the night went black.

Chapter 24

The sun burned bright, reflecting in the watery corners of Hume's eyes. Leaning up on one elbow, he wiped away the grogginess and surveyed the surrounding landscape, trying to remember where and how he got to where he was. Then the dull memory of the night began to emerge, bringing him to his feet.

Recalling dimly, as though through a scrim on a stage, behind, which actors performed, the night came back to him as he slowly turned his head toward the tree line. Uneasiness stirred in him as he made his way over to the edge of the woods. He poked his head into the dark coolness of the shady forest while his body remained outside the tree line, and he peered in the direction where he thought the dream, or whatever, had taken place.

Just as in the memory, his body entered the tree line, though not fully wanting to. He moved quietly through the trees. His head pivoted with every creaking sound the forest made. He had an unsettling feeling that he was not alone but he continued, slowly creeping deeper into the woods. Nearing a big grandfather oak, he had the distinct feeling he had been there before.

He stood behind the old tree, heart pounding, gathering his nerve to have a look at what might be behind it. Slowly, he peeked around the massive trunk and what he saw, he halfway expected. There in a clearing, was the charred blackened ground where a fire had been. Easing out from behind the protection of the tree, he edged over to the rim of the fire ring and inhaled the odor of burnt grass and wood.

Slowly, he bent over and felt the ground inside the ring. The warmth of the earth in the circle caused his hand to jerk back as he quickly stood. He scanned the scene several times before something on the other side of the burned ring caught his attention. He walked around the circumference and arrived at the other side, closing on the object until he was standing above it. Between his dusty boots lay a large, brown feather, measuring about an inch in diameter and perhaps three or four inches long. Reaching down to retrieve it, he suddenly thought better of it.

No, he would let it lie. For some reason, he felt he did not want to have anything to do with the feather. Best to let it remain in the dream.

Cutting across the land on his way back to the house, Hume came upon Daisy and Walt, sitting out under the shade tree.

"Mornin, Mista Hume. Care for a jar of cold well water?"

His tongue and mouth were as dry as sandpaper when he responded.

"Reckon I do. Thank you, Walt."

He took the Mason jar, full of cool water, and took a seat in one of the metal frame chairs.

"Morning, Daisy," he began, timidly.

With the dream of the owl was still on his mind, he thought this might as well be as good a time as any to broach the subject with her.

"Daisy, seems like somewhere, in the back of my mind, I remember an old wives' tale, something about—if you hear an owl call your name out, bad luck gonna come your way. Ever hear *tell* of that?"

Daisy stopped her sightless knitting.

"You *know* somebody who heard their name called out by an owl?"

"Well, no, not really... In a dream, maybe... Somebody who..."

"That *somebody* best not be foolin round with that stuff. That ain't no child's play."

"Why is that?"

"Cause, it just ain't. The owl lives—part in the real world, part in the spirit world. The owl be a messenger of secrets and omens. Somebody dream about an owl, death may be on its way. Somebody *hear* an owl call out they name, means things a-gonna change. That person's time on this earth may be nearing the end, that's for sho."

Hume sat motionless, the Mason jar suspended in his hand, the color in his face fading to a chalky tint.

"Appreciate the water."

Hume attempted to disguise his panic as he set the jar on the ground beside him.

"I believe I'll be on my way home."

"Nawsuh—that ain't no child's play. Somebody hear they name called by an owl, dey gonna come across some bad times, for sho," her voice followed, as Hume disappeared down the draw.

Chapter 25

Weary, he stepped into the backyard and stopped, hands in his pockets, and surveyed the familiar scene. All was quiet. It occurred to him it was Saturday, which meant Ellen and most of the kids would be sleeping late.

Crossing the yard, he stopped and bent down to pet Dixie, stretched out on her side beside the back steps, relaxing in the shade on the backside of the house. As he gently pulled her long ears, the hound looked up at the man gratuitously before plopping her head back to the ground.

"Dix, ol girl," he said smiling down at the devoted friend. "I reckon you and that mule of mine about all a man can depend on to be constant. Ain't that right, ol girl?"

The back screen door opened, filled with Ellen, her hands behind her back.

Glaring down, she rolled her eyes.

"I guess I don't have to ask, do I?"

Standing, he attempted to defend himself.

"Now, Ellen, wait a minute. You don't know what happened last night, and I ain't so sure I do either."

"No, I don't guess you would, when you're blacked out from alcohol."

"Yeah, I reckon you're right, Ellen. You always *are*. Ain't no use arguing with you, once you get something in that head of yours."

Her right hand emerged from behind her, and she threw the brown envelope down the steps, hitting him on the side of his face.

"You know, I'm finding it harder and harder to feel sympathy for you, Hume. Time was—the news that's contained in that envelope would have broken my heart, knowing how hard it would be for a man like you to lose his damn, precious land. But now days, I'm not so certain you don't *deserve* it."

He gazed down at the envelope.

"I don't reckon I need to open this to know what's in it, do I? When's the sale?"

"Week from Tuesday."

"Well, I guess that's that, isn't it?" he said, taking a seat on the bottom step.

"I *guess* it is! Least we can keep the roof over our heads. Tenser can *have* the land for all I care,"

"That's all you *care* about, ain't it? You always did want to live back in town, where your folks came from. You and your daddy always looked down on this way of life. I *know* that."

"You think that, Hume? You really *think* that about me? My daddy is another matter. But *I* didn't move out here, raise nine children, get tobacco juice caked all over my hands just to have you—now that you're losing your land—say something as untrue as *that!*"

She sighed, angry.

"You know, Hume, I'm stuck in this too. I'm *trapped* and would love to find a way to leave all this! Our marriage is not what I had thought it would be at this stage of our life, but I haven't walked out on you yet, have I? But I'm not so sure I can say the same for you. Sometimes I think you've already left."

As she turned to go back in the house, he spoke out.

"You know Rhody goes with the land, don't you?"

Ellen stopped in her tracks, turning.

"No, I didn't know that."

"Yep, the land, tobacco barn, the pack house and all farming tools and machinery. That includes my mule."

"What on earth would Tenser want with a *mule*? Make it a house pet? I wouldn't doubt it, considering the common sense of the man."

"I reckon the new buyer would have an interest in Rhody," he answered. "That's a damn fine mule."

As her husband turned his head back in the direction he'd come from, Ellen descended the stairs and took a seat on the step behind him. She looked at the backside of his head and couldn't help but reach out to gently tousle his hair.

"I reckon I'd better tell Walt and Daisy about what's to come. Need to give them as much time as possible to sort out what they're gonna do. God, of all the people that are gonna find out about this, I think telling Walt's gonna be the hardest of all. It just don't seem fair, all the way around.

"I know this is gonna be hard. But we can make it through this! Give it some time. Get back on your feet, and maybe someday you'll own land again, some *new* land. Maybe, this time raise some milk cows."

Turning his head back toward her, he glared at his wife.

"You're already talking bout a new life, when the old one ain't even ended yet! I still gotta swallow the prospect of someone else working my land like I've done for the last twenty-five years. What's wrong with you, woman?"

He remained sitting on the back steps, bracing his head with his hands, after Ellen got up and walked back into the house, but not before she turned and responded.

"I don't think much of a man, going off and pulling a drunk, letting his wife have to handle the news that came in the mail yesterday, all on her own. I could have used your shoulder," she said as she disappeared into the house.

Burying his head in his arms, he mumbled to himself.

"Ain't careful—gonna lose more'n your land."

"Have a seat and set a spell, Mista Hume. I'll pull up a fresh jar of water," Walt said, cranking the handle and pulling up a bucket of cold water from the well.

"Thanks, Walt. I think I could use that about now," Hume said.

Walt handed Hume the Mason jar, already sweating from the humidity. The two men sat under the span of the old oak tree, facing each other, not saying anything.

"What's wrong, Mr. Hume. You look a bit peek-ed."

Hume rubbed his palms back and forth on his thighs.

"I'm afraid you're right Walt, I am peek-ed... with what I gotta tell ya."

"Well it can't be as bad as you be lookin right now. Can't *nothin* be that bad! We been through a lot over the years, you and me, and we still came out the other side."

"We'll I'm afraid this one has only one side, and you and me ain't coming out the other side," Hume half-groaned.

A few heavy seconds passed before Hume explained.

"I'm losing the farm."

"You doing *what*?" Walt responded.

"I'm losing the farm, and there's nothing I can do to stop it."

Hume stood and walked out a ways from where they were seated. He put his hands on his hips, surveying the view of his tobacco field from what had been Walt's perspective, through all the years.

His dragged his right hand across his face, accompanied by a soft sob. With his back still to Walt, he struggled to say the words.

"God, I'm sorry, Walt!" Then softly, to himself— "I guess I'm just like my daddy, after all."

Taking a deep breath, he turned to face his old friend.

"I don't know what to tell you... as far as what you and your family will do. I guess maybe you should just stay here until the new owner takes over, and you can see what he has in mind. Maybe y'all can stay on and keep doing what you've been doing all these years. I just don't *know*, Walt."

The two men stood, facing each other, not knowing what to say.

"Yeah well, that's about it, Walt. That's what I come to tell ya. So I guess I'll head on back to the house. Tell Daisy I'm very sorry for all this. And that she was right."

"Right about *what*?" Mista Hume.

"About what she said about the owl calling my name."

"Mista Hume?"

"Yeah, Walt?" Hume answered, turning back to face him.

"I believe there's *always* the other side, and we'll make it there, somehow. Sho nuff! When times gets bad, my people don't know nothing else to do, but wade across the river to the other side. Don't you worry bout us."

"I hope you do, Walt. I really do. You deserve that. If this damned world don't give you anything else, you deserve to survive and come out the other side."

Hume had turned his back on Walt and started down the trail when Walt did something Hume had never heard him do. Walt broke out in a rich, deep, baritone voice and sang the words to an old Negro spiritual Hume knew from childhood.

Wade in tha water,
Wade in tha water, children, now,
Wade, in tha water.
Wade on over to the other side."

"Jordan's water is chilly and cold
Wade on over to tha other side.
Chills tha body but not the soul.
Children wade on over to tha other side.

Chapter 26

Tuesday arrived after an unusually quiet eight days in the Rankin household. Hume and Ellen spoke only when necessary. The relationship was limited to cold, polite exchanges. The children, picking up the tenseness, dispensed with excessive conversation as well.

Hume dawdled around the house that morning, appearing not in any hurry to get to work at the warehouse.

"Are you *not* going to work today?" Ellen inquired, detached.

"Yeah, just looking for my pocket watch. What'd you do with it?"

"Oh, I took it and pawned it yesterday. I figured you'd eventually lose your job by not showing up and we would need the money."

"You're real damn funny, woman," Hume glared as he turned to go back upstairs.

"Try looking on the dresser by your bed. That's where I saw it last," she shot back at him.

There was not a whole lot to do around the warehouse late in the month, since the tobacco auctions ended the middle of October. General housecleaning, moving the wooden pallets the tobacco was displayed on, and catching up on who sold what took up most of the day.

The farmers still came in, not on a regular basis, but more as a thing to do when there was nothing else to do. Farm life filled their world from spring to fall, and once the climax of the sale was complete, the farmers were at a temporary loss about how to spend their time. Thus, the warehouse served as an extension of their world, but on a social level. For the first time in his life, Hume became an outsider, keeping to himself, gathering bits and pieces of news on how well or how not so well the other farmers fared.

On that Tuesday afternoon in October, as he swept the concrete floor, near where he had sold his final pallet of tobacco, he discreetly listened to some of the other fellows discussing their season, when one of them suddenly bellowed,

"How *bout* old Worth Baker! Ain't he the *sly* one! Buying Rankins' land at foreclosure for fifty cents on the dollar! He bought the damn farm for *half* what it's worth!"

"Naw, you don't *say*! I never heard about that," another farmer replied.

"That's just the *thing*—seems like nobody heard nothing bout the sale, except for Baker. That's what I'm *saying*—he's about as sly as a fox, creeping up on a henhouse. He and that Yankee banker must have been in cahoots, somehow."

Hume stood transfixed, with the broom stopped in mid-sweep.

What he had just heard passed into the earlobe fine, but as it worked its way past the outer ear and through the auditory canal, into where the words *should* have found their seat in the temporal lobe of his brain, the words did not settle.

The message rebounded against the walls of his skull, causing a reverberation of sound that made it difficult to hold onto. The sound grew louder, like a freight train in his head, causing him to drop the broom and cover his ears so as to try and dim the noise. Hearing the broom handle slap on the concrete floor, the farmers turned in unison and observed Hume Rankin, his mouth agape, his head bowed over with his chin on his chest, both hands covering his ears.

"I'll be damn!" the farmer who broke the news shouted out. "I didn't know he was standing there!"

"Well, hell, you knew Faucette put him on the payroll till he gets himself back on his feet again," the other farmer said.

Hume's head spun and his breath became shallow. The interior of the warehouse containing the group of men swirled round and round him, as if he was on a merry-go-round. He dropped to his knees and tried to slow his breathing by taking deep breaths. It had worked in the past, and the technique seemed to be working now. The room finally stopped spinning and the freight train passed on down the tracks. Several of the farmers ambled over, except the one who announced the acquisition, to see if they could be of any assistance.

Faucette, who had witnessed the breakdown from his office high above the floor, bolted down the steps and arrived where Hume sat on both knees.

Bending over and patting him on his back, Faucette extended a hand.

"Hume, you all right? Anything I can get you? A glass of water?"

Embarrassed at his display of weakness in front of the other men, Hume called off his employer's concern with a wave of his arm.

"Naw, I'm okay. Preciate it, Faucette."

Then he looked up at the men gathered in the semi-circle around him and asked, "Is that true? Did Baker *really* buy my land?"

"I heard tell of it earlier this morning, but this here confirms it, I'm afraid. I'm sorry, Hume. I know you and he had your differences. This news must smart," Faucette replied.

Rising, Hume protested.

"Smart! Hell! He's the one who's gonna be smarting after I'm finished with him. Sombitch! This just ain't gonna happen. I'm gonna *kill* the bastard for this!"

The gathering of men cast worried glances at one another as Hume broke through a pair of shoulders and left the building. His pickup truck spit gravel as he disappeared in the gritty dust.

Chapter 27

Cyrus and Mason Baker arrived at the front door the morning following the sale, hats in hand.

"Morning, Mrs. Rankin. Is Hume home? We need to speak with him."

"He's not here. Never came home last night. But I know why you're here. Bessie Washington's phone finger is faster than you are. She called and gave me the news last night. I'm sure that has a lot to do with him staying out all night. Is there something I can do for you?"

"We'll, no Ma'am, there's not, to be rightly honest," Cyrus responded. "In fact, coming by the house here, is just a courtesy call by my brother and me."

Pulling the newly prepared deed from his front pocket, he offered it to Ellen for her inspection.

"I don't need to see that. Just tell me why you're here."

"Well like my brother just told ya," Mason stammered, "We came by the house as a courtesy. We didn't want to show up at the barn without first letting you know. But Mrs. Rankin, our brother aims to take possession immediately and he sent us over to collect any farm equipment there might be in the barn behind the house there. And I'm afraid that includes Hume's mule."

"Couldn't wait for the dust to settle could he, that brother of yours," Ellen answered through slightly quivering lips. "Well, I reckon this is as good a time as any, since Hume isn't here. But you aren't going out there all by yourselves. Hold right here and let me get Alford to go with you. I don't want you all taking anything that isn't, as of just now, rightly yours."

"Yes, Ma'm. We'll wait *right* here, Mrs. Rankin," Mason assured her.

———

"Y'all make it quick, now. I don't want my daddy showing up seeing y'all taking his mule and tack. He's had that harness since he bought his second mule. And that mule you're harnessing there is like taking a member of his family," Alford said.

"We will, Alford. This ain't real pleasant for us either, ya know. Me and Mason always got along with your daddy. It's just him and Worth that can't seem to gee and haw," Cyrus said.

"Well, in the Rankins' eyes, your brother don't stand very tall. Seeing as how he ain't man enough to come take it himself speaks that of him, don't you think," Alford scoffed.

Mason, slipping the bridle over Rhody's head, answered over his shoulder.

"Oh, but he *is* man enough, I'm afraid. He wanted to come over here with us in the worst way, but we told him it would be a might easier if we came, just us two."

Standing aside, Mason scanned the barn.

"Anything else? Transplanters? Sleds?"

"All that's down at the tobacco barn. All's left here will be crib storage up in the loft. You two will have taken everything of any value with you when you leave here."

"Well, I reckon that'll be it, then. Good day Alford."

Mason led the creature from its berth, walking it out of the barn.

"I hope that will be it. But I kinda *doubt* it," Alford muttered to himself while gazing at the empty stall, held in the barn's fading light.

Hume sat in the family living room, his silhouette outlined in the dim afternoon light. He did not make a sound as he entered the front door, and he took a seat in his rocking chair, sitting there, not rocking. Ellen entered the living room from the kitchen and had started across the room to turn on a lamp when she caught his dark form out of the corner of her eye.

"Oh my God, Hume! You *scared* me! Where have you *been*? We have been worried sick about you. George Faucette called yesterday and told me what happened at the warehouse. He said you had a spell—thought you were having a heart attack. Then he said once you started coming around, you started talking about what you are going to do to Baker. What happened?"

"Just felt a little light-headed there for a minute or two, once I heard *who* bought my land. I guess you heard?"

"Yes, I did. And what's this about what you're going to *do* to him?"

Staring blankly into his wife's face, he answered.

"What the hell you *expect* me to do? Help him set his crop next spring, on *my* land? That bastard!"

"Hume, you can't go around saying things like that in public, around other people."

"Don't you go lecturing me about nothing, you hear? I just don't wanna hear anything you have to say right now."

"That was *not* a very smart thing to do," she insisted.

"You better stop with the lecture, Ellen," he retorted. "I ain't gonna hear it!"

The heated exchange brought Alford, Fredericka and Mary Ellen to the doorway. The other children—Emmaline, Eleanor, Mirabelle, Johnny, Jackie and Tommy descended the stairs and perched there, their faces framed by the spindles on the stairway.

"What's going on in here," Alford questioned, while Fredericka turned and shooed the young-uns back up the steps.

"Y'all get on back upstairs. Y'all don't need to hear this!"

Hume remained in his rocking chair, now rocking ever so slightly, saying nothing.

Alford stood his ground.

"Daddy, I *asked* you a question!"

His aggression brought Hume up from of the rocker. He walked over to his son and planted himself in front of him before he responded in a low, near growling, voice.

"Boy, I've been beat down bout as low as a man can be beat, and I ain't gonna be beat down no lower. Not by you, Worth Baker, or *her*!"

"Hume, it's that we care about you. The four of us were out looking for you last night. After hearing what Lambeth said, we feared for what you might do."

Looking through weary, blood-shot eyes that exposed his obvious inebriation from the night before, Hume sneered.

"Oh, I *saw* y'all! I was watching the whole time while I was hiding in the bushes, so y'all wouldn't find me, laughing at all of ya—acting like y'all cared if I ever came home or not."

"Well, that'll be the last time I do it, I can tell ya *that*!" Alford sneered.

Both men stared each other down, face-to-face, fists clinched, as Mary Ellen started crying.

"Y'all stop that now! You hear me? *Stop* it!"

Slowly, Hume broke the locked glare at his son and turned his head toward his daughters and wife. And then he looked back to his son.

"This'll just about *do* it. I've seen it *all* now. The man takes my land and the four of you turn on me! Is *that* what you and him discussed that day he paid you a visit to collect his stewed apples, Ellen?"

"Hume, you keep sinking deeper and deeper and I can't bear to..."

"To hell with *all* of you," he said, his hoarse voice just barely filling the space around them.

 Stopping at the back door, he turned once more.

"All my grown life, all I've done is try to provide for this family! And *this* is what I get?"

The screen door slammed as the four stood silently, looking at each other in the fading afternoon light.

Chapter 28

Crossing the backyard, headed for the livestock barn, Hume walked past the coop and observed the chickens were acting up and in a state. He felt a kinship with their mood.

"To hell with that fool nigger woman and her damned *superstitions*! Sure as hell didn't know what she was doing when she worked *my* spell. My ruination is what it was! Asked for a little rain, and what'd she give me? A damned hurricane landing right on top of my crop, *that's* what!" As he entered the barn and stopped just inside the door, an overwhelming sense of emptiness overcame him. He held his gaze straight ahead for a moment, until his eyes began to betray him by slowly turning right, toward the stall. The betrayal was completely realized as he gave in, turning his head to fully observe the empty cubicle. Shafts of sunlight bathed the stall floor, where his mule should have been. He was not prepared for the ache that followed. A wave of emotion came barreling up from deep in his gut.

Bending forward, clasping his stomach, he fell to his knees, a groan emerging from the depths of his being. His upper body spilled over, the top of his head butting the barn floor, both arms spread out before him as his fingers clawed in a futile attempt to cause damage to the hard-packed dirt. Tears fell from his eyes, mixing with and becoming one with the unyielding soil.

He drifted away, falling into a merciful sleep, dreaming of open land and living, growing things. The part of the dream he would recall was the memory of him as a younger man, out in the fields, the sun low in the sky. The crop was mature, close to harvesting, as he walked toward the setting sun, both arms out, tenderly brushing the tops of the plants. The wind began to pick-up, gently at first, then mounting into a steady blow. Carried within that wind, a message blew across the swaying field, as if saying: *It is harvested. It always was. It will be harvested without you.*

The young man was confused.

"I don't understand," he said as he cast his voice out into the wind. "Tell me what you *mean*! It is all up to me! The crop will *wither* without me. I'm the *farmer*!"

"It is. It always has been. And it will be, without you," the voice spoke again.

And at that moment, the wind ceased. The sun dipped below the tree line, and the young farmer stumbled out of the dream, prone on his stomach, his cheek pressed against the barn floor as he lay there, gathering his wits.

Life as he knew it had changed. He knew for some time in his mind that he was going to lose the land. He knew his mule and the tack and other equipment were to go with it. But it never registered in his gut until he saw the empty stall!

Seeing that made it real! Now he not only knew it, but he felt the loss. He pushed himself into a sitting position with his forearms and wiped the drool from his lower lip. Sitting in the silent, empty barn, he pulled his legs into his arms and rested his head on his knees. He felt alone—as alone as he had ever been.

Seeing the upstairs bedroom light go out, he slipped in the back door. He had been sitting at the edge of the woods, watching the warm glow in the house slowly extinguish itself. The late October night had grown chilly, and he wasn't wearing a jacket.

Silently, he crept into the living room and lay down on the sofa, pulling an afghan, knitted by Ellen, over his chilled body. He felt tired, a profound tiredness one felt from inattention and abuse of one's own body and soul. And probably from a sadness that followed him nowadays, like a shadow.

He awakened with the couch cushion being depressed on his backside. He rolled over and looked up into the eyes of his wife, sitting at the edge of the couch.

"Hume, we *have* to talk. Will you be here this evening when I get home?"

"What do you want to talk about, Ellen?" Hume asked, rubbing the back of his hand across his mouth.

"I can't get into it now. The children are off to school and I've got to catch the bus for work. I want to talk to you when I get home."

"Now! Tell me now, and get it over with."

"Hume, I don't think we should be together right now. I think I want you to go live with one of your brothers until we can get a hold on this thing. It's destroying you and starting to get to the children."

Looking up at his wife, it occurred to him how lovely she looked in the morning light. A loveliness, he thought, that emanated from somewhere deep inside her, *from an inner strength and goodness that he knew he needed and depended on. Without it, he was less of a man.* Inside, he knew that. Always had, he figured.

Sadness crept over him. He wished he'd acknowledged and appreciated her more than he had. And, it seemed, future opportunities were waning. He just didn't know right then, but the rising pain and accompanying anger at once overcame the sadness.

"Well, if that's the way you *feel*, Ellen, you just go the hell on! What else can I lose now? That just about *does* it!"

"Hume, we'll talk about it this evening. Please be here."

The Blue Goose announced its arrival outside on the hardtop.

"I've gotta go now, Hume," she said, hurrying out the front door. "*Please* be here when I get home."

"Morning, Ms. Rankin. Looks to be a pleasant day, don't it?"

The inside of the bus held the usual riders. Two older, colored men sat hunched side by side, talking in hushed tones in the rear. In the middle, on the right, side aisle sat Juanita Walker, silently reading the *Grit* newspaper.

Forcing a smile, Ellen dipped her head to acknowledge her fellow passengers and took her familiar seat.

"I don't know about that, Charles," she muttered, more to herself than to him.

Moments later, her thoughts drifted across the rural landscape, and for some reason, worked their way to town, and settling on Tom Spence. Maybe she should arrange another meeting with him, perhaps that very day—to discuss Mary Ellen's curious fixation.

"Of course, Ellen—I would be *very* happy to see you today."

Tom Spence's voice resonated at the other end of the phone line.

"Let me check my calendar. Oh, okay. I have a block open this afternoon at three o'clock. Would *that* work?"

"I think I can make that, Tom. I can wait and take my lunch hour then," Ellen replied.

"Oh, I hate to make you miss your lunch. Shall we have lunch together and discuss it, then? Or would you prefer our meeting to be more private? *What* was it you needed to talk about today? You sounded rather dire."

"Your office would be fine," Ellen blurted, embarrassed and yet a bit surprised at her sudden boldness.

As the morning passed, she was in a nervous state. She made more mistakes during that one day than she had since she started. She just couldn't keep her mind on her work. Her thoughts centered on her meeting with Tom Spence and why she wanted to talk to him.

Was Mary Ellen the *real* reason for arranging another meeting with Tom? Or was he and his enchanting world of knowledge a destination to escape to?

The sudden, honest acknowledgement of such a possibility caused her breaths to come in short staccatos. Her jitters morphed into a light-headed dizziness, causing her to search out a desk and chair in a quiet corner, beside a window.

Sitting there, she gazed out the dirty window onto the quad below. Happy students, giddy in their uncomplicated world, laughed and touched as they made their way along the walk. As Ellen stared with envy at the happy parade of undergraduates beneath the window, lightly fingering the ends of her shortened hair, she made her decision.

She had to call Tom Spence and cancel the meeting. She knew the real reason she sought him out lay just beneath the surface of her consciousness. In an emotional state, a wave of embarrassment grew, filling her with shame.

"Oh, Mrs. Reed," Ellen stammered, relieved to hear Jane Reed's voice. "This is Ellen Rankin. I had an appointment with Tom at three o'clock today, but I'm afraid I'm going to have to cancel it. Something has come up at home that I need to attend to."

She listened for a moment.

"No, I don't want to reschedule right now. I'll call back later. Please apologize to Tom for any inconvenience I may have caused him. Thank you, Mrs. Reed."

Ellen's hand rested the phone back in its cradle, Grateful that she'd been able to abandon her misguided plan before it birthed, she turned her attention toward home.

Chapter 29

Hume left the empty house just after Ellen left for work, thinking thoughts of quiet desperation. He'd had enough of the losing end. He couldn't even the score, but he wanted, at least some, to tilt the tabletop back in his direction. He wanted to strike out at the injustices in his world. And sitting at the top of those injustices was the man who owned his former life.

Walking the old worn path through the woods, a pint of *Southern Comfort* in his back pocket, he made his way to the perch above the field. He felt a need to go there, to reassure himself that the land was still there, as it had been when it was his.

The afternoon sun had eased over its apex and started its slow glide down the western sky. Reds, oranges and yellows and all the shades in between, flamed in the afternoon sunlight, lining the field in a picture frame of color. He remained motionless for several moments, breathing in the scene below, before reaching around to his back pocket and extracting the bottle. He broke the seal and took a long pull. The sting in his belly and the immediate numbing of his soul produced a comfort that conflicted with his viewing of his relinquish land.

He took another long, slow pull on the half-empty bottle, and then he took a seat on the ground beneath an apple tree and studied the scene below, recalling days and seasons passed. The older children had grown up, spending their summer days on that patch of ground. The younger ones played, while their elder siblings worked. But for sure, all had handed up bundles of green stalks that were tied up to be cured golden in the barn. All had connected with the land. And though all else had failed, *that* was good.

That, he hoped, would never change. *If the soil ever got under a person's fingernails, it was sure to get into the bloodstream and eventually find its way to the heart,* he thought. *And I gave em that!—Me and their mother. Me and Ellen's toil made this land what it is. What it has meant to this family. And nobody can take that from us, I don't suppose.*

The thought, buoyed by the alcohol, was making him feel somewhat better, when a figure wearing a broad-brimmed hat appeared in the field to the right, coming from the New Ground, behind a mule and trailing a plow.

Hume knew the animal right off, even though his vision was slightly blurred from drink. He knew that creature by its stride, by the bobbing of its head and by the slight hesitating hitch in its front step—it was Rhody.

The driver popped the mule repeatedly on its flank with the reins, urging it over the roadbed that divided the New Ground and the older, established tobacco field. Once across, the man set the plow and again, he whipped the creature on as the spade bit into the earth, ripping the bare, spent tobacco stalks from the ground. Hume flinched with every snap.

Who the hell is *that* behind my mule? he said to himself, confused.

Closing one eye, he set his sights on the man. He should have known, but his dulled state had delayed the obvious when, not so much from the visual recognition, but from an instant recall of the state of things, the name Baker suddenly exploded, white hot in his head.

The man down there, beneath the broad-brimmed hat, was Worth Baker, and he was abusing Hume's mule on Hume's land. Vile emotion charged through his body, and his limbs shook from a rage that had suddenly possessed him.

The brown liquid was drained from the bottle by the time Hume arrived back at the barn. He entered the quiet structure and walked to the far corner, where he removed something from a recess in the wall.

The nickel-plate gleaned in the soft shafts of sunlight that found their way through the cracks in the barn, as he removed it from its worn leather case. Ellen had insisted he keep it out of the house, hidden away from the children. He'd obliged her wishes by hiding it in a niche in the far wall of the barn, covering the crack by stuffing it with an old hemp cord.

He propped the double-barreled shotgun against the wall, and then he climbed the ladder to the loft where winter hay was stored. He had taken to stashing more than one bottle of his elixir in the front bales, so as to not run out when his anger needed company.

He arrived back at the precipice and walked tentatively to the edge and peered over. Baker was still working the mule in the field below. Bringing the weapon to his cheek, he sighted down the two barrels and took aim on the figure, but he realized the shotgun spread would not span the distance.

"Down! Got to go down to the creek in order to get a shot at him," he mumbled to himself as he left his perch and stumbled, hurrying. He fell at one point, crossing a wash-out, his gun skipping along the marble size rocks down the trail ahead of him. He picked up the gun and made his way down the switchbacks, toward his intended subject.

He needed to obtain a better vantage point, before his target moved further out in the field, out of distance from the cover the creek bank would provide. Halfway there, he caught his rationale.

Cover! What the hell does *that* matter? *If he is out of range from the cover of the creek bed, I'll just walk out and shoot the sonofabitch, point-blank. Then he would know for sure who sent him to Hell earlier than expected*, he thought.

But Hume knew he didn't have it in him—much as he hated the man, to shoot someone point-blank and watch whatever expression, rise and fill the eyes of a man who knew his days had just ended. Besides, the field was in clear view of Old Reidsville Road. Anyone who just happened to be passing by would have a clear view of the deed. And Walt and Daisy's house was just over the knoll. Best to do it the way he planned.

When he reached the bridge, he crossed it and turned left, making his way along the far side of the creek, crouching behind the underbrush so as not to be seen by Baker. His foe was several rows out now, still working his way back and forth near the edge of the creek.

Arriving at what he calculated to be an appropriate distance, Hume stopped and squatted behind a thicket, as he watched Baker reach the end of the row. Turning, the man and mule headed back to where Hume waited.

Heart quickening, Hume hunkered lower, because after he made the turn, Baker would be staring down the row in the direction where he hid. It was getting late in the day and moving on towards dusk. Hume would only have a few passes before Baker would call it quits and take to the barn.

Rhody's head bobbed in its familiar manner as the mule drug the imbedded plow toward him. Peeking through the bush, Hume's heart pounded when Baker, for some reason, suddenly stopped, looked up the row and cocked his head slightly to the left, in Hume's direction.

Instinctively, he fell backward, the limbs threatening to reveal his hidden position by noisily switching back and forth into place. He lay motionless, daring not to move, not knowing if he had been seen and if Baker was coming in his direction or not. Lying on his back, attempting to press his body deep into the earth, out of sight, he stared straight up through an opening in the tree limbs, his view drawn to the Evening Star, perched in the sky directly above him.

Emotion stirred as he looked into the heavens and the dusty words came back to him as he silently mouthed, "Star light, star bright, first star I see tonight..."The spontaneous mental recitation of the old childhood poem stirred a memory of him and his mother, when she would gently sing the stanza into his ear as he lay back, sitting on her lap, mother and child, under the spreading elm in the front yard, looking up into early evening's silvery firmament.

That soft memory of those rare moments shared, when he had his mother to himself, without having to compete with the other siblings— protected from his father's iron, remained within him and came to him at that moment, wrapping him in a sad, yet comforting longing. How far away that seemed!

Fixated, his lips completed the refrain, "...wish I may, wish I might, have this wish I wish tonight," as the star dissolved in his misty eyes.

Pop! Pop! The slap of leather reigns on mule hide interrupted the moment.

"Come up, mule! What are you looking at?" Baker bellowed.

While Hume was on his back, Rhody had continued up the row, bringing both man and plow to a midway point in the field where the mule suddenly stopped dead in its tracks without its master's command. The mule turned its massive head to the left toward the creek bed and shook it back and forth, flaring snorting nostrils and pawing the turned soil with its hoof.

"Come up, you!" *Pop! Pop!* "Come up or I'll step into the woods there and pick myself out a tree limb and beat you over the damned head with it! See if *that* don't get your attention and soften that hard-headed skull of yours," Baker yelled.

The situation escalated in a flood of trepidation. It sounded as if Baker was very, very close. Hume wormed his way on his side, back to the shrub row, and he peeked through the limbs, careful not to disturb them. There, directly in front of him, about twenty feet out, Rhody was stopped in the row, looking in the direction where Hume hid.

"Damn you, Rhody! Not now. Don't do this now! Move on! Move on," Hume softly pled.

But the mule held its gaze.

"I told you! Now see if I don't mean what I say!"

Baker laid the reigns down on the top of the plow handle and started for the edge of the woods, directly toward Hume.

Looking to his left and right, and then back again to where Baker was advancing, Hume realized there was no way out without Baker seeing him flee. Pulling the shotgun toward him and cradling it in the crux of his right shoulder, Hume silently moved the safety to the off position, exposing the ominous red button, while lightly touching the cold metal trigger with his right index finger.

He didn't want to have to do it eyeball to eyeball, but it if it came down to it, *so be it*! As Baker moved closer to the tree line, the mule searched the edge of the forest until its coffee-colored eyes found what it had sensed. Looking between the straggly limbs, the farmer and mule locked eyes and held the stare for what seemed a dangerously long time.

"Please, old boy. Please. Move on. Don't make it happen this way," Hume begged softly.

Baker closed to within several yards, looking upwards with his pocket knife in his right hand and scanned the hanging tree limbs for just the right thickness, while the mule continued to stare into its former master's eyes. Baker was closing the distance and would be right on top of Hume in seconds, when the mule suddenly broke the stare, turned his head back down the row, and let out a piercing high-pitched neigh before bolting down the row, dragging the plow, tumbling on its side.

Turning at the commotion, Baker yelled,

"You sonofabitch! Whoa mule! Whoa. I'm gonna end up *shooting* your sorry ass as sure as I stand here."

He ran after the mule that had slowed to a walk. Bending to grab the reins dragging in the dirt, Baker yanked backward with such force that the bit pulled the mule's head straight up and back, bringing the animal to a halt.

Baker secured the reins by wrapping them around the plow handles and then proceeded to the side of the mule's head. He halted and removed his father's absconded Masonic ring before closing his fist into a bony club, and struck the creature with a wicked blow just below the ear. Hume flinched at the thud.

"That's it. Soon as he makes his turn and comes back this way, he's a dead man," Hume said to himself as he checked the safety to make sure it was still in the off position.

Baker arrived at the far end of the row and pulled hard on the left reign, circling the mule in a wide arc, bringing him around, facing in the opposite direction.

"Come up now!" Baker hollered and the creature started its slow, rhythmic plodding back toward where the man hid, waiting.

Hume checked the safety again. Droplets formed and ran down his brow. Both mule and man continued the procession toward Hume, unimpeded.

"Just stay low and wait till he passes. Give him three paces past you, and then let him *have* it— the left barrel first, and if need be, give him the right one to finish him off. You can *do* this!" Hume said in a hushed attempt to steady himself.

Scanning the sky, he observed it was true dusk, practically dark.

"This should be it. One more pass, and he's done."

His heart was pounding such that he feared Baker would hear it when he made his pass, and the alcohol was affecting his vision. He closed one eye to get a better bead on the man in the field, regretting he had consumed as much as he had, but he knew it was necessary it in order to get to this point.

Nearer! The target closed to within yards. Hume's breathing started to come in short, fast pants. The pounding in his ears consumed his aural, and a wave of dizziness rose and floated in his head, which he shook, trying to stabilize himself.

Close! The man and mule were now in front of him, about twenty yards out in the field. Time slowed. Movement was drawn out. It was an oddity to Hume that he found his attention focused on the side of Baker's face and noticed he needed a shave. As if looking through a pair of binoculars, he could see individual gray hairs mixed in with the rest of the stubble. And oddly, that bothered him.

After he was dead, somebody he don't know was gonna have to shave him before they put him back together for the viewing, Hume predicted.

At that moment, Baker's back was to Hume.

"If I'm gonna do this, *now* is the time!"

Standing from his crouched position, Hume raised his gun. The brakeman was asleep—the freight train that was rumbling through his head was wide open. Now! As he sighted down the barrel, Baker's red flannel shirt filled his vision.

You've got him in the bead. Now! Do it!

But the gun did not respond. Instead, it began to shake uncontrollably in a fit of buck fever. His rapid breathing, inhaled and exhaled through gritted teeth, caused dizziness and spinning in his head. Bearing down, he tried to fight through the state he was in and re-focus on the red-plaid target. Again, it appeared behind the bead at the end of the gun barrel.

Attempting to focus on the moving, swirling red target in front of him...

Now! Pull! It was the last thought he heard amid the roar in his head, just before the sky went black.

Chapter 30

Dawn broke with the creek full of voices, waking him on the bank where he lay. The alcohol was wearing off. His dulled mind attempted to sort out the night's events. He sat up, rubbed his head and thinly recalled what he remembered.

Damn! I did it again! Pulled another one! Ellen will be beyond caring at this point. She'll probably have my bag packed by the time I get home.

Home—the word ached in his soul. It was something he once had, something he could call his own and seek refuge there, but no longer.

Damn you, man! What the hell is wrong with you? You keep messing up. You're like a rock rolling downhill that just keeps tumbling over and over and can't stop!

Cautiously, he attempted to sift through his actions the night before. Sometimes he could remember. Most times though, it was like looking at a wall, where words should be written, but it remained totally blank. It was like trying to read the newspaper in his sleep. He just blanked out and for the most part and couldn't recall.

The urge to pee pressed in his loins. Placing his right hand beside him to boost himself up, his palm settled on something cold, which felt out of place in this setting of weeds, grass, and shrub. Slowly, he looked down at the object under his hand, and it all came flooding back to him. The comprehension shook his entire being as his mind began to gather itself around the day before.

My shotgun! Oh no! Dear God! Help me. Did that really happen last night? Or was it just a drunk dream?

His mind worked back into the murkiness and recalled his instructions to himself—*the left barrel first, and if need be, give him the right to finish him off.*

With trembling hands, he fumbled with the lock and after several attempts, broke down the double barrels of the shotgun, praying he would find two unspent shells nesting in the chambers. Staring wide eyed at the opened cylinders, what he saw buckled his knees. The left chamber was empty. The right one contained the bright-red plastic encasement of an unspent shell.

Dear Jesus!

He dropped to his knees and frantically groped the underbrush for a spent shell, but there was none to be found. His mind raced with possibilities.

I never checked the chamber. I just figured two shells were in there from the last time I used it. Maybe there was only one to begin with!

His thoughts diverted from the shell as he turned his head toward the field.

Is he lying out there? Maybe I missed or just wounded him and he's still alive!

His memory cleared, and he recalled where Baker had been positioned, with his red-flannel back to him and where he would be lying if he had actually shot him. He would have been just outside the tree line, several yards out, directly in front of him. Hume remained in place, not wanting to journey from the cover of the woods.

Breathing slowly, he took two last deep breaths, and then he forced himself through the underbrush and burst onto the newly-plowed field. The brightness of the morning blinded him for an instant as he covered his eyes with cupped hands. After a moment, he spread his fingers and his sensitive, blood-shot eyes searched the sun-drenched landscape directly in front of him. He slowly turned his head left and right, but he saw no body, sprawled on its belly, in the dirt.

Maybe it wasn't a clean shot and Worth had crawled further out in the field, trying to escape his end before his blood ran dry and death overtook him?

He walked to the center of the field, shielding his eyes as he scanned the perimeter. From that vantage point, he could see the entire field. Still, he did not see what his eyes searched for. His heart began to beat in short, staccato steps of excitement.

Dear God, maybe it was just a dream—maybe I imagined this whole damned thing!

But it all seemed so real! He couldn't be content until he walked the entire field in expanding circles. Still, he found no body.

———————

The smell of bacon remained, wafting through the still house. The children were off to school and Ellen was on the bus, headed for her job in town. Looking around the quiet house, Hume had the abrupt thought, *I can probably still make it to work by nine and only be an hour late.*

In that instant, his job was important to him, as was his marriage and his relationship with his children. All seemed worthwhile and salvageable. Last night's nightmare must have been a sign or warning. He felt he had been given a reprieve, and perhaps he still had a chance to put his life back together and save his marriage before it was too late.

It was as if he had been standing for some time, teetering drunkenly, on the edge of an abyss, and save for the grace of God (whom he never liked to give much credence) or some other benevolent entity, he had been allowed to come as close as a person was allowed, yet not fall off. For the first time since he could remember, he felt the long ago snuffed out, spark of hope sputter in him.

He turned the white, porcelain, hot water knob in the tub to let it heat up and then walked over to the lavatory and turned on the hot water there as well. Bending over, he cupped both hands and slowly brought pools of lukewarm water to his face. The act of cleansing was renewing as he remained bent over the sink. He dipped his face into the cupped water, letting it wash over his tired face and eyes, over and over, until the water was too hot to touch. He reached up, eyes still closed, searching the rack for a hand-towel but found a washcloth instead.

That'll do, he thought to himself as he straightened and pressed the cloth to his face, wiping the water from his eyes. He stood, facing the mirror, and opened them. What he saw startled him.

Staring back was a face that was bruised and battered—scratched repeatedly on the forehead, cheeks and chin, from the night in shrubs and briars. But the visage behind the scratches disturbed him even more—an image on an aged and distressed canvass, onto which brush strokes worked their way into a painting, whose colors ran and blurred. Yet the loss and loneliness in that face still bled through, dousing the sudden spark of happiness and optimism he had felt only moments before.

He put both hands on the lavatory and leaned forward, bringing the scarred canvass closer and looked deeply into the sad face that was staring back at him. Closer, he drew his face to the image and felt himself drawn to, and then immersed, in the overflowing brown pools that gazed back at him. Strangely, he felt a surge of compassion for the misbegotten image in front of him.

The journey that face had traveled was lonely and sorrowful, yet there was a humbling beauty that was woven through the struggle that face had endured. It dawned on him that perhaps the *world* was not out of balance. It was *he* that was out of kilter. The world still revolved in balanced perfection. And it was this understanding that led him to the realization that he had arrived at a point in his life—and he could go either way from there.

Step over the line and walk in the light, or remain where he was, lost and rummaging around, groping in the darkness, as he had been doing for some time. He made the decision then and there. It was time, as his daddy used to say, to "straighten up and fly right."

And he would, by God, just as soon as he figured out just how to do that. At that moment, he wished his daddy were still around *so he could ask him just how a man goes about making such a change*. He felt a desperate need to see Ellen and tell her of his decision.

But first, he needed to get to work.

Chapter 31

"Ellen, before you say anything, sit down here and let me talk to you. Please. I have something important I want to say," he pleaded as she entered the room, where he sat at the kitchen table, waiting for her arrival home from work.

He stood and pulled a chair out for her and then waited, hands in his pant pockets, while she studied his damaged face and decided whether to fill the empty chair or not.

"I won't even ask what happened," she said as she laid her purse on the table and took her coat off before taking a seat. "Now days I would ask what happened if there *weren't* scabs on your face."

"Ellen, I know you're fed up with me. And clearly, you have a right. But please, just hear me out on this. I want to tell you what happened last night."

Just as he was about to tell her about his perceived epiphany, Etta chimed happily from the living room, interrupting

"Daddy, Sheriff Bull is here, and wants to *talk* with you."

Hume stopped in mid-sentence, the color ebbing from his face. His paleness did not go unnoticed by Ellen.

Bull Roberson, a large, rotund man with not a speck of hair on his pate, was actually the township Constable, appointed by the Sheriff. He was a loveable man who sported a wide, gap-toothed grin and had the propensity of handing the children of the community a shiny penny, accompanied by a smothering hug, when he greeted them—but not *this* time.

He must have forgot, Etta thought, her delight dampened.

The gregarious man usually kept his pistol in its black leather holster, hidden from view, inside his coat. But just now, he wore it in full view, strapped on his side. Bull was lovable indeed, but he also had a serious side. And that was the side he was wearing as he approached Hume and Ellen.

Hume entered the living room and greeted the constable, his dry throat cracking.

"Evening Bull. What brings you out tonight?"

Bull looked from Hume down to Etta, who was still standing in front of the large man, looking up, hoping he might remember what he'd forgotten.

Picking up on the intended message, Hume cleared his throat, before speaking to the child.

"Etta, why don't you run on so Sheriff Bull and I can talk."

"Okay, Daddy. Goodnight, Sheriff Bull."

"Goodnight, honey. You sleep tight and don't let the bedbugs bite. Okay?"

"All right, I will. I mean, I *won't*," the child responded, giggling as she ran up the stairs.

"Bull, have a seat," Hume offered.

"No Hume, I'm afraid this ain't no social call. What I got to say won't take long."

"Something *wrong*, Bull?" Ellen asked, standing behind her husband, leaning against the doorframe with her arms wrapped around her waist.

"Well, I'm afraid there *is*, Ellen."

Then, turning back to Hume, he fixed a stare before speaking.

"Worth Baker was found shot dead in the creek on what used to be *your* land, just up from that parcel you bought from your brother. He didn't come home last night, so his brothers went looking for him. They found his body late this afternoon, hung up on a fallen tree limb down in the creek. He was shot-gunned in the back, and by the looks of it, from close range."

Announcement made, a degree of compassion returned to the constable's eyes.

"Now this is all preliminary, but I know there's been *bad blood* between you two for years. And seeing as how Baker owns your land, there is *motive*. The Sheriff wanted me to tell you—until this investigation is complete and someone is charged, he don't want you to leave the county. I hate to put it to ya like this, Hume, but it's a *serious* matter."

The dryness in Hume's throat left him without a voice. Unable to respond, he shook his head to indicate he understood.

"You'll probably be hearing from him in the next day or two. Good night, Mrs. Rankin. Sorry to have had to barge in on you with this," Bull Roberson said somberly, as he closed the door behind him.

Turning, Hume looked toward his wife. Her one hand now covered her mouth, the other arm remained around her waist, as if attempting to protect some small part of her inside, not yet wounded. The color had drained from her face.

Hume's stunned gaze fell to the floor.

"Oh my God, Hume! *Tell* me! Hume—*look* at me—What's this is all about!"

Hume's vacant stare remained fixed on the hardwood.

"*Tell me* you don't know anything about what Bull Roberson just left here in this house. *Tell me* you had nothing to do with that and this will all go away!" she managed, just before her voice evolved into a sob that filled the room.

"I... I... I don't know, Ellen."

"What do you *mean*, you don't know? You don't know *what*, Hume?"

"I just don't *know*, Ellen. I don't know if I did it or not. For a while, I didn't think I *did*!"

"Hume! Stop this nonsense and tell me what it is going on!"

Hume's gaze left the floor and climbed the distance to her eyes.

"Where do I *start*?" he asked.

"The end, the middle, the beginning—I don't care! Just tell me what is going on!"

Hume fixed on his wife's frightened face.

"He had it coming to him, whoever did it. And I ain't sure *who* done it. But I gotta tell ya Ellen, I *did* have the intention."

"Hume! We're talking bout *murder*! You wouldn't... you couldn't!"

"I was out at the precipice yesterday," He interrupted. "I wanted to see the land. I don't know why—I just wanted to see it. And that's when I saw him, on my land, working my mule way too hard. And it got away with me, Ellen. You know how I get when I'm drinking?"

He paused, remembering.

"And I got mad... *real* mad. I came back to the barn and got my shotgun. I went back, and *planned* on killing him... to end this damn pain he put inside me. I drank some more and got purty drunk."

His words confirmed the fear in his wife's eyes.

"I took aim on him, Ellen. I *did*. But I don't remember, cause I think I had one of my spells and blacked out. But this morning, when I came too, I searched the field, and I didn't find his body. I didn't see any blood or any evidence that he may have crawled away. And there were no spent shells around me, so I thought, maybe I *didn't* do it. That it was just a bad dream."

His gaze awakened and took life, filling his eyes with a pleading fear.

"I reckon it looks as if I did it, Ellen. *My God!* I'm not a murderer, am I, Ellen?"

He rushed across the floor into her open arms, as both attempted to shield one another in a heartbroken embrace.

Chapter 32

The knock at the door shook both Hume and Ellen from their feather-light slumber. It was too early for social calls. And the immediacy of the knock foretold what was to come.

Hume was the first out of bed. He pulled his pants on with a tug, while sitting on the edge of the mattress. He draped a flannel shirt over his shoulders as he made his way to the door. Before leaving the room, he paused in the doorway and turned to look at his wife and the room they had shared for so many years—the room the last three boys and four of the girls had been conceived in. Sitting on the side of the bed, Ellen looked up and cast a sad smile toward her husband. He sent it back and walked out of the room.

The large constable filled his view when he opened the front door.

"Hume," the big man addressed him.

"Bull?"

The large man moved slightly to his right, motioning over his left shoulder with his thumb, where the smaller High Sheriff appeared behind him.

"Hume, Sheriff Gibson here wants to *talk* with you."

"I understand, Bull," Hume whispered, looking past the constable.

"I know why you're here, Sheriff Gibson. But can we talk out here? I'd rather spare the family as much as I can," he said, as he stepped out onto the front porch.

"Makes no difference to me. Here's as good a place as any," the Sheriff replied.

"Mr. Rankin, ever since Mr. Baker's body was found yesterday, I've had some witnesses come forward with some pretty incriminating evidence against you."

The sheriff seemed to be studying Hume's expression and reaction.

"Seems *some* folks heard you make threats against the deceased. His brothers have signed sworn affidavits saying they heard you tell Worth Baker, after an altercation at his barn, that if he ever came on your land again, you were going to *kill* him. And some farmers over at the warehouse in Burlington heard you threaten to kill him after he bought your land at auction. They've signed affidavits as well. You got anything to say in your defense?"

Hume's face turned ashen as the porch started a wide, arcing spin, and the men in front of him started to recede.

"I... I don't *think* I did... I don't know if..."

His breathing became more rapid as he attempted his defense. Through the wavy panic, he felt his body moving out further from shore, into waters unknown to him. Sensing he was failing and sinking farther, he thought better of it.

"Sheriff, I think I'd like to talk to a lawyer."

"Fine. Bull—you wanna take this man into custody?"

The sheriff moved out of the way.

Looking at his neighbor with a sad disdain, Bull Roberson grasped the farmer by the arm.

"Hume, under your fifth amendment rights, you don't have to talk to us but..."

The rest was lost, as the inside of Hume's head reverberated with the sound of metal train wheels screeching and locking against metal tracks, in a futile attempt to stop the momentum. The sensation of his body being turned around and bent forward became real when the cold metal clasped around his wrists, grabbing a chunk of flesh with each click, while a pair of hands violated his upper and lower body.

Looking up from his stooped-over position, the image of his wife in the hallway, covering her mouth, sobbing, her body shaking, was etched in his mind... and would be forever. The scene seemed strangely disjointed as his oldest son stepped in where Hume should have been, wrapping his arm around his mother's shoulder in an attempt to console her.

———————

The smell of urine and stale vomit permeated to the outer waiting room. The drab, pea-green walls were scuffed and scratched with feeble attempts at words of angry, vulgar messages and slogans aimed at that, or those, who were responsible for the various authors' predicaments.

Ellen looked through the pall, at the miasma of hate, anger, and hurt that had been inscribed on, and into, the concrete wall, as she thought of what utensil she might have in her purse to scribble her own message.

But she did not know what her message was or who it would be for. She couldn't direct it and had no control over it. The emotions inside her pooled in swirling eddies, as caldrons of moving liquid— like the dark green water holes that formed in the mighty, rushing mountain rivers her daddy used to take her to up at Hanging Rock, near Walnut Cove. The family would sometimes picnic on Sundays after church, in retreat from the summer heat, to the dark, protective coolness of the mountain.

The creaking of the cell door, as it opened, intruded into her private space and snapped her back to the moment.

"Mrs. Rankin," the jailer said, looking directly at her. "You'll have to leave your purse with me before you go in."

He glanced toward Alford, standing next to her.

"Is *he* with you?"

"Yes. He's my son."

"Well, only one's allowed in at a time. He'll have to wait out here while you go in."

Ellen shuddered at the bare, exposed feeling of going into that strange, scary world by herself.

"Oh, please, officer. *Can't* he come? He's my oldest son, and quite frankly, I've never been to a place like this and I'm so... It would be of such comfort to me, officer."

Taking notice of the fear in her eyes, the jailer looked from her, to Alford, and back into Ellen's pleading eyes.

"Well, I reckon I could stretch the rules this one time," he said. "But you, I'll have to search," he told Alford. "You wait here ma'am. This will only take a minute."

Alford and the jailer disappeared behind the closing cell door.

Ellen went back to the wooden bench against the wall and took a seat. Moments later, the thick wooden outer door opened and the familiar beige shirtsleeve of a deputy sheriff extended out beyond the edge of it, ushering in new visitors.

"Y'all have a seat in here, and I'll buzz the jailer soon as he's finished," he said in a manner more gruff than he had used with Ellen and Alford.

A rotund woman with a bandanna scarf covering her head— Aunt Jemima came to Ellen's mind—proceeded into the room, followed by a smaller, older colored man, who was followed by a wild-eyed child who looked to be in her early teens. The threesome took a seat opposite Ellen, who sat nervously, with her hands entwined and tucked between her legs in the fold of her dress. She stared down at the stained concrete floor, trying to avoid the curious eyes of the large woman across from her.

The heavy silence in the small room was broken by a low, baritone voice.

"You got someone in here, *too*?" the woman said, from the opposite side of the room.

Ellen's eyes remained fixed on the floor, not sure how to answer a question that she had never been asked before.

She did, but not really, she thought. It's all a mistake and soon, it all would be straightened out, relegated to a dream, dreamed in a fog, a bad dream that would be over soon.

"Ah, uh... I do, but it's all a mistake..." she stammered, barely looking up. "We're just a victim of a bad mistake."

"Ain't they *all*?" the large woman retorted in a huff while attempting to fold her arms around her large girth.

"Excuse me?" Ellen asked as she looked up and into two tired, large, brown eyes stained with red spider veins.

"I mean *mistakes*," the woman explained. "They all need to have a *victim*, someone who pays. That's why you and me be sitting here talking this very minute. We both be at the mercy of things we have no control over. We be victims," she said, moving her meaty arm across the waiting room so as to encompass all its inhabitants. "Same as my boy they got in there. Maybe he did it. Maybe he didn't. Don't matter none. They gonna do with him what they want. A mistake was made, and to make that mistake right, it need a victim. And he gonna be the victim so the mistake can be made right."

She leaned forward, lowering the volume of her voice.

"Now who you got in here? Who *your* victim?"

"My... my husband," Ellen stammered.

The large women bent forward and said in a gentle voice, just above a raspy whisper.

"Good. Now you be better to deal with whatever is to come. You said it out loud—now you *own* it. The fact that they got your husband in there... right or wrong—he still be in there and you be out here. Things done changed in your world. You and he ain't together, and that ain't what's natural."

The door opened again, and the jailer appeared, holding the steel cell door with one hand, while motioning for Ellen to come with the other.

"Mrs. Rankin, this way ma'am."

She removed her hands from between her legs and straightened her dress as she rose, crossed the floor and stood over the large woman, taking the woman's dark hands in her own.

"My best to you and your family. I hope your son will fare well."

The burly, black woman gazed up into Ellen's face.,

"You take care, now. You gotta be strong."

Alford was waiting down the hallway with a disgusted look on his face as Ellen and the jailer approached him.

"Y'all follow me this way. The visitation room is right down here at the end of this hall."

They followed the jailer to the end of the hall, where another imposing cell door stood. The jailer stopped and fingered the round ring, containing numerous keys with large, square teeth. Finding the right key, he inserted it into the key slot and, with a quick twist, the door slowly swung outward. On the other side of it, they passed into a small room, where one empty chair faced a wooden divider, topped with a glass partition.

"Ma'am," the jailer motioned, pulling out a chair.

Hesitating, Ellen moved forward and sat down, sliding herself up to the glass. Alford stood behind his mother as she looked down, fidgeting with a wayward thread that dangled from her overcoat. Finally, when the cell door behind the thick glass opened, her glance turned upward in anticipation.

The brown-shirted deputy entered first, followed by a smallish man who was bent slightly forward, his hands held together in front of him by a pair of shiny handcuffs. She didn't recognize the man at first, but when the figure before her raised his head and his weary, brown eyes found hers, the sudden recognition brought a slight gasp from her lips.

Her husband was not a big man, but this slight, stooped figure bore little resemblance to the proud, attractive man she married. His lower face was covered in day-old sprouts of a beard. It seemed to her they were grayer there than she recalled. The rest of his face bore the worried look of an older man. His sad eyes were sunken, a hollow gaze emerging from the sockets.

When the deputy pulled the chair out, Hume shuffled around to the front, bending over and lifting both bound arms, as if praying, as he sat. His state of incapacitation brought a nervous smile to his lips as he sat down behind the glass in front of his wife. Both locked tired, moist eyes, saying nothing. The fingertips of Ellen's right hand instinctively reached up and gently touched the thick glass, meeting the responding fingertips of her husband's shackled hands.

Hume looked up at his son.

"How are ya, Alford?"

"I'm all right, Daddy. How are you doing?"

"As well as can be expected, I reckon. The foods not the best—certainly not the fine fare I'm accustomed to eating," he said, tears swelling as he looked toward his wife.

"I appreciate you stepping in and taking care of your mother, Alford. I really do."

"No need to thank me."

"Well, still, I do. I just wanted you to *know* that."

"I know it, Daddy," his son replied, the welling tears causing the young man to turn his head.

Not letting on that he saw, Hume turned his attention back to his wife.

"Ellen, how are the young-uns? They holding up?"

"Okay, under the circumstances. Jack and John are real confused. They don't understand. But I guess that goes for *all* of us. Hume, I just have to know this. *Did* you?"

Surveying the room, looking both left and right, he answered in a soft voice, so as not to be heard by unintended ears.

"Like I told you, I just don't *know*. I *did* have intention, but Ellen, I know *me*. And *you* know me. I ain't got that in me. That's what I've got to go on while I'm in here. I just ain't got killing in me. And that knowledge keeps me from going crazy right now. That's what I'm holding on to."

"I know that. We *both* know that," Ellen responded. "But the fact is you were drunk and don't remember. And you *admit* you had the intent... That frightens me, Hume. I'm scared. *Real* scared. Scared like I've never been before."

"Me too, Ellen. But I hang onto that thought. And *you* need to as well. When you get real scared, think, 'That's just not Hume. That ain't in him.' That's what I do, Ellen. And believe it or not, I get a small slice of peace when I think that. Cause I guess I know that all the way down to my soul, if there is such a place in us."

He glanced briefly toward his son as he continued to speak to her.

"I know I ain't been much of a pleasure to be around the last few years. Things got beyond my control, out of balance. But try to remember me *before* all this. *That* is the man I am. *That* is the man I want to get back to, if I have another chance."

He paused.

"*Remember* the other night when you came home, when I started to tell you something in the kitchen, just before Bull came to the house? Well, I had a feeling in me that I might have changed. When I woke up in the woods by the creek, I sure thought I'd killed Baker. I got up and looked around for any spent shells on the ground, but there weren't none. And then I poked my head out of the woods, to where I thought he would have been if I had of done it. And I gotta tell ya Ellen, I was real scared. But again, he wasn't there. I searched the field all over and still didn't find any sign of him.

"Then I came home and cleaned up, and that's when this feeling came over me. I felt I had been given a second chance at life, and for the first time in I don't know how long, I wanted that second chance—to get it right. But then Bull came to the door and all that hope vanquished, exploded into tiny pieces there on the front porch."

Ellen stared at the man in front of her as she listened to her own soul, which *she* knew existed in all people, letting her heart decide whether Hume did this thing or not. But she was just too tired and worn out to be able to come to that conclusion herself. After hearing him out, she found herself leaning toward his innocence. His nature was not that of a killer. But her mind battled with her heart. There were too many variables, too many unanswered questions, which pointed to his having done it.

"Hume, look at me. Look into my eyes."

He lifted his head from his palms, complying with her request.

"I have to tell you, it would almost be easier if you told me you *did* it. That is a real possibility for me to consider, and that possibility is like a dagger in my chest. But add to that burden, the fact is that all things point to you having done it. And with me here, still hearing you and somehow believing you, having to weigh both sides of this—it's just tearing me in two. It's as if I'm being split down the middle. I think, maybe the dagger would be less painful."

The wounded, broken look that crept down his face did not go unnoticed by his wife. Tears streamed down her cheeks and pooled in the corners of her mouth as she continued.

"Hume, I'm sorry. I just don't know how to *do* this. I need you now, to help me with this—like we always did throughout our life together. You were strong, and I always depended on you. But you can't do that now. You're over there and I'm over here. And just like this glass wall that separates us just now, so does the truth."

Ellen buried her sobbing face in her hands, stood up and turned into the arms of their son.

"Ellen," Hume called out to her.

His plea stopped her, but her back remained to him.

"I understand what you just said. I understand the confusion of your heart. I take responsibility for doing that to you. Even if I didn't do this thing to Baker, my behavior in the past has led up to this moment. And for that, I'm sorry. You do what you have to. You have a pure heart, Ellen. Always have. And I reckon if your heart were my judge and jury... well, I'd be fortunate for that."

And after saying that, he was alone, with only the sound of his wife's muffled sob settling in his mind, long after she was gone.

Chapter 33

The mercy of sleep was hard won in jail. The occupants, held deep in the barred catacombs, welcomed the blackness that accompanied it. Men being corralled in such confines produced a cacophony of night sounds. Nightlong sessions of staccato snoring, coughing, and the flutter of gas being expelled, kept a man awake into the wee hours. The fortunate could catch sleep early and ride it into the darkness before the other inmates got there. For Hume Rankin, the soft, hiccupping sound of men crying bothered him the most.

He was enveloped in that darkness when the dream came to him. Hovering above him, sitting on a log, was a little man, dressed in a rough-made vest that was bound at the waist by a thick leather belt. His feet and legs dangled over the side of the log and were bound in boots, made from the hide of an animal that looked to be deerskin. The curl of smoke wafted upward from the corncob pipe he held clinched tightly in the corner of his mouth. Hume's attention focused on the rising smoke.

It remained there as a whitish-gray cloud, held captive by the jail cell's ugly green ceiling. He watched the billowing smoke bounce along the ceiling, seeking an escape. The search enthralled him for some time, when strangely, the ceiling began to disintegrate. Stars, embedded in blackness began to emerge, filling the space where the confining ceiling had been, allowing the clouds of smoke to rise into the darkness and join with puffy white clouds, floating above him in the night sky.

———————

The crackle of the fire and its light illuminated the forest around him. Turning his head slowly, he realized he was deep in a forest of hardwoods that had shed their leaves, on which he now lay. The fire danced upward, encircled by a pit, lined with river rock. Its warmth made him a bit woozy as he stared into the center of the flames.

He held his gaze there for some time, when all at once, he sensed a presence across from him. Cocking his head sideways, he glanced through the fire as the little man, who had appeared in his jail cell, emerged and took form, sitting on a log on the other side. Peering through the blaze, the visage of the man came to him in orange, distorted waves, but the slight smile and the twinkle in his eye was steady.

The two locked eyes and remained that way, not uttering a word, studying each other through the crackling fire that danced between them. An inkling of recognition had just begun its walk toward Hume when he heard the man speak.

"Hello, old friend."

Startled, Hume looked around the fire-lit circumference, but found no one had entered the encampment that could have uttered the welcome. Eyeing the surrounding woods and its empty silence, he turned his attention back to the little man, whose previous smile now beamed through the fire. His cherub-like face held a wide grin, framed by a white beard, exposing little, square, brown-stained teeth that gripped the pipe in the corner of his mouth.

Hume attempted to get up from his resting place to confront the diminutive man, but he could not. His arms and legs betrayed him, paralyzed, unable to assist.

"Why don't you just stay put awhile? We need to talk," the slight fellow seemed to say through the steady grin, though he never moved his lips.

"You say that? How the hell'd you *do* that?" Hume asked, perturbed.

"We can do things in this world that you can't, or forgot how to, that is," was the reply.

"You wanna *talk* to me, you can start by moving your damn *lips*, you little boron!"

His bumbling of that last word bewildered him, just as the little fellow's thoughts again came to him.

"No, I am not a moron, my friend. But *you*, at times, have certainly acted like one. But I will not dishonor you by calling you names. And I'd appreciate it if you would refrain, on your *own* accord—with no assistance from me—from calling me names in the future. I am known in this world as Jebeddo."

Again, the little man's lips did not move, and Hume realized the man was filling him with thoughts, not words. Relenting somewhat, Hume relaxed.

"So what is it you think you and me need to *talk* about, Mr. Jebeddo? And I ain't got all night. Got somewhere I'm supposed to be right now, and you're putting me in jeopardy."

"The night will cover your absence. Don't worry about your previous engagement. There will be time enough for that."

"Just what *are* you anyway? You one of them *gnomes* my daughter always talks about seeing and talking to?"

"Ah, Mary Ellen—such a dear, trusting child. You and your wife did a fine day's work when you first thought of *that* one."

"You keep my family outta this, or so help me I'll..."

"Well, I really can't *do* that now, can I? After *all*, it was Mary Ellen who first opened the door for you and I to meet, didn't she?"

"What the hell you *talking* bout? I ain't never met or known about you till this *night*! And Mary Ellen ain't sitting round this fire tonight."

"I'm not speaking of our meeting tonight. I speak of our previous encounters."

"Ain't so. I never met you till tonight, and I wish that honor were still yet to come."

"Really? Perhaps you don't recall, or just don't want to. But, my dear sir, we have encountered each other numerous times before—those times in the fields, in the barn and beside the creek. In the evenings you love so, when the light of night and day marry and hold you in that timeless moment of neither male nor female—when there are no opposites and all is in harmony—we've met. As much as you wish to suppress it, we are not strangers, you and I. It is *you* that allowed Mary Ellen to open the door for the possibility of us.

"And as much as you want to think that every time she spoke of us, every time you heard us speak to you from the creek, every time you heard a rustle in the field, or you thought you were being watched in the forest—you *thought* you turned your head away from the possibility. But each time, you turned you're head back around, unsure, but curious. Searching! And *that* is what makes you worth saving, my friend."

"Naw. Afraid you got the wrong man. I lost my chance at salvation a long time ago, and that was *my* choice."

"That was *not* your choice. That was the circumstances of your life, and the circumstances of other lives that made the choice. You just responded and went along."

"You don't know who you're talkin bout—bout salvation and such. You're preachin to someone who may have just *killed* a man. And if you're so damn smart, and you know so much bout the inside of me, why don't you answer *that* question, and maybe we can all cut the chase and go home."

Silence followed as the two sat across the distance, staring at each other, neither speaking until Hume, glaring back through the blaze, concluded.

"I *thought* so. Look, I know this is all a dream, and you ain't really sitting over there talking to me through the top of your head. And I have to admit, I believe I've dreamed about your damned, little, munchkin ass before—like the dream with you and your wee friends dancing around a fire and the owl spouting its nonsense up in the tree."

"Good! You remembered."

"Least this'd *better* be a dream, or else I'm gonna be in a world of trouble when they find I broke out through the ceiling of that jail and am not there when the jailer makes his rounds."

Allowed to stand, Hume brushed the leaves from his pant legs.

"Yeah, I remembered. I remember a lot of things. Like I better get my ass back now—with your permission, of course. A new day bound to be on the rise back there, and coming soon."

"Yes, it is my friend," the little man said, as his kind, knowing smile floated across the lowering fire.

"A new day is on the rise. And it is your time. The owl has deemed it."

The filtered light of morning mixed gray with the cell wall. Hume rolled over onto his back, rubbed his dry eyes and recalled the dream from the night before. A sense of disappointment took up space in the cell with him. The freedom he'd experienced in that dream came back to him, and the mystery of the night reminded him of childhood nights, spent camped around a roaring fire, filled with the spirit of the unknown. In a very real sense, he acknowledged to himself that he would have embraced the night if it had indeed, been real. But he knew it was just a dream.

He heard the jailer making his rounds down the hall, rousing the prisoners from their hard-earned sleep, as he rolled out of bed and walked, stiffly, over to the sink to wash the night's dream from his face. Standing before the washbasin, he stretched, arching his back, and tousled his tangled hair. And at that exact moment, he detected the faint but distinct odor of wood smoke, as a portion of a broken leaf floated to the floor behind him.

Chapter 34

"You've got a visitor, Rankin," the jailer announced through the bars.

He had just finished his breakfast and settled back down on his cot to try and take a mid-morning nap. He allowed perhaps, that the dream might return and he might, once again, escape to the freedom of the forest.

Standing, he faced the jailer, wondering who his visitor might be.

"Your *lawyer*—" came the response to the unasked question.

Roy Callahan was a well-known criminal attorney in Greensboro, who took mostly high profile cases, interspersed with the less glamorous, run-of-the mill, garden variety of breaking and entering, assault and occasional moonshine cases, in which his pay sometimes included a Mason jar of the clear, potent spirit.

Hume's two brothers, Mose and Sanders, hired the man and paid his retainer. As was his nature, Mose objected to the outlay of cash without a certainty of results. The idea of a retainer was new to them and seemed like a pretty shabby way of doing business.

The jailer inserted the large, square-tooth key and, with a twist, the door slowly swung open.

"Hold it here while I put these on," the jailer demanded as he detached a pair of the silver cuffs from the back of his belt.

"Deputy, do you *have* to do that? How am I going anywhere? Every time you do that, those cuffs try to take out a chunk of my wrist."

"Sorry, Rankin. It's procedure. Wish I didn't have to, but I do. If the lieutenant sees you in the visitation room without these on, he'll put me in them just before he *fires* me. I'll fasten you in the front. That way, it won't pinch as bad."

"I preciate that, Deputy."

The top of Roy Callahan's silver hair was the first thing Hume saw when he entered the visitation room, as the attorney was bent over, studying a file.

"Have a seat, Mr. Rankin and I'll be right with you," Callahan said, looking up. "I just came from court and haven't had a chance to review your case."

In spite of his hands being clasped, Hume pulled out a wooden chair and eased himself down into it as he waited for the attorney to review his file. The waiting made him nervous, just as it had when he had to wait for Tenser to review his file at the bank.

His experience was that files usually contained matter that was not beneficial or helpful to him or his situation. Most often it was harmful and required him to defend the actions of the contents, so the silent, initial examination made him feel uneasy. He supposed it was the reason he didn't go to the doctor as often as Ellen wanted him to. Just the fact someone was looking on the inside of something concerning him made him ill at ease.

"Mr. Rankin," the lawyer finally sighed, catching Hume by surprise. "I have reviewed the charges in your file and the state's case looks substantial in its evidence against you. Although it is largely circumstantial, it's pretty damaging."

"They have several affidavits here," he continued, "signed by people who heard you threaten to kill the deceased. You and he appear to have a history of conflict, including your trespassing on his land and assaulting him. At this stage, my thoughts are to attempt to plea your case. Plead guilty to a lesser charge, such as second-degree murder, and place yourself at the mercy of the court. You'll do considerable time, but it beats the electric chair."

"Mr. Callahan, you haven't even *asked* me whether or not I did it. Don't you want to *know* that? Isn't that important?"

"Not really, Mr. Rankin. You see, my job is to defend you and in that, it doesn't matter to me whether you killed him or not. I don't really *want* to know, because if you did—and you told me you did—I would be required by law, as an attorney and an officer of the court, to advise the court of your admission and remove myself from your case."

"Well, let me ask you *this*: The evidence is that Baker was supposedly out turning under the land just before he was killed. Does anybody know, or has anybody looked into just where Rhody... my mule, where he was after they found Baker's body? Was he out, wandering in the field, dragging the plow? Or was he back in Baker's barn? If he was back in the barn, then Baker made it back home that evening."

"How did you know that, Mr. Rankin?"

"Know what?"

"Know that Baker was out plowing his land when, or just before, he was shot?"

"I... uh... heard that... I thought..."

"You *see* now, Mr. Rankin, how the law can work? How information can work against you? Knowledge about the circumstances of a crime, even though you think that knowledge might exonerate you, can be turned around and used against you. Sometimes it's best to know nothing and say nothing. Just require the state to make its case. That's the way it's done in our system of justice. But, in *your* case, I'm afraid they have done a pretty good job of doing that."

"Just like that? It's over, Mr. Callahan? That's *all* I get?"

"Well, Mr. Rankin, you have threatened, in front of witnesses, to kill him. And you have admitted you were at the scene, with a weapon in your possession, on or about the day he was murdered. Now *what*, Mr. Rankin, would you propose I build your defense on?"

"I... I... don't know, Mr. Callahan. I know the circumstances are stacked against me, but I was drunk. I think I may have passed out or blacked out or something. I've been having episodes. I just remember seeing black, then waking up the next morning."

Hume felt a sense of desperation setting in.

"I looked for spent shells, but there were none. And I've been having these spells... nervous spells where I... Look, Mr. Callahan, I know this sounds pretty stupid, but I *know* me and against all this evidence, I just *know* I couldn't have done such a thing."

At that, the lawyer looked up from the file and incredulously eyed his client before taking off his glasses and rubbing his eyes with his thumb and forefinger.

"No. No, not stupid at all. Forgive me, Mr. Rankin. I am obviously not doing my job here. Forgive me for not picking up on that earlier. Since I did not consider that defense and you did, perhaps I should be paying *you*. You know, the more I think about it, the more I think *that* just might do it."

Callahan's voice took on a mocking tone.

"I can just see it, 'Ladies and gentlemen of the jury, although the state has done a fine job of presenting its evidence against my client, at this time I would like to offer our one and only piece of evidence, one that the state cannot argue against and one that will

set my client free. And that is, ladies and gentlemen of the jury—
Mr. Rankin did not commit this murder. The reason being, Mr.
Rankin *knows* himself and through that intimate knowledge of
himself, he just knows he could not shoot a man in the back. Thank
you for your attention. And now, if you don't mind, my client and I
will take our leave of the courtroom, because I can see in your eyes
you agree that he could not have committed such a crime, even
though the evidence, circumstantial as it is, is stacked against him
up to his eyeballs."

The attorney stood.

"Think about my advice to you, Mr. Rankin You have no alibi. I
can't put you anywhere. I can't take you away from the crime scene.
You have admitted you were at the scene, but you just don't *think*
you did it."

He began collecting up papers in the folder.

"I'm a very good criminal lawyer, Mr. Rankin, but I'm not *that*
good. Think about it, and if you are so inclined, I can present it to
the prosecutor and see if he will be willing to accept a plea of a
lesser charge. He may not, and if so, we are stuck with the hand we
have been dealt. But if he will, it may just save your life. Good day,
Mr. Rankin. Have the deputy call my office if or when you decide.
Jailer! I'm done here."

"Come on, Callahan, you know I ain't gonna do that. I've got a
case against him that, even without an eyewitness, is about as solid
as any I've had since I was elected by the good people of this
district. Besides, you don't have your client's authority to make
such a deal."

Burl Cline, the young solicitor, was standing in his office,
responding to the attorney's offer.

"True, but if I went back to him and told him you might be
amenable to an offer, he might agree to it."

"Naw, Callahan. I can tell you right now that I'm not going for
that. Shot in the back like this was the Wild West? And a *white* man
at that! The public ain't gonna like this one at all. They're gonna
demand your man gets the chair."

Chapter 35

Granite faces filed into the jury box as jurors stood before assigned seats, waiting for the judge to tell them to be seated. Each took a cold glance at the accused, as if curious as to what kind of animal could shoot a defenseless man in the back. The jury selection did not take as long as Callahan estimated. He had explained to Hume that a lot of lawyers felt the *voir dire* was the most important part of a criminal trial, especially in a murder case.

"Get one juror who just *can't* make a conscious decision to put a man to death, and he could hang up a jury, and that would be it. A hung jury and the judge would declare a mistrial."

And in this case, Callahan was hanging particular importance on that slightest of possibilities. Although the jurors responded that they could deliver a guilty verdict if the evidence so warranted, two did seem to hesitate initially, so Callahan focused on those two.

"Ladies and gentlemen—you may be seated."

The gray-haired judge spoke over the half-glasses, resting on the tip of his nose. Judge Douglas Brinnon was not the judge that Callahan had hoped for, but he was better than some. Steeped in the tradition of the role, he was fair, but he went strictly by the book. He didn't allow his court to get sidetracked by theatrical defense lawyers, a role in which Callahan had earned his reputation.

People said Callahan never met a jury he couldn't connect with. They might not have always gone his way, but seldom did a juror leave the courtroom at the end of a trial without breaking a grin over the lawyer's good ol boy antics and homey analysis in matters of law and common sense.

The trial opened with the state presenting Hume Rankin as a cold-blooded killer, who had shot Worth Baker, a well-respected man in the county, and with whom he'd had a long-running feud, in the back. The latter was not a matter of law pursued by the state in the presentation of its case, but it was simply used for the drama, to plant in the jury's mind when it came time to deliberate.

Behind Hume and Attorney Calhoun's defense table sat Alford and Ellen Rankin. In the row behind them, Walt Neal, in his best bib overalls, a white tee-shirt, and the only pair of lace-up shoes he owned. Walt was certain of Hume's innocence and knew it only a matter of time before the entire courtroom knew that as well. Walt was certain Hume would be set free of the charges he could not have committed. His nervous presence at the trial came from a sense of loyalty to the Rankin family.

The state put on its first witness, Cyrus Baker. After being sworn in, Burl Cline began his questioning.

"Mr. Baker, if you will, please tell the jury about the events on the night of May the tenth, specifically at the deceased's barn."

"Well, me and my brother, Mason, had stopped by the barn that night to check on Worth. His hired help was putting in the year's crop and it was getting late, so we stopped by to see if he needed any help. The three of us were there at the barn talking, when all of a sudden we hear this commotion over in the corner and we saw Mr. Rankin, here, stumble out and fall onto the ground. He was a might drunk—stumbling drunk, I should say. And he accused Worth of calling on his wife earlier that day. Anyway, the two of them got to arguing and one thing led to another and they got to fighting."

"Now, Mr. Baker, what, if anything, did the defendant, here, say to, or threaten your brother with, that night?"

"Objection, your honor! Mr. Cline is leading the witness."

"Sustained," the judge ruled.

"Mr. Baker, what, if anything, did you hear the defendant say to your brother after the fight broke up?"

The witness looked toward the judge before responding.

"You may answer," the judge advised.

"Well, once we got them apart, Rankin told Worth that if he ever came on his land again, he would *kill* him," Cyrus said, his voice breaking with emotion. "And I reckon that's just what he did!"

"Objection, your honor! The witness is drawing a conclusion!"

"Objection sustained, as to the last sentence..."

Looking over his half-glasses at the jury, the judge gave the instruction.

"As to what the witness heard the defendant say, you *may* consider. As to the statement, 'that is just what he did,' you must not consider. That has not been proven, at this point."

The silence that followed the remark spread out over the courtroom like a blanket, as Callahan looked at the jury to read its reaction. It was obvious jurors heard and were interested in the remark. From man to women, they all looked over at Hume with obvious disdain.

Cyrus was then excused and his brother, Mason, took the stand. Though he had a hard time of it, and his emotions got the best of him at times, he told the exact same story his brother recited.

The witnesses from the warehouse were less emotional, but they also repeated the threat Hume made when he found Baker bought his land at auction. George Faucette, the warehouse manager, was the most damaging, as he clearly struggled with the solicitor's questions. It was obvious to the jury that the man was having a difficult time, hanging his friend.

"Tell the jury please, Mr. Faucette, what, if anything you heard the defendant say while in your presence, about what he was going to do to the deceased—once he found he had bought the defendant's land at public auction, which by the way, is a perfectly legal way to acquire land in this state."

"Well, Hume, he, he was pretty upset, as you can *understand* he would be."

"Mr. Faucette, please just answer my questions and do not add your own references as to the defendant's supposed state of mind."

"Okay, I'm sorry," Faucette stammered. "Well, Hume, ah... err... Mr. Rankin had just heard some of the men talking about how Baker bought his land for fifty cents on the dollar and now owned his land... and he... it got to him pretty bad..."

"And just what did he say, Mr. Faucette?

"When? Ahh, at which time?"

"When the defendant found out Mr. Baker was now the owner of the land? What, exactly, did you hear him say in front of other workers, that he was going to do to Worth Baker?"

"Well... ahh... uhh... he said he was going to *kill* the sonofabitch," he answered, glancing down at the floor in front of him.

"I'm sorry? I didn't quite get that," the solicitor asked, for emphasis.

"He said he was going to *ki*ll him," Faucette answered.

"I have nothing further, your Honor."

"Mr. Callahan?" the judge offered.

"No, your Honor. We have nothing at this time."

"You may step down," the judge said.

Rising and stepping from the witness stand, Faucette paused to tuck his shirttail in his hind side and when he did, his eyes met Hume's. The look in Faucette's face said he was sorry. Hume's look was accompanied with a sad smile that forgave his friend, relaying he understood and held no animosity toward him.

The judge pulled his pocket watch from under his robe.

"It looks as if at this point, it would be a good time to recess for lunch. I'll remind the jury—you're not to discuss this case with anyone. The court will recess for two hours. Be back by two o'clock."

The bailiff rose, his voice booming.

"Oh yes, Oh yes—the court is now in recess. God save this court and this honorable state. Court is adjourned until two o'clock."

Ellen, seated just behind her husband in the front row at Callahan's request, was numb from the overwhelming evidence. Leaning forward, she spoke to the lawyer.

"Mr. Callahan, can you arrange for me to speak with Hume. This is not good. I cannot believe what's happening. He is going to be convicted for this and sentenced to death!"

Turning in his wooden chair, he responded.

"I understand your concern, Mrs. Rankin. I'm concerned, too. I tried to get your husband to agree to pursue a plea bargain, but he said he was not certain of his guilt. His defense was simply that he knew himself and he did not think he was capable of doing the crime. I guess if I was in his shoes and had to admit to something I wasn't convinced I'd done, it might stick in my craw as well. I'll see what I can do, though."

Walt remained in his seat as the crowd filed out for recess. Alford looked down at Walt as he escorted his mother, who dabbed at the corner of her eyes with her handkerchief, out of the courtroom, a worried look on his face. This, Walt thought to himself, was not going as he figured it would. A worried crease furrowed his brow.

Her husband appeared smaller than ever, sitting in the lawyers' conference room, just behind and off to the left of the courtroom.

His hands were cuffed in front of him, attached to a menacing thick chain that surrounded his thin torso.

"Hume, *something* has to happen! This thing is not going well at all. It's going just awful, to be honest. Please, let Callahan go to the solicitor and try to plea bargain your case. Let him try to save your life," she sobbed.

Hume stared for a time before responding.

"Ellen, how would that be any *better*? Second-degree murder carries a minimum of twenty-five years. I'd be an old man by the time I got out, and you'd be long gone. I just can't see the attraction in that. If I can't walk out of this courtroom and take up living my life again as a free and innocent man, then I'd rather end it. I don't want to spend the better part of what life I have left behind bars— not to be able to lie down with you at night, and you being the first thing I see when I awake? Or not be able to see the kids on a whim? To feel concrete under my feet and not be able to feel the land shift beneath my boots as I walk free across the land? Or not be able to see the colors across the evening sky, after the sun drops below the horizon. I don't believe so, Ellen. That ain't no kind of life."

He leaned forward, as much as his constraints would allow, and asked, "I know that may be selfish of me, but please try and understand, Ellen. If you do, maybe the strength we get from that understanding... well... maybe we can better handle the outcome of this thing. "

Sobbing, she reached out for him, but she stopped when the bailiff stepped in and intercepted her thin, quivering fingers.

"I'm sorry, ma'am. No contact with prisoners allowed. Time's up anyway. Let's go, Rankin."

Standing, he gave his wife one long, last look, as if he were a drowning man taking a last, slow breath of air before going under the surface, before being turned and led away by the bailiff.

Balking, he spoke over his shoulder.

"Ellen, maybe this thing is beyond our control anyway. Maybe the ending to all this has already been written."

"What you mean by that?"

"The owl called my name out, Ellen. After all this is over, go talk to Daisy. She'll explain."

"Hume!" Ellen implored. "I don't know anything about what you just *said*! But as far as your freedom and the rest of your life— you do what you have to. I'll understand."

The farmer, his back to her, lowered his head in gratitude.

"Oh, yes! Oh yes! Please stand as court is now in session! God save this court and this honorable state," the bailiff roared as the judge entered the courtroom.

The judge seated himself and poured a glass of ice water from a freshly-placed pitcher.

"Bailiff, bring in the jury,"

Once again, the jury filed in, stone faced, avoiding eye contact with the defendant. Callahan knew it was not a good sign.

"Is the state prepared to continue with its case?"

Standing, the solicitor for the state of North Carolina replied.

"We are your honor. At this time the state would like to call to the stand Mrs. Earlene Wyrick."

The blood drained from Hume and Ellen Rankin's face as the spinster approached and took the stand.

"Mrs. Wyrick, would you tell the court your name and address?"

Perched as haughtily in the witness chair as a hen looking over its roost, Earlene Wyrick surveyed the courtroom. A beehive, piled proudly on her head, swiveled upon her long, skinny neck.

"I will. My name is Earlene Bodsford Wyrick and I live on Route Five, Hicone Road in Brown Summit, North Carolina."

"And Mrs. Wyrick, where is *that* with regard to where to the defendant Hume Rankin lives?"

Attorney Callahan offered in a weak attempt to do something to earn his fee.

"Objection, your Honor—irrelevant,"

"Overruled," the judge responded. "You may answer, Mrs. Wyrick."

She smiled with satisfaction, replying.

"I live three houses down from the Rankins."

"And living so close, do you or did you have the occasion to visit or call on the Rankins?"

"I did," she answered. "That is, I did until they became such *rude* neighbors."

"Objection, your Honor. That is an irrelevant and unproven conclusion!"

"Sustained. Mrs. Wyrick, answer the question and nothing more. There is no need for any qualifying or opinionated statement from you," the judge instructed.

Straightening her back, she preened the pleats of her cotton dress and grudgingly offered, "Well, all right. I just thought..."

"That will be enough, Mrs. Wyrick," the judge admonished. "The court is not interested in what your thoughts are."

The solicitor continued.

"All right, Mrs. Wyrick. And on the date in question, did you have an occasion to visit the Rankins? Just a yes or no will do, Mrs. Wyrick.

"Yes, I did."

"And on that date, did you have an occasion to hear the defendant here, Mr. Rankin, say or have a conversation with his wife?"

"I did. I was standing..."

"Yes or no, Mrs. Wyrick," the solicitor intervened.

"Oh my goodness... yes!"

"Now, if you would, Mrs. Wyrick, would you tell the court what you heard and how it came about that you heard it?"

"Well, I had walked down to the Rankins to visit with Ellen and perhaps have a cup of coffee and catch up on things—just as I do with my all my neighbors from time to time... We had always been a close knit community... Well, we had been before..."

"Please, Mrs. Wyrick, stay with the question I asked you," the solicitor directed.

"Oh, well now, let's see... What was the... oh, yes. Now, I recall the day I arrived at the Rankin's back door and saw Hume ...uh... err... Mr. Rankin there, and Mrs. Rankin, standing in the kitchen, and it quickly became obvious they were in an argument of some sort. At first I really didn't know what it was about, because I'm not that kind of neighbor. I don't concern myself with other people's matters... but as I stood there, preparing to knock, I saw Mr. Rankin grab his wife by the shoulder and raise his fist, as if to hit her. Now I froze and was horrified, because I'm not used to that sort of thing."

"Mrs. Wyrick, please do not stray. Just stay with the question," the solicitor insisted.

"Well, I saw him rare back and then one of the little girls came into the room... I believe it was Mary Ellen—sweet, poor little thing—anyway, she came into the room and saw what her daddy was about to do and screamed at him to let her mother go. And Mr. Rankin was caught at that point, so he had to let her go. I just can't imagine how many times that must have gone on in the family. I knew he was a mean man, but I never thought..."

"Objection!"

"Enough! Mrs. Wyrick! If you do not maintain yourself in my courtroom I will hold you in contempt of court! Limit your answer to the question the solicitor asks you and nothing more. Is that understood, Mrs. Wyrick?"

"Yes sir. I mean, your Honor."

"Now, Mrs. Wyrick, if you would, continue by telling the court what, if anything, you heard the defendant here, say to his wife concerning Worth Baker," the solicitor proceeded.

The witness swiveled her neck back around and stared with cold, detached eyes at the defendant and held the stare for several heavy seconds before calmly answering

"I clearly heard the defendant tell his wife that if Worth Baker ever came on his land again, he would... *kill him*."

She emphasized the last two words in an acidic tone that was just above a whisper.

A hush consumed the courtroom as the jury's attention was directed at the defendant.

"Does the defense wish to cross-examine the witness," the judge followed.

"Just a moment, if you please, your Honor," Callahan responded.

Callahan leaned over and whispered into his Hume's ear,

"Who is this lady and is what she says the truth?"

Sitting still as a board, Hume's faced turned toward the front of the courtroom as he whispered from the side of his mouth

"Afraid so. She's the neighborhood busybody. One day, when Ellen and I were having an argument, she showed up."

"Why did you threaten to kill Baker during *that* argument?"

"He paid Ellen a visit and I found out. I was just mad."

"Well, *this* is a hell of a way for me to find out!"

"Sorry, I reckon I just forgot about it. I'm sure the solicitor didn't have to look far for her."

"What do you mean?"

"I'm sure she searched him out. Couldn't wait to spill her guts. She's the community gossip."

"Right. And the community gossip just happens to show up at your backdoor just as you raise your hand to strike your wife and threaten to kill the deceased? Just great!"

Standing, Callahan rose and answered, "No, your honor."

"Very well then. The state may continue."

The solicitor stood and faced the judge.

"Your Honor, at this time, the state rests its case."

The entire courtroom seemed to sit back for a moment, taking a collective breath.

"Okay then. Mr. Callahan? Are you ready to proceed with your defense?"

"Your honor, at this time, the defense would like to..."

At that moment, the door to the courtroom opened again, as it had throughout the trial with curious spectators coming and going—at one point causing the judge to pound his gavel and threaten to seal off the courtroom if the visitors could not enter and leave in a quieter fashion.

Court spectators turned their attention to a white-haired negro, in bib overalls, making a commotion as he clomped down the aisle in ill-fitted shoes, hurriedly leaving the courtroom.

Judge Brinnon resumed his pounding.

"Order! Order in this courtroom!"

Frustrated by the constant eruptions, the judge stood and pulled out his pocket watch, pounded once more with conviction and declared,

"This court will stand in recess until tomorrow morning, at which time the defense will present its case. Court is now adjourned!"

The bailiff stood beside the judge's chair and repeated his refrain.

"Oh, yes! Oh yes! The court stands adjourned until tomorrow morning at nine o'clock. God save this state and this honorable courtroom!"

The jailer entered and applied the leg cuffs to Hume, while his attorney began to gather papers to file in his briefcase. With one hand on a stack of papers and the other holding the briefcase open, he turned his attention to his client.

"I'll see you back here in the morning. I need to file some papers with the clerk's office. Hume, before I open with your defense in the morning, I may still be able to work something out with the solicitor. Are you still *not* willing to consider a plea bargain?"

Callahan paused, and getting no response, he continued.

"I have to tell you this. Although their case is built on circumstantial evidence, I have seen men get the death penalty on less. And my read of the jurors' faces disturbs me. Will you at least *consider* it, overnight?"

"I appreciate your concern, Mr. Callahan. But I have talked with Ellen, and she says she understands me on this. And with that understanding, she has sort of set me free. Ya see, I just ain't convinced I did it. I know you don't think much of that argument, and I'm probably the only one, except Ellen now, who buys that, but that is all I have."

He shrugged.

"And ain't nobody proved to me so far that I done it—just an old busy body, two brothers and some out of work farmers over at the warehouse heard me say something in a state of anger. You ever said anything when you were mad that you didn't mean and wished you hadn't said, Mr. Callahan?"

The attorney searched Hume's eyes, seeking an answer, a habit he had developed over the years, looking for a clue, when all else failed to give him some feel for the truth of his client's guilt or innocence. A slight smile parted his lips.

"More than once, I'm afraid."

He placed a gentle hand on Hume's shoulder.

"I just hate to see you face what could possibly be the result of the lack of a defense. I guess I just don't feel you're fighting hard enough."

"You may be right, Mr. Callahan. Maybe the fight has left me. I don't have my land anymore and that alone, is enough to bring a man to his knees. And I've put my family through an awful lot. They don't deserve to deal with twenty-five- years-time. I just reckon if I can't walk out free now, I don't want to walk out in the future, on the weak, bowed legs of an old man. And in the end, I want you to know—so you don't have to stir around in your conscience, questioning that you hadn't done the best with what you'd been given. *I* know you have. And I consider myself represented by a very good attorney and a good man."

"I'll remember that, Hume. I'm afraid I'll need to. Thank you."

Chapter 36

"Can I help you?"

The jailer stared at the black man with a degree of suspicion.

"Yessa. I need to speak with Mista Hume Rankin."

"And just *what* is your business with Mr. Rankin," the jailer said, with a smirk.

"I work for Mista Rankin, and I need to talk to him."

The jailer looked at the clock, hung high on the green wall.

"Well, visiting hours are over at six and it ain't six o'clock yet. You think he'll wanna see you?"

"Yessa. I believe he *will*."

"Well, wait right there. I'll need to send a deputy down to see if he'll see you. What's your name?"

"Walter Neal."

After a longer than required wait, the deputy returned to the jailer.

 "Well, Rankin said he'd see him."

He turned toward Walt.

"You know we'll have to search you before you go in, don't you?"

"That'll be fine with me. I ain't got no gun or knife on me."

"Well, *we'll* have to be the judge of that. Turn around, put your hands on the wall and bend over," the jailer ordered.

"Okay. He's clear. No weapons or contraband. Deputy, take him down to the lawyer conference room. All the visitation rooms are full right now. Bring the prisoner out. I want him shackled, both hands and feet. Get Deputy Johnson. He's big as a house. I want you two to stand guard outside the door. I don't want no jail break on my shift before they sentence him tomorrow."

"Yes sir," the deputy saluted.

Walt was seated in the conference room at a long wooden table when a knock preceded the opening of the door. He jumped. The door was filled by a very large, crew-cut deputy.

"You Walt Neal?"

"Yessa, I am."

"Stand up and put your hands against the wall."

"Yessa, but they done searched me out there."

"I don't care what they did out there. You're in here with me now, and I'll rest easier knowing for myself that you ain't got no weapons or other jailbreak tools on you. Now get over to that wall."

Walt did as he was told, and after the search, he turned around to find Hume seated at the table, surrounded by two sets of chains.

"Mista Hume! I wasn't expectin to see..."

"How are you, Walt?"

"I be doin all right, I expect."

"I've saw you in court. I appreciate you coming, Walt."

"Well, that ain't nothin, Mista Hume."

"Well it *is* to me, Walt. And I thank you for it."

"Mr. Hume, I gotta tell ya. I'm not a liking what I'm hearing in that courtroom. I figured you'd be outta there and home by now, cause I know you didn't do it. But it ain't looking so much like that, right now."

"Well Walt. Maybe you better prepare for the worst, because I really don't have much of a defense, other than the fact I know inside me that I didn't do it. Only problem is, they want me to prove it, and I can't. The set of circumstances I'm presented with didn't come with any proof of innocence."

"Lawd, Mista Hume, I don't..."

"Let's do something here, Walt. How bout you drop the 'Mister' and just call me Hume. We're not out in the field anymore. We're more... alike now."

"But Mista Hume, I don't believe I can do that... not after all these years."

"I guess so."

"Mista Hume, life done me wrong—pulled a switch on me. I don't know where, but somewhere along the line, I became somebody else—somebody that other people were afraid of. They thought I was mean, and I *was*. I am. But that ain't who I started *out* to be. My momma used to say I was the sweetest child... sweetest of all my brothers and sisters and cousins. 'Sweet Tea' is what she called me. But somehow I got mad. I was made mad."

Walt rambled on.

"And justice? There ain't no justice for the likes of me. You. You *got* some justice. You got a trial, at least. Me. If I'd done what they accused *you* of, I'd get a rope around my neck and they'd be done with it. I'm scared of the white man's justice. You don't know how my legs shake when I walk in that courtroom and that justice just surrounds me. Like air that's hard to breathe."

The old man shook his head.

"That justice don't have no place in *my* world. In my world—you take it into your own hands and make justice. And that's what I've done most all my life. And they call me mean, for that. And I guess I am. But what they *don't* know is I've lived my life scared. I'm scared of the white world, and I reckon that is what made me who I am."

"I'm not sure I get where you're going with this," Hume said, a little confused.

"And sometimes I feel like I'd like to go back and be that sweet person I started out to be. I know some of it might still be in me. Mary Ellen. I feel it in there at times when I'm around her. She brings it out of me, so I know it must still be in there."

"Walt I..."

Standing, Walt put both hands into his bib pocket and continued.

"I've been afraid most all my life, and I guess that's why I haven't done what I should of done before this."

He extracted both hands from his pockets and leaned in, both fists on the table.

"I'm ready to wade in the water now, Mista Hume. There really may not be the other side for me, but I'm ready to do this to find out."

With that, Walt opened both fists, his hands now flat on the table.

"Mista Deputy—I expect I'm ready."

Walt stood erect and put his hands back in his pockets.

"Maybe *this* will be your proof of innocence," he said as he turned to leave the room.

On the table, under where his right hand had been, glistened a gold Masonic Ring.

Chapter 37

Roy Callahan was running late. He had called the Clerk's office and asked that court be delayed until he got there. He said that the judge would understand once he arrived and was able to explain. He had just set his briefcase on the defense table, beside his already seated client, as the bailiff bawled.

"All rise!"

After the judge entered the courtroom and took his seat, the bailiff followed.

"Be seated!" which the rest of the court's occupants did.

"Are we prepared to resume?" the judge inquired.

Both solicitor and defense attorney rose simultaneously again.

"We are, your Honor."

The judge turned to the bailiff.

"You may now seat the jury."

One by one, the jury filed in, avoiding eye contact with the defendant and his attorney.

"Mr. Callahan. Do you have an excuse as to why you delayed my court this morning," the judge inquired.

"I do, your Honor," Callahan replied.

"Well, it'd better be good. We'll discuss it in chambers at recess. For now, let's get started. Are you prepared to offer your first witness?"

Nervous, Callahan glanced toward the front of the courtroom.

"We are, your Honor. At this time, we would like to call to the stand... Mr. Walt... uh... Mr. Walt Neal."

Standing, the solicitor protested.

"We object to this witness, your Honor. He was not on the defense's witness list and we know nothing about who this man is, nor his credibility.

The dark man, standing in the witness box was stooped slightly at the waist, with shoulders hunched forward, an effect that was either caused by him being bound in chains or the result of years of enduring the heat and hostility of life in the South.

Callahan rose to meet the state's objection.

"Your Honor, the state still objects to..."

"Gentlemen," the judge admonished. "I would like to see you *both* in my chambers before we proceed any further."

In short order, the lawyers disappeared into the recesses behind the judge's imposing chair.

"All rise!" the bailiff declared as the judge took his seat.

"Be seated."

Looking down at the defendant's table, the judge folded his hands under his chin and pondered, for what seemed to the defendant and his attorney an eternity, before he addressed them.

"Mr. Callahan, this is highly irregular and it is my inclination to deny this witness's testimony. I have researched in chambers and I find, however, no case law disallowing the valid testimony of a last minute or heretofore unknown witness. This man may have information pertinent to this very serious case. You may call your witness. Bailiff, have the witness sworn in."

The courtroom began its low-pitched buzz again as the bailiff followed the judge's instructions.

"Raise your right... uh... place your left hand on the Bible and raise your right hand, if you can. I believe you can, if you bend down a little more."

The witness bent over further and placed his restrained left hand on the Bible and raised his encumbered right hand.

"Do you swear to tell the truth, the whole truth and nothing but the truth, so help you God?" the bailiff asked.

"I do."

"Then you may be seated."

Callahan remained seated, holding his yellow, Number 2 pencil by the point, rhythmically bouncing the eraser up and down on a white legal pad as the witness situated himself in the witness chair.

"Now Mr. Neal, would you tell the court your name, address, occupation and age?"

"Walter Neal. If I had a middle name, I done forgot it. I lives in a house down by the tobacco field that Mista Hume owns, and I help him in tobacco and anything else he needs. And the last thing... Oh—my age—I's afraid I ain't too sure of that, either."

"All right. Thank you, Mr. Neal. Are you comfortable? Would you like a glass of water before we continue?"

"I believe I would."

The bailiff poured a glass of water.

"Now Mr. Neal, on the day in question, I believe you have some information about the events of the evening of October 31, 1959. Would you tell the court, in your own words, what you know to be true," Callahan began.

"I will. Well, earlier that afternoon, I seen Mista Worth Baker bring Mista Hume's mule, Rhody, across the lower yard from the New Ground onto Mista Hume's land. I thought that a might peculiar, but I just went on with my bidness splittin wood. So I stayed out choppin till my wife called me to wash-up fo supper. We ate supper, and I was tired from the wood splittin, so me and her went to bed shortly after supper."

"Mr. Neal. If I may ask, who is 'we?' "

"Say what?"

"When you say 'we' went to bed, who are you referring to?"

"Oh. Me and Daisy, my wife. Me and her went to bed."

"Thank you for that clarification. You may proceed."

"Well, anyways, we went to bed, and it was a warm night for that time of year and I had the windows open. It was a full moon out, and it was so bright, it was causing me to sleep fitful when..."

With that, Walt told the court what took place at his home that night:

"Nettie! Nettie! You in there," came a whisper. "Come on out here, girl. I got a *present* for ya."

Moments later, a shadow appeared at the back corner of the house, in the darkness of the overhang of the tin roof. Slowly, the shadow emerged into the shape of a young girl, crouched and creeping on tiptoes toward an old oak tree that stood sentry out at the edge of the yard.

The girl had arrived at the tree, when another shape suddenly stepped out from behind it, a much larger shape, a figure wearing a broad-brimmed hat. The figure towered over the girl and reached out and planted both hands on her shoulders.

"You know I brought you that present with me, don't ya. And I know ya want it now, don't cha," the figure said, looming over the girl, swaying her back and forth in front of him, as if surveying his prize.

"Please... I don't wanna..."

"You don't wanna *what*? You know I *own* this land now. I told ya—it's different now than before. You hold out on me, and I'll throw you, your daddy, your momma and your sisters out. And your daddy won't have no work and *won't* have in this county again. And what will your family do? Pack up and walk down the road to the next county over so he can find work and maybe a shelter for y'all to live in? That's a long way for Bessie, all knocked up and full as a July watermelon, to have to walk. And it'll all be *your* fault. Now you gonna lie down and spread them legs or not?"

In fear, the girl relented, and the large man mounted the small girl. He was about press his member again, into her dawning womanhood, when suddenly, a yellow light from outside the front door filled the yard with eerie shadows.

"Who's *out* there! Who the *hell* is out there? You better answer fo I fill yo ass fulla buckshot," came a raspy voice from the front steps of the house. The coon hounds were penned-up behind the house, near the edge of the woods. The noise from the disturbance caused the dogs to arouse and fill the night air with their bawling howls.

From behind the tree, the big man put his large hand over the girl's mouth and nose, whispering.

"Don't you say a word, or I'll break your damned neck."

Stepping off the cinderblock front step, the demand from the porch was issued again, and this time the warning had drawn closer to the large tree.

The girl, becoming dizzy from lack of oxygen, began a frantic life struggle. Summoning what strength she had left in her, she violently jerked her head sideways and her mouth momentarily escaped the smothering hand as she gasped, taking in a gulp of night air before the mitt-sized hand recovered.

"I *mean* it, girl. You're dead if you make another sound!"

This time, the threat was accompanied by the cold, sharp tip of an object, pressed firmly against her throat.

The outline of a thin man, holding an oblong object out in front of his body crept out from the house across the yard toward the oak tree.

"Who be there! I hear ya breathin, back there behind that tree. I smell ya, too. I knows ya there. Come out from round there or I'm gonna blow yo ass to kingdom come! I ain't gonna tell ya again."

The rustling of leaves and the jingling sound of metal belt buckle followed the last threat. The man with the gun now moved quickly toward the commotion and stepped around the wide, old tree. The vision of his youngest daughter lying on the ground, her head resting on a pillow of gnarled tree roots, with her blue-plaid nightgown pulled up over her waist, revealing thin, dark thighs that led to her exposed young nest confused him and distracted his attention from the escaping figure that was limping away into the darkness, with his pants bound around his ankles, his belt buckle jingling, trailing and bouncing along on the ground behind him.

The man rotated his head twice, from his child on the ground, to the figure, before raising the oblong object and training it on the backside of the retreating shadow. An orange-red flame erupted from the end of the shotgun, simultaneously illuminating a mix of cloth, flesh and red-pulpy material, exploding outward from the back of the figure—like water, plunging upward and around a large rock that had been dropped into the surface of a still pond.

A sticky substance covered the gun barrel and the trembling hands of the shooter as the smell of gunpowder floated in the still night air.

The courtroom was quiet, save for the soft crying of Ellen Rankin as Callahan continued.

"And now, Mr. Neal—would you please tell the court what you did next?" "Well, when I seen who I'd done killed, I was scared! Real scared! I done killed a *white* man! And not just *any* white man. And I knowed what that meant. A colored man kills a white man—his next date not gonna be with his wife. His next date be with the electric chair," he explained.

Callahan nodded, encouraging him to continue.

"So my only thought was to get him away from my house, and so I drug him down to the creek over on Mr. Hume's tobacco field, and that be where I left him."

"And who, Mr. Neal, was that white man, violating your daughter, that you killed that night?"

"It was, it was, Mista Worth Baker."

"And *how* was it that you came to be in possession of Mr. Baker's ring?"

"We'll, when I got him down to the creek, I started to turn to come back to the house, when I noticed the ring on his finger. It was shinin in the moonlight. And I just thought, *he sure ain't got no use for that ring now.*"

"And?"

"For what he done to my daughter, I slid it off his hand and put it in my pocket."

Looking down at Hume, who sat with his face buried in his hands, his elbows resting on the defendant's table, Walt spoke directly to him.

"I'm sorry Mista Hume. I just didn't know what *else* ta do."

And so the black man seemed alone in the still courtroom— exposed, afraid, and wide-eyed—sitting there on the witness stand, his toothless mouth and sunken jowls moving in and out, making soft puffing sounds with each breath.

The room remained void of sound, as if needing time to take in what had just transpired.

Finally, Roy Callahan rose from his seat.

"Your Honor, the defense rests its case."

He smiled.

"In addition, we respectfully make a motion the court dismiss all charges against my client, Mr. Hume Rankin."

Judge Brinnon stared for a few seconds, down at the man who had just told his unexpected tale. After a moment, he broke from his thoughts.

"Mr. Neal, you may be excused. Bailiff, return this man to the holding cell."

Then the judge turned his attention to the solicitor.

"Mr. Cline. Do you have anything more?"

The solicitor slid his chair back and stood, slouching.

"We do not, your Honor."

"Very well, then. And before I proceed, may I say that the state is free to pursue charges against *this* witness, but I would advise it would probably not be in the state's best interest to pursue its case against this man in my courtroom."

Standing, Judge Brinnon brought the wooden gavel shoulder high, and with one emphatic strike, ended the matter.

"Case dismissed!"

Chapter 38

Sitting, now on the *other* side of the glass partition, the visitor waited. He felt the strangeness in the reversal of fate, yet the effect was still not real, as he waited for the prisoner to be brought out. He had known the feeling of meaningless anticipation that the man on the other side would be feeling as he was led down the drab-gray hallway to the visitation room. A shudder ran through the visitor's body.

The shuffle and the clinging of chains preceded his entry into the small room.

"Mista Hume! What *you* be doin here? I thought you'd be home with your family."

"I will be soon. But I needed to see you first."

The two men, who had shared days that ran into years, out under the sun, good days and bad—in an unspoken but understood bond, sat quietly, eyeing each other, not sure how to proceed.

Finally, Hume made the attempt.

"Why, Walt?"

"Why what, Mista Hume?"

"Why did you *do* that? I mean I understand why you defended your daughter, but you almost let me go the electric chair. And then you stepped in and saved my life."

"I didn't know what to do, Mista Hume. Like I told ya—I was scared. But then I got mad, too. Me and my family... my race... we been kept down and stepped on all my life—and will be that way for my daughters' lives too, I suppose. But I done *cleared the world* of a bad man. *You* a good man, Mista Hume. Been good to me and my family. Gave us a place to stay, with a roof over our heads. Gave me work, so I could feed my family. It was good the day I met ya— an omen of good things to come. And we *did* have our good days. Plenty of them. So, I couldn't betray the spirits that set this all in motion. It just couldn't end that way."

"But it *did* end, didn't it, Walt? And *I'm* the one responsible. I brought that end on. If I just coulda just held on to..."

"No, Mista Hume. *You* didn't end it—time ended it—change ended it. That new man at tha bank and his new ways of bankin ended it. Remember that night, year fo last, when we was out under the sky, by the fire? We passed the bottle that night, you and me—

first time. And ya told me change was a-coming. I told ya my people *wanted* change—that change weren't nothin we was afraid of. And then *you* told me to watch out what I wished for, cause I might wake up and find that wish sittin on my front steps, and that wish might be done taken the form of a wolf?"

"Yeah, I remember."

"Well, Mista Hume. That wolf did come to my house, sho nuff. Only it didn't sit on my front steps. It was slinky, sly and cunnin. Didn't come out in the open. Nope. It hid itself. And it come ta take one of mine away.

Walt's eyes glazed over as he continued.

"Called her out of the safety of where she stay, out into the darkness of night, and told her if she didn't do what it say, didn't go along—now that it owned the world around her, it'd take her and her family's life away from em—theys life, as they was accustomed ta."

He sighed.

"And that *wolf* came in the form of Worth Baker, Mista Hume. And when that wolf done took over your land, a power come with it. A bad power. I reckon power come with gettin bigger and ownin more. Bad power, sometimes. But just listen to me. I don't know nothin about that. I don't own nothin, so I don't know nothin bout power—just what I see from a distance, lookin in."

"Sounds to me like you *do* know something it all Walt. Even if you've had to see it from a distance... from looking *in*."

"So you see, Mista Hume—its bad power had to stop. It shouldn't ruin yo life, like it done ruint mine."

"Maybe not, Walt. Callahan said he would represent you on the murder charge. He said he thought he might be able to get that charge dropped, given the circumstances. You may have to do some time on a lesser charge, but at least it wouldn't be murder."

"Well, I sho nuff preciate that. Lord, Mista Hume. I don't deserve such..."

"But you *do*, Walt. And here is what I'm trying to digest. What you gave me today was... was... freedom. Me—a white man—got my freedom from a colored man. Freedom—something my people haven't been able to give your people yet. Oh, maybe in talk and some laws, but not real freedom. Not like *I* got today. Imagine *that*,

Walt. I'm indebted and owe my life to a Negro. Will *that* do, for now? Is *that* change enough for you?"

The toothless mouth parted slightly in a shy smile.

"I reckon it's a start."

Chapter 39

Hume arrived again at the precipice overlooking the land he once owned. It was late in the day, and he was torn. He knew his family waited for him at home, but he was not ready.

Maybe it was because of the man he had become in the last few years—and all he had put them through. And what exactly awaited him and where he was headed with his life was still not certain. He hadn't had much time to contemplate such matters of late.

Even so, he suspected those thoughts had ridden with him for some time. Since before the trial, and a good time before that even, he supposed. He was not sure when he became aware of it all. It was just that now, he was.

And so, he felt the precipice was where he needed to be. Not home. Looking behind him, he found a clear spot on the ground and brushed away the few twigs and dried leaves before crossing his legs and lowering himself to sit. But not before removing the brown paper bag and its contents from his rear pocket.

Holding the small bag with both hands, his forearms perched on his knees, he surveyed the land in front of him. But his mind contained no thoughts, not just yet. And that was fine with him, because the void bathed him in a soothing wave of numbness. No thought. No feeling. There was just the sense of melding—similar to the feeling when his soul was reclaimed in those moments during a sunrise or sunset.

The comfort of the "in-between" time prompted him to think, *this must have been what it was like. To rest, suspended in that dark nesting place before being thrust, naked and exposed, into the world.*

His thoughts fluttered and came to rest on his mother, a soft soul, whose only fault was in being too gentle to fend for herself against the trolling ill wills of many—and the additional burden of not being able to fend for *him*, as a child, when he was in peril of injury from those harmful souls. It was if she had sat, hands folded in her lap, smiling sadly, sweetly, as the blood that was let by those, trickled down his back.

She reminded him of Mary Ellen. Hell! Mary Ellen reminded him of himself in some ways, a chain of vulnerability, spawned by the succession of generations.

The absence of pain was the first thing he noticed when his mind decided to wake and reclaim itself. The seal on the bottle remained unbroken, yet that feeling of numbness bore a resemblance to the cure in the bottle held in his hands.

Thought returned as he looked down at the land that lay in front of him. His right hand instinctively removed the bottle as the finger on his left hand met the movement, peeling the seal from the neck. The sensation of pain reawakened, and he lifted the cure to his lips, taking a long, slow pull.

The sound of dried leaves rustling behind him brought him around in a defensive pose to meet the intruder.

"Ellen! I didn't know..."

"The children are waiting for you. Alford got angry and left. When you didn't come home, I figured you'd be here."

She stepped around him and looked out across the land, her arms folded across her bosom.

"Yeah, Alford's mad at me, again," he said. "We're just two stallions, corralled in the same pen."

"Hume, you *have* to let go..." she said, her voice trailing off as she saw the bottle cradled in his lap. She peered at her husband with silent disdain.

"What, Ellen? A man can't do a little celebrating after he's just been spared the electric chair and his life was given back to him?"

"Perhaps, but I thought you would want to celebrate with your *family*—not a bottle. I was hoping some things might change, now that you... *we*, have our lives back."

Looking up at her in the fading light, he pondered her words, *Now that we have our lives back.*

As in coming back after being away—as in finding one's way back home—the words remained in his head, resonating with familiarity until he heard Ellen's voice again.

"Well, I'll be going now, Hume. You stay out here and get blind drunk again, if that's what you want to do. Maybe I'm starting not to care."

She halted and turned toward him.

"Just one thing, though. We aren't going to *look* for you anymore. We've been through that enough. Maybe it's time you looked for *yourself*. And I hope you find yourself, Hume. I really do.

But you can do that from your brother's house. Not ours. Not anymore."

Ellen turned and started back toward the house, when Hume called out from his sitting position, his back still to her.

"Ellen! Come back! Please."

She stopped, and a silence visited the precipice before he stood and turned, facing her back.

"There is something... some *things*, I need to tell you. Please come back and let's talk. It's been a long time since we've done that—since long before bars and glass separated us."

Something in his voice, perhaps vulnerability, held her there. With her back toward him, she spoke.

"What is it Hume? What is it you wish to tell me?"

"Please, come. Let's sit here and talk for a while."

"I can't, Hume. The children..."

"The children will be fine. Fredericka is there. She and Emmaline can put them to bed. This time is for *us*, Ellen—this evening, this moment. We owe that to ourselves. And if we don't grab hold of this minute, right now, it may pass us by, and we may never have the chance again. I *know* now. Second chances are one thing I reckon I *should* know about. Maybe I shouldn't be asking for more second chances, but unless I get this one, the first one just ain't as important."

The full moon crested in the horizon, just above the treetops, and lit the landscape, lengthening the tree line, its shadows extending and creeping further out into the field.

"Ellen, what I'm about to tell you, I don't know where it comes from, but I know it to be true. But the funny thing is, it's a truth that really ain't truth, but a lie. And it's been kept inside here," he said, pointing to his chest.

"It's been there for some time, welling up, getting bigger and bigger, taking up more space than I had room for—till there was less and less room for me. So it had to come out. It had to come out before it took up all the room that was left, and if that happened, I would be no more. I'd wither up and be blown away by the first breeze. And I reckon that is where I've been heading for, all along."

"Today, I let some of that out, so I can make room for me again. Walt came to see me in jail the day he gave me Worth's ring, and he taught me some things that day—things that are common in some men. This is hard Ellen, because a man don't need to be sniveling and talking about such nonsense. But I'm not much of a man anymore, so I guess it's all right. I'm not so sure I can express what's in here, but I'll *try*," he said, pointing at this chest again.

"Comes a time in a man's life, when things start to change *around* him. And try as he may, he can't do a thing to stem that change. And though he don't want to admit it, that's fearful. And the more things change, the more fearful he becomes. Eventually, the changing ain't the problem no more. It's the fear and doubt that the change *started*—taking root, growing inside the man. And if those two feelings together stir round in there long enough, it ends up blinding the soul so it don't know itself anymore. It took a *colored* man, in a fearful, unknown world to him, to show me what courage is."

He bowed his head.

"And then, it appeared to me, that's what happened. I woke up one day to find that fear and doubt had blinded me, causing me to go down the wrong trail. I'd somehow gotten off the one I knew— the one that was familiar to me. I don't know or recall the exact day it happened—just that it happened. I don't wanna spend the rest of my life trying to find that path. But if that's what it takes, I'm willing. You still got in your heart to walk with me Ellen, until I find the one I knew?"

His wife stood, facing the man in front of her, searching deep in his eyes for some recognition of the person he'd once been. Traces of that man seemed to be emerging, as if arriving from a far journey, making his way back home. In the glimmer of her mind's eye, she recognized him, dirty and tattered, walking toward her from a distance, up a slope to where she stood, on top of a grassy hill, the breeze blowing her shiny black hair back and forth, in and out of her face. She saw him wave shyly, and that young-boy's sweet smile that she knew from so long ago--broke from the distance.

"I never turned the light off, Hume. You kept trying to, but it's still on," she sighed.

"I know that, Ellen."

Staring longer, as if to make certain he was not an apparition of what she so desired, she smiled, took his arm and said, in a whisper.

"Let's go home."

And the two turned and walked arm in arm through the darkening forest, the moonlight casting a glow throughout the night woods, illuminating a tree stump that looked a whole lot like a little figurine, standing there smiling at them from the shadows.

They left the world of the woodland and arrived in silence at the edge of the backyard, when Hume suddenly stiffened and stopped. Ellen looked up at her husband, alarmed at his balk. He stood rigid and erect, a glow illuminating his face. Ellen stared curiously at her husband before turning her head, following the direction of his gaze.

Across the yard, the back of their house was washed in golden warmth that made its way through the windows and spilled out into the night yard. She felt his ever so slight tremble and patted his hand resting on her forearm.

"Remember when you told me that an owl had called your name and you told me to talk to Daisy?"

She paused to make sure he remembered before continuing.

"Well, I did. And then I called Tom Spence. His version was similar, but a little different from Daisy's. Tom explained the call of the owl is a lore that came from the Indians. They believed that when the Holy Spirit comes down and takes the earthly form of an owl, and that owl calls out your name, it meant the process of the death of the old had begun, and the rebirth of the new would evolve. The death Daisy spoke of was actually life being changed and renewed—of the soul coming back home."

She turned away from her husband and looked across the backyard.

"That's home, and it's waiting for your return. Are you ready to come home, Hume?"

The tears ran golden down his check as he held his gaze on their home place.

"I reckon I am."

CPSIA information can be obtained at www.ICGtesting.com
Printed in the USA
BVOW03s0117111113

335967BV00001B/4/P